JOHN ELLSWORTH

THE CONTRACT LAWYER

VINCI
BOOKS

Vinci Books

vinci-books.com

Published by Vinci Books Ltd in 2024

1

Printed and bound in Great Britain by Clays Ltd, Elcograf S.p.A.

By John Ellsworth

THE THADDEUS MURFEE LEGAL THRILLERS

The Defendants

Beyond a Reasonable Death

Attorney at Large

Chase, the Bad Baby

Defending Turquoise

The Mental Case

The Girl Who Wrote The New York Times Bestseller

The Trial Lawyer

The Near Death Experience

Flagstaff Station

The Crime

La Jolla Law

The Post Office

The Contract Lawyer

THE MICHAEL GRESHAM THRILLERS

The Lawyer

The Defendant's Father

The Law Partners

Carlos the Ant

Sakharov the Bear

Annie's Verdict

Dead Lawyer on Aisle 11

30 Days of Justis

The Fifth Justice

Lies She Never Told Me

Girl, Under Oath

Lawyers in Gray

SISTERS IN LAW

Court Order

Hellfire

The District Attorney

Justice in Time

Prologue

San Diego

Her phone pulsed. Text message. She pulled it from her shirt pocket and absently—she was busy tracing radar system schematics—scanned the screen. It was as if she had been electrocuted: she cried out in her cubicle and dropped the phone. The image was unspeakable horror. Another worker, Anna Marie, next cubicle over, asked Nancy if she were all right. But Nancy had scooped up the phone and there, in block letters, she read: DO NOT CRY OUT! DO NOT MAKE A CALL!

She slumped back in her chair. She watched the screen as the message lengthened.

WE HAVE YOUR SON. YOU ARE THE LEAD ENGINEER ON THE AN/SPY-1 RADAR SYSTEM AT LOCKHEED MARTIN. WE WANT THOSE PLANS. NO ONE IS TO KNOW. BRING TO THE AVION KITE SHOP ON A THUMB DRIVE. SIMON WILL BE RETURNED. TELL NO ONE.

1

The image materialized on her iPhone. Her son's face, three running sutures across each eye, sealing his eyes shut.

"Nooooo!" she moaned.

Hyperventilation brought her close to passing out right there in her cubicle in San Diego, California on that bright April day. But she fought it down, grabbing up the empty sandwich bag out of her wastebasket and breathing in and out. She asserted her mind and stilled her shaking hands. Even as she brought her physical body back under control, her mind was flying, analyzing, as only the mind of a master's level computer engineer might analyze a problem.

She would need software code to bypass the system's cybersecurity if she were to remove the secret AN/SPY-1 military documents from Lockheed. Her mind was already writing the code, solving, solving, as she stared again at the iPhone image of her son with three running stitches across each eye.

She couldn't look at any more of his face, but she knew.

She knew he was howling, as only a four-year-old could howl.

For his mother.

Chapter 1

Special Agent Damon McDowell displayed the 8x10 glossy to the team. They paid close attention to the person they were going to arrest since she—Nancy —was the sister of Thaddeus Murfee, and it was going to be all-hands to make this arrest stick. The SAIC held it high above the table so the other four agents could memorize their prey. McDowell had to admit she was an attractive enough young woman, around 30 years old, with soft brown hair, wide eyes with a "please don't hurt me" look, the look of someone who'd been dunked in deep water a few times. But she was much more than that.

The FBI agents knew she was a senior software engineer with Lockheed Martin in San Diego. They also knew she had been selling military secrets to a corporation in San Diego that would take the secrets, build the same radar systems, and sell them back to the Navy at half the price. Failing that, the corporation would sell them to the Iranians or the Russians or the Chinese. In other words, in the world of corporate intrigue, it was business as usual, and the FBI agents had an urgent case of national security.

The perpetrator was Nancy Murfee Bergholzer. She was married to a lawyer named Jeff, and they had a four-year-old son they called Simon. The crime she was going to commit that day was the crime of treason. It was punishable by death.

The agents put their heads together and discussed how to proceed. Nancy Murfee Bergholzer had one thing in her favor that overshadowed everything else. She was the sister of Thaddeus Murfee. She would walk free nine times out of ten, thanks to her brother, the Super-lawyer. Murfee meant to the FBI agents that this would be a tough criminal case to make. Thaddeus would fight them to the bitter end to secure a defense verdict. So, the senior FBI agent in charge and his four underlings would make a perfect arrest that afternoon in San Diego. There could be no lack of probable cause, no misidentification of the target, and no unwanted civilians' involvement in the arrest. There would be eyeballs recording the crime, a high-speed 4k camera. The FBI agents felt the case was airtight on paper, but McDowell knew better from long experience. Once a case became lodged in the federal court system, anything could happen and usually did. So, this time, not only was he being meticulous about making the arrest, but he was also covering his butt.

McDowell, still holding the 8x10 glossy photograph above the table, asked, "Is there anyone here who hasn't memorized this pretty woman yet?"

Andy Lerner, the newest agent out of the Academy, raised his hand. An act which was never necessary for these pre-mission briefings.

McDowell sighed. "Yes, Andy, what is it?"

Andy pursed his lips as if considering whether he should ask his question, but then he plunged ahead. "Is there any chance the target will be armed?"

The agent to Andy's left, wearing khaki shorts and a UCSD T-shirt for the role he was going to play in Seaport Village, picked a scab on his thumb. "Cardboard boxes. Cut myself with an X-Acto knife. Bitch hurts." The agent's name was Jim Smithers, and, of course, he went by the name of Smitty. "No guns, Lerner, so please, for hell's sake, don't take yours out."

At the head of the table, senior agent McDowell shook his head. "Smitty, I know this must be boring you out of your head, but please recommit to your job as an FBI agent just for the next two hours, if that's possible. There are no dumb questions. If anyone should know that, it would have to be you, who still holds the record."

Smitty shrugged and stuffed his hand into his cargo shorts. "I'm on it, boss, locked and loaded." He would be standing an arm's length away from the handoff, armed with a Glock pistol capable of taking out everyone in sight. And he was every bit as good as his gun.

"In answer to your question," said McDowell, "we have no expectation at all that the subject will be armed. Of course, as you learned at the Academy not so long ago, we're always prepared for anything. That goes to say that even though *she* may not be armed, *we* will be. We will be armed to the teeth just in case anybody wants to rock 'n' roll with us."

Smitty pulled out a cigarette and stuck it squarely between his lips and began speaking without lighting up. "Marty making the buy?"

The senior agent looked directly across the table at Ronnie Martinez—Marty.

Ronnie Martinez was 32 and had been an agent with the FBI since the age of 21. He was quiet, unassuming, and knew every rope there was to know. All the men agreed they wanted Ronnie at their back when the shit got bad. He was the one who would be making the actual hand-to-hand purchase of the stolen military secrets from Nancy Bergholzer. He wasn't a pushy kind of guy, never crowded other people in their space, never tried to talk over others, and was wise enough to know most people would hang themselves when confronted by an FBI agent if the agent only had the sense to let them speak. Today, he would be the one passing the $5000 in marked bills to Ms. Bergholzer.

"Marty, you ready for your part?"

Wearing a new pinstripe suit, white shirt, and Brooks Brothers Regimental tie, Ronnie Martinez looked like any businessman would look—normal. Nothing flashy, nothing uncommon, nothing that would stand out. He even wore a pocket square to match his necktie. "I've got the five-thousand dollars cash in my left jacket pocket. I signed them out, countersigned with her name, Nancy Bergholzer, dated it, and checked every Benjamin against the list to make sure all serial numbers matched. It took me all morning, but I'm ready."

The senior agent looked to the end of the table at the last man, an African American named Darius Longmont. "Darius, you ready with the cameras?" Darius nodded and lifted the pocket of his T-shirt where an ink pen was clipped. He held it up until the senior agent nodded.

"You're going to get me a video of the buy with your fountain pen camera—we're still good with that?"

6

"I'll be in the store before she arrives, looking like any other customer at Seaport Village in my baggies and T-shirt and sandals. I'll fade into the blackground. You hearin' me?"

"Blackground, does it never end?" countered McDowell.

Darius shook his head and carefully said, "Don't get me goin', boss. You really don't want a piece of me today." As he spoke, he was smiling playfully.

Senior agent Damon McDowell clapped his hands once and said, "All right then, ladies, let's go arrest someone."

The agents rode the elevator to the parking garage. They piled into a van and slid the doors shut. They headed southwest and cut over at Harbor Drive then began making their way south to Seaport Village, a popular tourist attraction consisting of several buildings built contiguous to the bay and selling every type of tourist gewgaw imaginable, including beach kites. It was the beach kites store they would infiltrate since that's where the sale would take place.

When they arrived and parked their anonymous white van at the next building over from the kite store, the men waited while Smitty, wearing his cargo shorts and T-shirt, infiltrated the kite store. He wore his Glock beneath his shirt and would provide close-up firepower if the need arose.

Five minutes later, he was followed in by Ronnie Martinez, all Brooks Brothers clad, ready to make the hand-to-hand with his $5000 in marked bills. He clapped a Padres baseball cap on his head—the sign Nancy Murfee Bergholzer would be looking for.

Finally, Darius Longmont, with his fountain pen camera, moseyed toward the store. He would wait outside on the wooden bench until the target arrived, then follow her inside and, standing beside her, would pretend to be interested in kites. At the same time, his wide-angle camera would record every pixel of the sale.

McDowell and Lerner remained in the van where they would wait until young Ms. Bergholzer showed up to collect her money and pass her thumb drive to Martinez. Then they would assume positions at either side of the front door, ready to make the arrest.

Chapter 2

W hen Nancy Murfee Bergholzer logged out of her computer at Lockheed Martin, she also removed the thumb drive that she'd loaded with top secrets about the Navy's AN/SPY-1 Radar System. Ordinarily, the insertion and removal of a thumb drive would have alerted the system's operators to a breach, but Nancy was way smarter than that. She had written an algorithm to cloak the thumb drive activity, keeping the guardians of Lockheed Martin's data in the dark.

She shot a look around the office floor where she worked at Lockheed, the San Diego Bay only a couple blocks away. She glanced at the other cubicles around her, searching out anyone who might be watching her. She had access to every possible drawing, schematic, system circuits, warfare capabilities—everything most important about the U.S. rotary-wing aircraft. She also knew there were eyes in the sky—surveillance cameras planted in the ceiling—but she had positioned her body in such a way that the cameras had missed her taking the thumb drive and shoving it straight down into her panties. She then turned back to her computer and appeared to be shuffling the electronic schematics on her desk. The time was 5:05 p.m., time to call it a day.

Along with the other 423 systems analysts, programmers, and support staff, Nancy made her way to the exit of the cavernous building where she worked. Before leaving, all employees would pass through a screening station routinely where they would be scanned, and their bags searched. Approaching the station as she waited her turn, Nancy felt the cloying sensation of being squeezed in from all sides, the same feeling she'd had on the other nine occasions when she'd smuggled contraband from the workplace.

Then it was her turn. Amos McCarthy, a man who had worked at Lockheed Martin longer than Nancy's seven years, brusquely waved an electronic wand around her body. She then stood facing the screen, arms raised, while her body was scanned.

"Hey, Nancy," said McCarthy, "you stealing anything today?"

"Just the usual, a *Western Living* magazine and a pack of Juicy Fruit. How about you, Amos?"

"Get on out of here, girl, and have a good evening."

Again. He had missed it again because she kept eye contact and smiled her huge white smile.

Nancy's knees all but buckled as she passed through the exit doors into San Diego's blinding sunlight beneath the blazing disk that hung in the western sky. Again came the cloying fear that the guards would approach her at any minute and seize her for the thief she was. But as she made her way to her car, no one accosted her, and no one came to capture her.

Her step grew lighter as she traveled the asphalt parking

lot to the far end, where she had managed to find some shady parking under a Palo Verde tree. The keys in her purse signaled the door, the white Corolla unlocked, and she slid inside.

She depressed the starter button and waited while the engine took hold and ran for five seconds before she shifted into reverse and backed away from the curb.

She knew exactly where she was going; a text message was received: today's date, 5:30 p.m., Avion's Kite Shop, Seaport Village. The kite shop was only 15 minutes from her workplace, so she made her way up to Harbor Drive and headed north. She switched on her radio and listened to the DJ doing some routine about a walrus and an Eskimo. "You had to be there," she said and shrugged, missing the point of the joke entirely.

Traffic was heavy, bumper-to-bumper, as she crawled the three-mile route. She watched out carefully, looking for other drivers who might be paying too much attention to her. She also scanned the rearview mirror for cars following her, cars that never allowed others in between them and Nancy's Corolla. She wanted to talk out loud, to soothe herself with her voice, but she was afraid her car was bugged. She was scared she had been found out some time ago and was being watched every time she made a handoff, the FBI recording the sale and the purchaser's identity.

She opened her purse and removed a damp washcloth that she kept inside a plastic baggie. She removed her sunglasses and drew the washcloth across her forehead. She then brushed it down both cheeks and across her mouth, eliminating any signs of makeup. She placed the washcloth in the baggie and then the baggie back in the purse. Holding her bag open with one hand, she retrieved a black baseball cap that had NY on the front, but she put the hat on with the bill to the back.

At last she arrived at Seaport Village. She set her blinker for a left turn into a parking lot, just down the road from the kite shop. A kind soul stopped and let her turn across the oncoming traffic, and she thanked him with a wave of her hand. She pulled in where she had parked nine times before, next to a tilting Joshua tree, and rocked to a stop. Nervously looking around, she noted who else might be there occupying parked cars, but she was rewarded to see no one appeared to be giving a damn about her.

At 5:27, she reached down inside her panties and withdrew the thumb drive. She threw open the door and climbed out. She then walked up to the sidewalk and turned right, walking with the San Diego Bay on her left. After passing a seafood restaurant, she arrived at the kite store. She swallowed hard and went inside.

Was anyone watching? She shuddered when she saw the CCTV cameras sprouting out of the walls like teenage acne. That was the one thing she could not avoid, the cameras. If she ever got busted, the FBI would review thousands of hours of film to pick her out while she was making felonious sales over and over again.

She didn't know the messaging between her usual buyer and her cell phone had been intercepted by the SIGINT capabilities of the Department of Homeland Security. She didn't know the DHS had notified the FBI, and it was the FBI that had set up the meeting this time.

At exactly 5:30, Nancy made a right turn into the store and went all the way to the back wall lined every fourteen inches with shelving. She took the thumb drive in her right hand and reached the top shelf on the far right side. It was placed beneath a kite of red tissue with a picture of two boys running along the beach. Seven steps to the far wall and stop.

Nancy appeared to be examining kites when FBI agent Ronnie Martinez approached from the backside on her right and stuck the $5000 in cash into her open purse before immediately stepping away from her.

Throughout the transaction, Nancy never saw Special Agent Darius Longmont photographing her every move from two steps away. Nor did she see pistol-packing Smitty just beyond, his Glock weapon in readiness. It wasn't that she wasn't alert; she was. Only the FBI agents were so practiced, smooth, and perfect in executing their roles that very few people would've noticed them.

Sometimes, at the kite store, Nancy would select a kite, pay for it, and take it home to Simon, who loved kites and seemed to live for those times when mama and daddy assembled a new one with him while he danced from foot to foot, ready to tear outside and test the wind. Today wouldn't be one of those kite-buying days—but there was hope. It was her tenth and final drop. Excited wouldn't begin to say how she was feeling. Who could tell? They might even be waiting just outside with her little boy!

Her hands shook as she turned to leave the store. She and Jeff were frantic to get their beloved little boy back, and she would've sold not only the schematics to the radar system but to the whole damn helicopter if that's what it took.

A bolt of excitement ran up her spine. She'd lived like a zombie the last six weeks without him, constant worry and dread keeping her awake at night. She'd gone through the motions at work and home, mechanically eating, walking, talking, moving. She and Jeff would pass each other in the house like shadows.

Nancy and Jeff had already made arrangements for counseling tomorrow for the boy. It was anticipated by the child psychologist that he would be greatly traumatized and in need of serious intervention. She reached inside her purse for a tissue and lowered her sunglasses, dabbing away the tears from her eyes as she tried to think of anything besides her son's trauma. The tears were so often and so heavy that her eyes were forever red-rimmed like the eyes of a hippy toker.

She had now collected a half-dozen more kites in his absence. So she would have one waiting for him when he came home tonight. Hell, she thought, he could have all of them tonight. And it couldn't happen fast enough.

Nancy failed to see Special Agents Darius Longmont, Jim Smithers, and Ronnie Martinez exit the Avion Kite Shop ahead of her. Nor did she know they waited on either side of the front door, facing the bay, their backs to her. When the agents grabbed her and threw her to the ground, Nancy was shocked--and wasn't. She had known it could happen any time.

They weren't rough with her as they cuffed her--no knee pressed her head into the sidewalk. An agent on either arm pulled her to her feet. There was a momentary pause, and then Damon McDowell began reciting Miranda. "You have the right to remain silent," he first said, but then her mind shut off as he went through the rest of it, a latent drone in the background of her thoughts. Instead, she was crying inside, crying over the Simon she wouldn't see that night after all and crying over the career this blackmail had cost her whether she was ultimately guilty or not guilty. Tears flowed, and she hung her head without a word to the special agents.

The senior agent continued speaking. "Ms. Bergholzer,

we have to take you to jail now, and you will be allowed to call your lawyer from there. We have a pretty good idea who that will be, and if you'd like, I will place the call to him myself right now and explain what's happened here."

"You would call Thaddeus for me?"

"I would."

"Then make the call. Now, please."

"Number?"

"619…"

SAIC Damon McDowell began punching numbers into his phone.

Chapter 3

Thaddeus Murfee stood at the gate of Coconino's horse stall. Inside was Coconino, Thaddeus's horse, standing with his left rear hoof caught up in the hands of a farrier everyone called "Nasty" because of the horseshit, flies, anxiety, and kicks the farrier had to contend with while he removed horseshoes, clipped hooves, and re-shod his customers.

Thaddeus and Nasty would discuss the horse's shoeing fit before he was done today. A lot would depend on the first few steps the horse took after the shoeing concluded. The farrier would then check the horse's leg, foot, and hoof before cutting away any excess hoof growth and make sure the horse was balanced correctly.

Coconino turned his head around and looked directly into Thaddeus's eyes as if asking, "Are you sure about this?" The farrier clipped away another piece of hoof and threw it out of the stall. As soon as it hit the ground, the three Murfee dogs growled and sparred over who got the morsel. Tammy, Christine's black Lab, came up with the hoof cutting and ran away with it. From the end of the barn, she made slurping noises and profoundly satisfied sounds as she chewed the hoof and swallowed it down.

Thaddeus shook his head, unable to see the connection between eating a horse hoof and happiness. Just then, his cell phone buzzed inside his shirt pocket. He unsnapped the pocket and two-fingered the phone, pressing it to his ear. "This is Thad, your turn."

"This is Thaddeus Murfee?"

"Yes, this is Thaddeus Murfee. What's up?"

"Mr. Murfee, my name is Damon McDowell, and I am the special agent in charge of the San Diego FBI office. We have just arrested your sister, Nancy Bergholzer, and she asked that I call you."

"As her attorney, I am instructing you to attempt no statements from my client. You understand this?"

"We knew that's the way it would be. That's why we wanted to call and lay all our cards on the table."

"Thank you for that. Please tell my sister I'll be down to see her in about ninety minutes when you are finished booking her in. Metropolitan?"

"I'll do that, and thank you, Mr. Murfee. Metro, yes."

"If I may ask, what crime is she accused of?"

"Treason. Punishable by death, Mr. Murfee. Don't delay."

Thaddeus didn't bother to reply to that last smart-ass remark. Instead, he dropped his phone back into his pocket and headed for the house to change clothes. From the ranch house west of La Jolla to the Metropolitan Correctional Center downtown, it would take a good ninety minutes in the six o'clock traffic bumper-to-bumper on the I5 freeway that was returning workers to San Diego from the north part of the county. He quickened his steps when he realized how slow going it would be. Then he had a thought, and he hit the speed dial for Marcel Rainford.

"Marcel, please come over to my house, asap. We have a new case, and it's the most important one since we started together."

"I'm on my way, boss."

Thaddeus jogged to the ranch house, up the porch stairs, and strode inside.

* * *

Marcel arrived and parked at the side entrance to the Murfee ranch house. He climbed down out of his Dodge Ram and two-stepped the stairs up onto the porch and went inside without knocking. "Hello, the house!" he cried out.

"Be down in five ticks," Thaddeus called back. "Coffee's still warm."

"No thanks. I know the way you roll with that weak stuff."

Marcel was six-feet tall, dark-skinned, short black hair combed back, brown eyes, and a scar across his forehead, courtesy of a spy who had given it to him with the butt of a Walther pistol. He was wearing tan jeans, a Ralph Lauren pocket Tee, a blue windbreaker to conceal his Glock 19, and brown Roper boots. His sunglasses hung from his shirt by one stem. In his T-shirt pocket was a Sony recorder and a pack of Tums—he was never far from a handful of Tums.

Marcel walked to the coffee pot and tapped it with his finger. Cool to the touch. He walked back across the kitchen, reached above the stove, the second cabinet to the right, and pulled it open. The ever-ready bag of Coconut Creams was opened, and he took two and began munching. He nodded and took two more, slipping these into his windbreaker.

Thaddeus strode into the kitchen, adjusting his necktie

as he came. Like the FBI, he wore pinstripes on most days, but he wore his suit with thousand-dollar boots handcrafted in Colorado of synthetic fabric made to look like ostrich. Sunglasses were perched atop his head, Ray-Bans. He reached and pulled his cuff up an inch. "Damn, forgot my watch."

"No Mickey?"

"No Mickey, no Minnie. As they say, I'm out of time."

They took a seat at the round kitchen table. Thaddeus tapped it with two fingers, thinking. "All right, here's the deal. FBI arrested Nancy. They've put a charge of treason on her. I'm off to the jail to meet with her, so I need you to get to the scene and forensic the hell out of it."

"Photographs?"

"Photographs, video, measurements, canvass for witnesses, the whole nine yards. But that's after I have an address for you. So let's say you follow me to the MCC and park and wait outside. They'll produce Nancy and give me the location. I'll catch you up by phone, and you take off. Good enough?"

Marcel rubbed his chin. "Okay. How do you know the charge already?"

"FBI. SAIC Damon McDowell did me a solid. Treason, Metro Correctional Center, no interview will be attempted by the Fibbies."

"All right. Question of the year: why in hell would Nancy commit treason? I know she has secret clearance at Lockheed, but treason? Jeff's doing all right with the money angle, no?"

"Guess so. She knocks down a buck-fifty, he's a partner ten years, probably making half a million. No need for treason for damn sure."

"What about Simon? Who's with him?"

"I called Jeff. I expected he would go straight home to relieve the nanny, but he said a funny thing. He said, 'There's something about Simon I can't say over the phone. I'm sure Nance will bring you up to speed.' That was it."

"Something about Simon? Hell, man, let's travel."

They stood, and Marcel led the way out the door. Thaddeus jumped into his Mercedes 550, closed the top, and peeled out of the driveway. Marcel followed, also laying down a couple of feet of rubber.

Ten minutes later, they were merging onto the I5 freeway, headed south.

It was time to pay an official call at the Metropolitan Correctional Center. Thaddeus had been there so often the car knew the way. Marcel rode his bumper, sunglasses in place, anticipating what tools he would need at the scene.

Twenty-five minutes later, they drove the speed limit up Union Street to 808, where they turned in and searched for parking. There were federal officers everywhere and briefcases in a two-way parade.

Thaddeus climbed out.

Chapter 4

Thaddeus joined the lawyers and law enforcement officers and family members headed for the jail. He had retrieved a yellow pad of paper from the Benz' console and was ready to proceed with Nancy's meeting. He entered the correctional center and was greeted by a line at the conveyor belt. Lawyers were removing their shoes, belts, wallets, and watches and depositing them in gray trays that rode the conveyor through the X-ray machine. He watched, waiting his turn, shifting foot to foot, checking his watch that wasn't there, and praying his sister was all right. He had no idea except that she was in here someplace and was probably wilting by the minute under the stress of her predicament.

The security officer waved his wand around Thaddeus, ignoring the proffered bar card that should have let him pass freely through the security checkpoint. Without looking up, he said, "All right. Good to go. Move on, sir."

He made his way up to the Plexiglas window, where he was again required to show his bar card. The bored clerk on the other side of the Plexiglas yawned, covering her mouth with her fist, and then grinned with embarrassment.

"Up late last night?" asked Thaddeus.

"Who are you here to see, sir?"

"Nancy Bergholzer. She was brought here about two hours ago."

The clerk turned to her computer screen and began scrolling her mouse. Finally, she said, "Aha! Your girl's right here."

She picked up her phone, pressed two buttons, and spoke loud enough that he could hear her paging Nancy Bergholzer to conference room 3B.

"Go right on in, sir, and wait at the receiving station."

Thaddeus pushed through the double doors and stopped at the large circular desk. Again, he held out his bar card and waited while it was scanned. Then he was told to proceed to Conference Room 3B. He didn't need to be shown the way, so he made his way down the main hallway and then to the right down a second hallway to a conference room marked *3B Attorneys*.

Five minutes later, Nancy was brought into the room by a deputy matron with a kind smile and a nod to Thaddeus.

It was a long hug that lasted at least a minute, and Thaddeus could feel her tears dampening his shoulder by the end. He had to pull away to begin the conversation, but he regretted even doing that. When they were seated at a round metal table that was bolted to the floor, he said very gently, "I'm sorry for you. But I'm going to get you out of this. Tonight, you'll have to remain here in jail, but tomorrow we'll see a federal magistrate and have bail set. You'll be released at that time, have no fear."

He handed her his pocket square, and she dabbed at her tears. Nancy was an attractive woman, light brown hair like himself, with the same wide-set eyes and a mouth that ordinarily would present a beautiful smile to the world. Also, like her brother, she wore eyeglasses. But unlike him, she usually wore small silver hammered hoop earrings and a necklace, though this time the necklace had been seized and stored for her by the matrons upfront.

"I don't even know where to begin," she said. "So many bad things have happened, and I'm almost embarrassed to have to tell you."

He nodded solemnly and looked his sister in the eye. "Okay, let's start at the beginning. When did you make your first sale of Lockheed documents?"

"It's probably been six weeks now. I received a text at work, telling me Simon had been kidnapped. I made it home at eighty miles an hour and found he wasn't there, and his nanny had fled when the intruders entered the house."

"Any idea who it might be?"

"I think they are a corporation who consider themselves a competitor to Lockheed. Which is ridiculous—no one is a competitor to Lockheed."

"How many times have you passed documents or electronic files to these people now?"

"Today was the tenth time. After today, they promised to return Simon to Jeff and me. But now, that's hopeless."

Thaddeus jotted a few notes on his yellow pad, all the while thinking. Ten transactions equaled ten different crimes. If the government proved these had occurred, she could be looking at ten different counts of treason. It was a horrible thought since even one count of treason under federal law was a capital crime, which meant it was punishable by death.

He began slowly, saying, "Now I need to hear why you

did this besides the fact that the kidnapping of Simon coerced you. Was there money involved?"

"There was money involved each time. I didn't want the money. We don't need the money, but the kidnappers insisted on it. I still don't know why."

"Each time you made the exchange, was it with the same person?"

"No, it was always someone different. But my instructions were always the same. I was told to leave the thumb drives on the top shelf, right-hand side, of the Avion Kite Shop in Seaport Village. It never varied."

Thaddeus pulled out his cell phone and raised one finger. He hit the speed dial for Marcel and relayed to him what he had just been told and the location of the incidents. He ended the call and looked up at his sister again. "What, exactly, have you been delivering on the thumb drives all this time?"

"Well, I work in the Lockheed Martin division known as Rotary and Mission Systems. We support\Aegis Combat System integration testing. I'm working as a test and integration engineer. In my capacity, I have access to all test records, electronics, and capabilities of the radar system."

"How much of that have you turned over?"

"All of it." She sighed, dropping her eyes to the table. "Do you hate me yet?"

It cut him like a knife slicing his heart—hate her? He remembered when they were pulled apart by social services as small children. Separated, different foster homes. He hadn't been able to save her then. *Hate her now? I'll show you hate, whoever did this to my sister.*

"That will never happen. You did what you had to do, and no one can blame you."

A look of irremediable panic clouded her eyes before

she again raised the pocket square and dabbed. He watched her shaking hands and reached across the table to steady them. He said gently, "Brother's here. Now, let's talk about Simon. That's my chief concern right now, not that your case isn't important, too. But I know what I can do for you, and I'm happy with that. What I don't know is what I can do to help get Simon home. First, what's the name of the corporation your buyers are working for?"

"Catalina Systems Integration and Development. CSID for short. They're a couple of miles south of Lockheed and are known to be quite a comer in the avionics field. The people I've dealt with have all been men, except for one woman who came the second to last time. She looked nervous and out of place, and I wondered at the time if she was filling in for someone, or what she was doing was just scaring the living hell out of her."

"Maybe a little of both. Let me ask you this. If we were to go and sit outside that building and take notice of all people coming and going, would you be able to pick out any faces you've transacted with?"

"Probably. The woman, definitely. One, because she was so recent, and two, because I wondered where she got her hair done. Dumb as that sounds."

"No, it doesn't sound dumb at all. It's exactly the kind of observation I'm looking for that will help bring Simon home safe and sound. I'm going to ask that when I get you out of here tomorrow, we go directly to the CSID building, park ourselves outside the entrance, and begin seeing what we can see."

"Oh, Lord, it makes me feel so much better that we're actually going to do something. I've been sitting in here with my teeth chattering, I've been so scared. But I'm so relieved you're giving me hope in the middle of this desert where there is no hope. Thank God, I have you for my brother."

There it was again. *Save her. This one is yours.*

Thaddeus reached across the table and took her left hand in his. "How long has it been since we found each other again? Eight years, nine? And still yet today I haven't forgiven myself for letting the CPS separate us into different foster homes. I was your big brother, yet I was helpless to do anything. I felt, and still feel like I let you down that day. I don't want you ever to feel that I'm not there for you."

"I had no idea what they had done with you either, no idea where you'd been taken, and no one would tell me anything. I still don't understand what that was all about. Maybe someday we should sue them."

Thaddeus nodded violently. "I've long been thinking the same thing. Little kids should never be treated that way, and it's our responsibility to step back and step in when it does happen. In this case, we hold all the cards, and maybe if we hit them hard enough, word will get out to others like them."

"I'll be right there with you, brother. Am I going to be safe in here?"

"I'm going to demand that they single-cell you. I've got a pretty good basis for that demand, and they would be well advised to do what I'm asking. If they won't, I'll have the FBI agent who called me to call them, and we'll get it done by hook or crook. In the meantime, these facilities are carefully monitored and violent offenders far removed from the general population. You will be shoulder-to-shoulder with forgers, mail fraudsters, and ne'er-do-wells of all types. But the violent ones—the bank robbers and assholes who murder federal employees—you're safe from any of that.

Besides, I have a pretty good reputation down here. They generally listen to me."

"Whew, I feel so much better, Thad. Thirty minutes ago, I was thinking about hanging myself. But now I have a glimmer of hope. I'm going to spend tonight praying for Simon and asking God to give you the guidance you're going to need to get him back."

"That's the best idea in this situation." Thaddeus squeezed her hand across the table. "I think we're about done here. I want to stop by the main desk and make my demand for your single cell, then go meet up with Marcel and put our heads together, see what he thinks about the scene of the crime and discuss ways of getting to the bottom of CSID. Give me a quick hug, and I'll knock on the door and let her know we're finished in here."

They hugged momentarily, then Thaddeus turned and rapped the door with his fist. The steel door transmitted very little noise to the outside, but it was only a moment before they knew they had been heard, and the door came open. The same deputy matron guided Nancy to the door, then left with her without another word.

Thaddeus went forward and stopped at the desk. He was told she was already on her way to a single cell. It went without saying they knew who she was. He went outside and made his way to his Benz and let himself in. He pulled out his cell phone and dialed Marcel. They spoke briefly, making plans to meet at Seaport Village so Thaddeus could see for himself what the kite shop looked like. After he hung up, Thaddeus pushed the starter button and backed away from the curb.

Then he was out on Pacific Highway, headed north toward Seaport Village. He realized his eyes were wet, and he was shaking with fear for Simon and grief for his sister.

He knew her job prospects in the future were nil, even after she was found not guilty. Her record would be smudged forever by all this, and it would be impossible to erase, impossible for her to work again in a job that required secret clearance. This made him very angry at the asshats who had done this to his sister, and he vowed to take them down. All of them.

Twenty minutes later, he turned in at Seaport Village, parked, and headed for the kite shop. The earlier emotional trauma was no longer inside him and was replaced by an unerring sense of direction toward what came next. He was bound and determined to find a person or persons who had transacted with his sister when she was under such enormous duress and incapable of defending herself. What would he do, kill them? Or eat them alive in court?

Why not both?

Chapter 5

Thaddeus found Marcel standing at the cashier's counter in Avion's Kite Shop.

Marcel turned when he saw Thaddeus enter the store, shook his head, and said, "We got problems, boss."

Thaddeus walked up to the counter. "What kind of problems?"

"This lady here—Viola?"

"Yes, Viola." Viola was a woman in her late twenties, short blond hair, heavy black-frame glasses.

"She's the manager of the store. She tells me that the FBI has already been here and removed days of closed-circuit TV files. She definitely doesn't have the CCTV from your sister."

Thaddeus turned to Viola. "Is it true? The FBI took away your video records?"

"Sad, but true. I thought this was America. I didn't know the FBI could just come busting in your store and take away your records when you're not the one they are after. I'm really bummed."

"Then we'll just have to go downtown to the FBI and demand they let us look at those video records," Thaddeus said to Marcel. "Why don't you show me what you know about the store so far, and then we'll run back downtown. Viola, is it okay if I look around the store?"

"Sure, I have no complaint with you guys. Marcel says it was your sister who was in here?"

Thaddeus shot a look at Marcel. Why on earth would he tell anyone that? "Yes, my sister. Where is it, Marcel, back here on the right?"

"The top shelf there on the right. The red kite featuring the two boys running on the sand. She said that's where the FBI was looking. Evidently, the crime lab was up here dusting for prints last night. I can only assume this is the scene of the crime right here. At least, nobody told me any different."

Thaddeus turned and said back across the store, "Viola, did you happen to see any of what was going on back here yesterday?"

"I'm sorry, but I didn't. We were swamped yesterday, and I never got out from behind the counter to tell the truth."

"You have your pictures and video?" Thaddeus asked Marcel.

Marcel replied, "Yep, also measurements, and Viola is preparing a list for me of the people who were in the store between five and 6 o'clock last night. This is a list she's making up from her sales software. I expect to start contacting them when I'm done in here today. I can canvass them and see if anyone happened to see anything."

"That's excellent. Good thinking. We never know what that kind of extra attention for a case might dig up. All right, I've seen enough here. What say we step outside, and I place a call to FBI Special Agent Damon McDowell?"

"Who is he again?"

"He's the special agent in charge of the San Diego FBI field office. He headed up the team that arrested Nancy. He won't be in the office, but maybe I can catch him on a call."

They walked out to the parking lot and climbed into Thaddeus's Mercedes. Thaddeus found McDowell's number his "recents" list and punched his name for a call-back. The line began ringing, and after half a dozen rings, it was answered. "Yes?"

"Agent McDowell, this is Thaddeus Murfee calling. First, I want to thank you so much for the courtesy today of calling me when my sister was arrested. The next thing is, we are sitting outside the Avion Kite Shop in the parking lot and wondering why the FBI made off with all of the store's video records instead of just asking for copies. Can you enlighten me on that?"

"I'll have to talk to my guys about that and see what's up. Why, you want us to make you a copy of what we have?"

"That would be excellent. Can I drop by your office tomorrow and pick it up on my way to work?"

What time do you go to work?"

"Just give me a time. I'll be there then."

"How about nine? We can have it wrapped up for you by then, I'm sure."

"That would be perfect. What if I sent my investigator Marcel Rainford to make the pickup? Any trouble with that?"

"Let me write that down. His name is Marcel Rainford?"

"Marcel, just like it sounds, R-A-I-N-F-O-R-D."

"Sure, tell Marcel to drop by any time after nine, and I'll have a package waiting upfront. Can I do anything else for you gents, tonight?"

"Not that I can think of," said Thaddeus. He sat thoughtfully for a moment, perplexed about something. "You mind if I ask you another question?"

"Just don't ask me my age, and we're good."

"You've been very helpful and considerate with all this. I'm not used to the police or the FBI treating a defense attorney like this. What gives?"

"Simple. The case is open and shut. I could give you our entire file, and your sister is still going to prison, Mr. Murfee. I hate to be the bearer of bad news, but that's just how the cookie crumbles. Anything else?"

"I like a man who doesn't dance around. But I have to admit I see the case quite differently than you. When I take her home a couple of months from now with a defense verdict, please remind me how simple this case was. I'm sure you won't forget."

The agent's answering laugh was so loud Marcel could hear it through the phone and gave Thaddeus a disgusted look. Then he heard the voice on the other end of the line say, "Have a great night, Mr. Murfee. Sweet dreams."

After he hung up, Thaddeus said to Marcel, "The main office is on Vista Sorrento Parkway. Be there at nine tomorrow morning."

"I'm all over it, boss," said Marcel. "It sounds like you have some minds to change. I can't think of a better guy to do that job."

"Wait. I have one more question for Viola. Let's head back inside the store for just a minute."

They climbed out of the car, cut between two buildings, and hiked down to the kite store. As before, Viola was alone at the cash register while six or seven customers browsed. Thaddeus approached her with a smile, saying, "I do have one more question. What exactly did the FBI tell you when they asked for the video records?"

Viola smiled back. "They gave me ten dates and told me they wanted the video from those ten dates and nothing else. The forensics man hung over my shoulder and watched every step I did while I was making copies of what they wanted."

"Copies? I thought you said they took the actual video recording itself. Did I hear wrong?"

"I did? I guess I didn't mean they took the actual video recording. I still have those here in the back room on our server. Should I make you copies, too?"

"I'm just wondering why you told me they had taken everything. Do you remember what you were thinking then?"

"I guess I was missing what you were asking me."

"Or maybe you didn't want me to have those records? Maybe you're upset your store was being used for the sequence of ten criminal events? Could that be it?"

Violet shrugged, the smile disappearing from her face. "Guilty as charged. It really pisses me off your sister was in here committing felonies while I'm working hard, just trying to get through the day. It's not like I'm paid a lot. And I work sixty hours a week. As far as I'm concerned, she can go to jail for the rest of her life. I'm not what you would call a friendly witness, Mr. Murfee. Please keep that in mind. And, oh yes, I have Marcel's list of customers between five and six o'clock this evening ready for him."

She produced two pages stapled together and inserted them inside a white envelope. She made a production of handing this over to Marcel and not to Thaddeus, who was standing closest to her. Thaddeus couldn't help but smile. Friendly witness, she was not.

But who could blame her? He had to admit he'd be pissed, too.

After the men left the store together, Marcel told Thaddeus he would start calling the customers and taking statements that same night. He would email the results to Thaddeus before midnight.

They split up in the parking lot, and soon Thaddeus was headed northbound on the 163 freeway, heading for Vista Sorrento Parkway. He had a hunch that Damon McDowell might still be in the office. He wanted to talk to the guy face-to-face, and it didn't hurt to drop by, even though it was getting late, almost nine.

Forty-five minutes later, Thaddeus was headed home to La Jolla. McDowell had not been in the office after all, or so Thaddeus had been told.

When he got home, the kids were already in bed, so he kissed his wife and went right into his office to begin preparing legal documents that he would use in the morning with the federal judge to get bail for his sister.

He couldn't type fast enough.

Chapter 6

United States District Court Magistrate Peter
O'Reilly was in a good enough mood when he
settled himself onto his courtroom perch and
looked out over the crowd. The third case called that
morning was *United States of America versus Nancy Bergholzer*.
Thaddeus had previously provided the original of his
motion to the clerk of the court to set conditions of bail. He
had distributed the same to the Assistant U.S. attorney who
would appear on the case that morning. Judge O'Reilly
waited for the minor court clamor to dissipate and raised his
eyebrows at the parties. "Ready?" Thaddeus had come
forward with his sister, and they were waiting at the lectern
while the Assistant U.S. attorney finished conferring with a
colleague at her table. She then came forward to the lectern
on her side of the walkway.

"The defendant has the right to have counsel, and I see
Nancy Bergholzer is appearing with her attorney. Sir, would
you please state your name for the record?"

"Thaddeus Murfee, San Diego, California."

"Mr. Murfee, has the defendant received a copy of the indictment in this case?"

"She has your honor."

"Has she read it, and does she understand it?"

"She has read it, we have discussed it, and she does understand it."

The court then went into the other business of the initial hearing, rights were given and discussed, and all manner of procedural items were settled. Then the court addressed the defendant's motion to set bail in a reasonable amount.

"Defendant Bergholzer, your attorney Mr. Murfee has filed a motion to set conditions of bail. The court is ready to hear comments from counsel on this matter. Mr. Murfee, you may proceed."

"Your honor, I would like to say at the outset that Ms. Bergholzer is my sister. I know her situation well, and I know that she is a master's level software engineer, educated right here at the University of California in San Diego. She has many ties to the community and is not a flight risk. She and her husband live in Pacific Beach, where they own their home and where Mr. Bergholzer, who is a lawyer and could not be here this morning, has his own law practice. The defendant is ready to surrender her passport to the court. She has brought it with her this morning for that very purpose. On a more personal level, let me say that it has been brought to my attention that unknown parties have kidnapped the minor son of the defendant, and his whereabouts are presently unknown. The evidence is strong in this case because the FBI has done a thorough job in documenting its charges. But I want the court to be aware that none of this would've happened without the coercion applied by third parties to my client by kidnapping her son to force her to cooperate with them. Thus, the court and the U.S. Attorney's office are now on notice that the defendant's defense in this matter will consist of the affirmative defense of coercion from the outset. None of this would've happened and will not happen again because my sister is on leave of absence from Lockheed Martin now. Plus, it's now out in the open, so there will be no further contact with the third parties in the case. Moreover, since my client's son is missing, my client wouldn't leave the area for all the world, given that she wants only to remain here and continue looking for her little boy. For these reasons, the defendant asks the court to set bail in a reasonable amount, not to exceed $100,000. Thank you for your time and courtesy, your honor."

Judge O'Reilly then nodded to the Assistant U.S. attorney, and with a slight smile, said, "You may proceed, counselor."

The Assistant U.S. attorney, a youngish woman, wearing a gray pinstripe suit and her hair up in a bun, nodded to the judge and began speaking. "May it please the court, counsel, the U.S. Attorney's office objects to any amount of bail in this case for the following reason. The defendant has been filmed selling American defense secrets to what can only be described as foreign adversaries on nine different occasions. The sales have been recorded on the CCTV installed at the Avion Kite Shop in Seaport Village. There is no doubt from the video footage that the actor in this case who is turning over American secrets is Nancy Bergholzer, the defendant. The U.S. Attorney's office is surprised by Mr. Murfee's comments, so casually given, that the defendant seems ready to admit to the factual basis of the government's complaints and contend that the defendant's way out of this mess is vis-à-vis the affirmative defense of coercion.

In other words, Your Honor, you have before you a defendant who has admitted to nine different counts of treason, a crime punishable by death in our country. We are also putting the defense on notice that the U.S. Attorney's office will be seeking the death penalty in this case. Appropriate paperwork in that regard will be filed after today. Given that the defendant is facing nine different charges where a finding of guilt only once could send her to the death chamber, it is the government's position that this defendant is a high-flight risk and should not be admitted to the privileges of bail. For this reason, the government asks that the defendant's motion to set conditions of bail be denied."

When the parties had concluded their remarks, Judge O'Reilly consulted a book on his desk, slowly and thoughtfully reading through two pages before looking up again to address the parties.

"Counsel, the court faces a tough decision in this case, but one the court will render in an exercise of its judicial discretion. As a preface, let me say for the record that upon all arrests in criminal cases, bail shall be admitted except for punishment that may result in death. Having heard the comments of counsel and having read the indictment and considering the circumstances under which the indictable offenses allegedly occurred, the court will set bail of $100,000 per occurrence, for a total bail of one million dollars. The defendant also shall surrender her passport to the court's clerk this morning before leaving this room. Counsel, is there anything further?"

Both lawyers replied they had nothing further. Nancy was delivered into the custody of the court personnel for return to the Metropolitan Correctional Center, where she would be processed out that day after bail was posted.

Thaddeus waited until court was concluded so that he

could meet his sister in the hallway for a brief discussion, courtesy of the U.S. Marshal's service.

"Big brother, what can I say? Thank you for your incredible work this morning and the thoughtful legal workup you did in the motion you filed. My question is, what do you want me to do once I'm released from jail today?"

"I don't want to say right here with all these other people around, but I'd like you to come directly to my office where we can discuss what happens next. You take care now, and I'll see you later this afternoon."

Thaddeus then turned toward the elevators and was caught by Marcel, who had news of his own. Thaddeus and Marcel paused at the elevators, standing off to the side and speaking in hushed voices.

"Hey, boss, I got through about half the names on the list Viola gave me last night of the customers who were in the store at the time of the handovers. I found two people who think they recognize Nancy's picture. She appeared frightened, and her manner and expression seemed totally out of place in a kite shop. They said they watched her place a small object on the shelf, turn, and proceed to the far-left corner of the shop where a man brushed against her. They were unable to describe those people since their faces were hidden from view. Whoever we're dealing with is extremely well-versed in avoiding eye contact while at the same time avoiding the CCTV cameras inside the shop."

When the elevator arrived, Thaddeus led Marcel inside. Since they were the only ones riding, Thaddeus continued. "Great work, Marce, especially the parts about how she appeared nervous and under stress. Did you happen to ask if the people who brushed up against her were seen taking an object from the shelf?"

"Yes, both prefaced their comments by saying they had seen the entire transaction, the putting up and taking down of some small object that fit inside their hands, making the object unseeable. I have another dozen statements to review, and then maybe we can start making some conclusions, at least about her manner, her apparent fear, and how those support our defense of coercion."

"Exactly what we needed, Marcel. Please go on back to the office and finish up with your research. I'll be there shortly. For now, I received a call this morning from Damon McDowell at the FBI, and I'm meeting him at a Denny's. He says I deserve to know about Simon."

They arrived on the main floor, and the elevator doors swooshed open. Thaddeus held the door as Marcel stepped out. His investigator turned and said, "Simon? That has to be good news. At least, I hope. If they have any idea who took the child or where he might be held, please let's talk immediately. I'll be all over that."

"Yes, *we* will be."

Marcel turned. "Are you handling the bail for Nancy?"

"Contact Christine. Tell her to post bail ASAP. She knows which account to use in my bank."

———

THADDEUS RECEIVED the call from his lawyer-wife, Christine, an hour later. Bail had been posted for Nancy. She would be out of jail that same day.

Chapter 7

They met at the Denny's on Harbor Drive, three miles from the courthouse. Thaddeus arrived, went inside, and found Special Agent McDowell sitting by himself at a window booth overlooking the parking lot. He nodded when Thaddeus joined him at the table and said, "Thanks for coming. I hope I'm not about to ruin your day with what I have to tell you."

They ordered coffee from the frowning waitress, who appeared disappointed it was a coffee-only table. Thaddeus reminded himself that he would pick up the ticket and leave her a decent tip.

"Thaddeus, the FBI sometimes comes across information from unexpected sources, and sometimes that information can be frightening."

"Go on. I'm listening."

"Well, we think we have a line on the whereabouts of your client's little boy. Our contacts in Bogotá, Colombia, federal agents themselves, have become aware of a horrendous situation outside of Bogotá at a place long known as the Monkey's Paw. It appears to be a compound owned by a human trafficker by the name of Cárdenas. Children are being held there en masse. The DEA's contacts at the facility believe the children have been smuggled out of the United States. They passed along to us some photographs, and your client's son matches one of the children being held there. This is totally unexpected, and I don't know what you're going to do with this information, as neither the DEA nor the FBI have any jurisdiction there and have no plans to intervene. On the one hand, I know this must be difficult to hear, but on the other hand, your client can celebrate that her son has been found alive. At least the FBI believes it is her son. That remains to be confirmed by any American agency, so take it for what it's worth."

He then passed a single photograph to Thaddeus.

Simon. Thaddeus's heart pounded in his chest. The problem had just narrowed itself to a point on the globe. Now for the solution—Thaddeus's domain.

Thaddeus sat back in the booth while the waitress delivered two coffees and a silver creamer. The men smiled at her, then Thaddeus said to McDowell, "But what does this Cárdenas guy have to do with CSID? What's the connection? Why would Catalina Systems Integration and Development, a systems developer for military use, send American children to a trafficker in South America? Why would that company go to the trouble? Money? Something else?"

McDowell slumped back on the bench seat and rubbed his hand down his face with a deep sigh. "That's the part we don't know. All we know is somehow your sister's son is in Colombia at a known human trafficking compound. Either that or a child that looks almost exactly like him. What are the odds?"

"No, this photograph is my nephew. I'd know him anywhere."

"All right. So now you have a 'where.' But the connection between CSID and Cardenas? We're working on that."

"All right. I have a feeling about this—"

"Maybe a family connection is the line between the two. Maybe something deeper."

Thaddeus considered for a moment and then said, "They steal system designs from other companies and then sell them as their own, right?"

"That's correct."

"So CSID is crooked as a hound's leg. If they're stealing classified engineering data, then kidnapping and theft of those secrets by threats to a loved one—they wouldn't hesitate." He stopped and shook his head. "From there, it's an easy leap to selling the loved ones. That's probably where Cardenas comes in. Is he a known human trafficker?"

"He is."

"And you're taking no action?" Thaddeus felt his anger rising in his chest, hot and mean, that the government has no plans about these kidnapped American citizens. It was totally wrong and unheard-of.

"Your FBI is only authorized to pursue the matter of the stolen property from Lockheed and determine where its secrets landed outside of our country. And, of course, the prosecution of your sister, Nancy. There are many others just like her in different parts of the country and different slices of the defense industry. Not to mention the cybersecurity attacks all this has triggered. As we speak, Russia owns the United States' cyber-world, thanks to stealing computer system data from U.S. engineers."

"I think I'm following. But I have a question, and it's a simple one. What would you do if you were in my shoes and it was your sister's son that had perhaps been identified near Bogotá, Colombia? How would you handle it?"

"Difficult to say. But one thing I know, I would have to follow up. I could not rest, I could not sleep, until I did everything I could do to identify that child and, if it were my sister's son, to exfiltrate him."

"I think you just pressed one of my buttons." Thaddeus took a sip of coffee. "My head is spinning. I see no way of getting into someplace in the remotes of Bogotá where children are being held as hostages and probably as shields against people like me who want in. What the hell do I do? How do I get inside there?"

"That we can't help you with. We don't even have an exact location for this compound called the Monkey's Paw. We've only heard of it through our contact. It could be anywhere in the jungles of Colombia. But if I had the means and funds, which I think you do, I'd go in there guns blazing and get the kid out. But you didn't hear that from me."

"This is beyond anything I ever imagined doing. But the bottom line is that this is my nephew, the son of my sister. I love her as much as anyone in this world. Long story short, I'll take you up on your offer. I'll go to Bogotá and make my plan for the Monkey's Paw and my nephew." It was an easy decision. There was no alternative for him.

Agent McDowell took a long sip of his coffee. He nodded and wiped a napkin across his mouth. "I knew it would come to this with you. I've heard a lot about you, Thaddeus, and I know that men like you don't just walk away." McDowell rose and offered his hand to Thaddeus. "I'll wish you the best of luck."

Thaddeus firmly gripped the agent's hand. He appreciated everything this man had done for him already. Even though he and his team would forge ahead to try to convict Nancy, Special Agent McDowell was definitely on Thaddeus's side for Simon. "I will bring this child home if it's the last thing I do. And thank you, Agent McDowell, this means the world to me, and I cannot express that enough. As far as my sister: you're in way over your head. I'm going to walk her out."

Pulling out of the parking lot of the Denny's, Thaddeus found his thoughts racing. *My God,* he thought, *can I really go through with this?* The answer came immediately, as it had just minutes before. He had no choice but to go through with it.

The only question remaining was how he would break this kind of news to Christine, the wife who expected him home every night by six.

She was not going to go along with this, and she would not approve, no matter how he approached it. So, the best thing would be to tell her his mind was made up.

The rest would be up to him.

Chapter 8

T haddeus, with lawyer-wife Christine, and Marcel, met in Thaddeus's office in La Jolla. The purpose of the discussion, he had told them in advance, was Marcel's infiltration into the Catalina corporation and the exfiltration of Simon from Colombia.

The first assignment for Marcel would be two-fold. Get proof that CSID was indeed the other half of the sales Nancy had been making and see if there was a connection between CSID and Cárdenas.

Thaddeus opened, saying, "When I spoke to Nancy earlier, she told me that Catalina Systems Integration and Development, CSID, is known to be a rising force in the avionics field. She has information from earlier contacts that Catalina was purchasing the Lockheed Martin radar systems package. There were eight men and one woman who made the purchases. Nancy thinks she can identify the woman if she ever sees her again.

"Marcel, your job is going to be to infiltrate CSID, make your way into the records of the CFO's office, and see what you can turn up in the way of financial transactions that prove CSID was purchasing information from outside sources. This won't be earmarked as such, but I trust your ability to read one thing and understand it might mean something else, which you excel at. It's my goal to file a massive lawsuit against CSID for the treason they coerced. It's a Civil Rights violation worthy of huge damages, and it's got RICO written all over its ugly face. It's my goal to wind up owning that company, and I will."

Marcel, sitting across from Thaddeus, lit a cigarette and cracked a window. He inhaled mightily and exhaled at the glass. For several moments, he thought about what Thaddeus had said before replying, "Can do. I will also obtain from personnel files the pictures of all women working security or any other related lines. I'm going to show those pictures to Nancy and see whether she can identify for me the woman who purchased from her. If we can get that done, and if I can turn her--make her work for us--then your lawsuit and Nancy's defense are going to go down one hell of a lot easier. You can trust me on this, boss. My head is already working on it."

"I know I can trust you, Marcel. As for the other matter--" Thaddeus hesitated. This was going to be the first mention of Simon and Colombia to Christine. He took a deep breath and continued, "I need you to find out if there's any connection between the Cárdenas' human trafficking cartel in Colombia and the trafficking of American children. The FBI has reason to believe that Simon has been handed over to Cárdenas for sale."

Christine gasped, but before either could interrupt him, Thaddeus said, "It's of utmost importance that we expedite that information to confirm that CSID sold Simon to Cárdenas. I'm ninety-nine percent sure that's what happened, but I need total confirmation." Thaddeus leaned forward in his chair. "And Marcel, I mean by any means necessary. We're totally limited on time."

Christine looked uncomfortable. Thaddeus studied her face. She was stolid, but he knew the lines at the corners of her mouth: she was angry as hell. Still, she kept her cool, and she was stony-faced when she asked, "Is the information about Simon solid? I mean, could the feds have gotten it wrong?"

Fair enough question. Christine was always on the ball. "Possibly, and that's why Marcel needs to get that confirmation. As soon as he does, I'm leaving for Bogotá to get my nephew back." He wanted to take Christine's hand, but her stance across the desk was screaming all sorts of walls at him right now. Thaddeus knew enough to keep it professional. For now. "Christine, your part in this will be to take over my law practice while I'm gone. It could be for a month, maybe two, however long it takes for us to find Simon. I really can't say. I could also use your stamp of approval in my doing this."

Christine, wearing her little black dress and black heels, turned to Marcel. "I wish to hell you wouldn't smoke in here. It's a dirty, disgusting habit, and I have to have my clothes cleaned every time I'm in a room with you. As for you, mister," she said, turning back to Thaddeus, "you're not going to get my stamp of approval for running off to South America. You're not a soldier, and I don't believe you're the one to be doing this. I would rather see you infiltrating CSID and see Marcel going to South America since he's worked before as an undercover agent. Tell me what's wrong with my thinking."

"I thought about this," Thaddeus said evenly. "And my only answer is this. If this whole thing goes wrong and something bad happens to Simon, it has to be on my shoulders. It can't be on Marcel's shoulders. That would be asking too much of my friend. Plus, I let Nancy down when we were kids. First, I couldn't save her from being abused, even though it was happening to me, too. Second, I couldn't do anything when we were separated into different foster homes. I won't let her down again."

"Horsefeathers," Christine spat out. "Brothers and sisters, or whatever else, you have my thoughts, and you have my disapproval." Christine then stood and stamped out of the office, leaving Thaddeus and Marcel alone to stare at each other.

"Well, boss, it wasn't the answer you were looking for, but at least it was an answer. Sometimes I pity the married man."

Thaddeus was unruffled. He had actually expected much worse. "Please hold the pity. She'll come around about the time I return to the States with Simon in tow. Sometimes a major victory is all it takes with her." Thaddeus smiled and shook his head. "Wow."

"All right, so I'm off to CSID. How do I get inside their four walls?"

"Hey, you're the infiltrator. That's for you to figure out. But in my magic crystal ball, I can see forged papers, a forged diploma from some accounting school, and a forged resume. How am I doing so far?"

Marcel nodded and flipped his cigarette out the open window. "Took the words right out of my mouth. I just wanted to know if it sounds as ridiculous to you as it does to me that a high school graduate can pose as an accounting nerd and get away with it surrounded by a bunch of financial analysts with their PhDs."

"Tell me if I'm wrong, but you've gotten away with much stranger fictions since we've known each other."

"True that. And I can do it this time, too. There's too much at stake here not to. I can promise you I'll do my best to pull this off, find the connection between CSID and Cárdenas and score some pictures to help Nancy identify the woman she dealt with that day during the exchange. I plan to get that woman's trust and get the names and identities of all of the other men, too. Never underestimate what an Englishman can do."

"Never. Never do I underestimate you, Marcel. All right, let's wrap this up so you can get started. I'm going to need to lay some serious tracks on Nancy's case before I leave. Lots of prep work and paperwork." Thaddeus smirked. "My favorite."

"I'll make some contacts yet this morning and hire some paperwork help. I'll let you know what I find out."

"Then we're done here. If you see my wife out in the hallway, please put in a good word for me. It's very likely she and I are no longer on speaking terms, and I can use your help."

"Haha, buddy, you're on your own with this one. I would never get between you and your superior. I'm not stupid."

"Superior? Ha! On the other hand--sheesh."

Chapter 9

P roblems between Thaddeus and Christine almost always escalated to a boiling point. There was no walking away and ignoring things with her. She refused to allow disagreements to bubble and do nothing about them. So when he got up the next morning and heard her downstairs, he knew this was going to be a tough cup of coffee he was about to pour for himself.

When he walked into the kitchen, she was at the microwave, and the smell of microwave bacon was filling the kitchen. He made as much noise as possible at the Keurig coffee maker, but she did not turn and acknowledge him or say good morning. His coffee was finished making in about sixty seconds. He then got his half-and-half and dosed the brew as he liked it. He went to the round table and sat down in one of the maple captain's chairs. He cleared his throat. She still did not acknowledge him.

Finally, he couldn't avoid saying, "Good morning to you, too. I understand you're quite upset with me. And that's for good reason. I would be very angry with you if you were about to run off to South America and put your life on the line. My days from start to finish would be nothing but worry and fear. I get that. But, Chris, I don't know what else to do because it's Nancy's little boy, and Jeff certainly isn't up to making the trip. While he's Simon's dad, he hasn't got what this is going to take."

Her head snapped around, and she fastened her eyes dead on his. "What's that mean, 'he hasn't got what it takes?' Are his arms broken? Is his head painted on? What exactly is his problem that he can't go to South America to retrieve his own son? He's a lawyer and every bit as smart as you, so I don't get why it has to be you, Thaddeus."

"I'm expecting there might well be the need to brandish firearms." It sounded like something a politician might say, but he didn't know how else to say and water it down at the same time, so he made it vague.

But she didn't buy it. "What the hell does that mean, 'brandish firearms?'"

Thaddeus sipped his coffee and considered his best answer. "There might come a need for me to display a gun to get Simon back. As you know, Jeff has zero experience with guns. Also, as you know, I do."

The Silver Star recipient from the Iraq War jumped all over that, saying, "Well, as you know, sir, I have more experience with guns than you will ever have. If that's the case, then it should be me going to South America and not you at all."

"I have to admit, your logic is right on. But there's one other consideration that controls the decision. And that's the fact that it's my sister's little boy, and therefore it falls to me to go to South America. Please understand, Chris, that I'm not doing this because I want to. It's the last thing I want to do. Quite frankly, Bogotá Colombia scares the living crap out of me because of all the drug lords and casual murders that go on down there. More than anything, my goal is to get home with Simon safe and sound. But on the other hand, I'm not going to hesitate to go in and use a gun if that's what it's going to take to get him out. Damon McDowell of the FBI told me that the next step for him is to be sold into child slavery. Well, that's not going to happen. If it takes everything I have, that's not going to happen."

Christine brought her bacon on a paper towel to the table and sat down and began nibbling. She pushed the towel toward Thaddeus so that he could join her if he wished. He ignored the proffer. "Child slavery?" she asked. "I didn't know about that."

"I'm sorry, I should've told you before."

"Well, child slavery is out of the question for anybody that you happen to find down there. What if there are other children in the same location as Simon? Have you thought about what you would do for them? Or would you just leave without trying to help them, too? And if that would be the case, and it might have to be, then what arrangements can you see yourself making for them? Did the FBI even go over this with you, this possibility?"

He had to admit the FBI had given him very little. The possibility had crossed his mind, but he had to some extent allowed it to remain ambiguous, telling himself that he would decide what to do about any other captive children when and if the problem presented itself to him. As it was, he didn't know what he would do if there were more than one or two children.

"You're going to need enough time on the ground with a helicopter to exfiltrate all of the children. I know you, and I know there's no way in hell you're going to leave even one of those kids behind. I guess that's the thing I'm furious about. The problem is about more than just Simon. What in the world are you going to do about stopping this company from continuing to do this with children over and over again? Have you even thought about that?"

"Maybe it's time I ask you to get involved," he said in all seriousness. "Let's think this through. What if you file a lawsuit against CSID while I'm gone, begin discovery, take depositions, and see how close you can get to their South American *finca* where the kids are being held. My guess is that you're going to find a thread there somewhere, maybe even in their financial records, and be able to trace that down. Tell me what you think about getting involved."

She shrugged and said, "I'm already in. I was just waiting for you to ask me. I'll have a lawsuit on file by Monday. While you're gone, I've got your back. The only missing piece is that you and I need to communicate while you're away. Not just because it scares the hell out of me that I can't talk to you, but also because we might need to compare notes on what we're doing in each of our own cases and see if any of it crosses over so that we can combine our efforts at that juncture. So, tell me, how do we communicate when you're in the middle of a jungle?"

He took another swallow of his coffee and reached and took half a strip of bacon. He began munching, thinking, wondering how in the world they could communicate when he was out in the middle of nowhere, Colombia. "You were in the military. Tell me what you know about SAT phones."

"I know that's the one way to keep our signal private for what we'll be doing. I think it's probably our best bet. I'll get Marcel going on that as soon as I get into the office this morning because he knows all about SAT phones."

Later that afternoon, Marcel and Christine entered Thaddeus's office, and Marcel produced a small box that he set on Thaddeus's desk "Open, please, you're going to like this."

Thaddeus opened the box and then looked up at Marcel. "What is this, a new wristwatch? I don't need a wristwatch. And it's kind of bulky. What's the deal?"

Marcel nodded and said, "It's a SAT phone. My friends at Interpol put me on to where I could score these. It can't be used indoors, but it can be used anywhere in the world independent of the restrictions a normal cell phone puts on a user. I think if you wear this one, and Christine got something of her own, you will have no problem communicating between South America and San Diego. Tell me you like it."

"I'm very impressed," said Thaddeus, removing his own watch from his wrist. He slipped on the new watchphone and admired it. "Like I said, it's pretty bulky, but it's better than anything else, isn't it?"

"Yes. Wear it in good health. Christine's also been filling me in on your upcoming adventure. I'm thinking it would be a good idea if you made room for me to go, too. I could have your back, and if it turned out there was a larger group of children to be exfiltrated, you would be quite glad you brought me along. What do you think, boss?"

"I like the idea. Maybe we can bring you in sometime after I get there and get settled."

Christine shook her head. "You need to take him with you now, Thaddeus. It's not going to get any easier down the road, and I would much prefer if you have Marcel with you from the get-go. He's got all the connections. Get a team together and get Simon the hell out of there."

"Roger that, Sergeant Murfee. And thanks for understanding."

They were in the air, aboard Thaddeus's private jet, four short days later. If there was any delay, it was only because Marcel had to quickly open and close the loop on CSID before leaving San Diego.

The hunt was on.

Chapter 10

Bogota, Colombia

The pilot called back to Thaddeus and Marcel over the intercom. "Gentlemen," he announced, "we have begun our descent into Bogotá, Colombia. We will be touching down in approximately twelve minutes."

Thaddeus folded his laptop and stowed it inside his backpack. Across from him, Marcel was yet asleep, mouth open, snoring softly. His leather jacket had flopped open so Thaddeus could make out the Sig Sauer handgun the investigator packed. Marcel had been awake for forty-eight hours before the flight while working undercover in San Diego at CSID. Many phone calls had been made from the plane in flight. Marcel was speaking with Interpol, while Thaddeus was busy making contacts and renting working space in Bogotá. Money, as he would say, doesn't talk, it swears. And his cash made things happen before they even arrived.

As for Marcel, he had gone straight for the jugular of

CSID, locating and confronting the head bookkeeper. A bribe had been offered, and photographs obtained. There was still more to come, but that was going to take time. Rather than wait, he had joined Thaddeus on the flight down. His efforts did not go in vain. Even though Nancy couldn't identify any of the pictures of the female employees that Marcel showed her, he was able to pay off the bookkeeper and track the funds from CSID to Franco Cárdenas—a new name, with a picture, associated with CSID as its contact in Colombia. And that was enough to get them airborne.

Thaddeus shut his eyes and drifted off.

Ten minutes later, he was jolted awake by the screech of airplane tires on asphalt. The Gulfstream jet bounced once violently then settled onto the runway, its engines thrusting in reverse, braking hard. The one stewardess on board swayed forward against her seat restraints while the co-pilot ignored the touchdown and taxi and made his way back to Thaddeus and Marcel to ask if they needed anything else before they deplaned. Thaddeus shook his head, thanked the man, and turned to Marcel.

"Any luck with Interpol?"

"Yes, I've had four talks with them on the way down. We're lining up a fairly good team. Have you had any luck putting together an assembly point for the crew?"

"I have a compound in the inner city, once used by the DEA during its cocaine interdiction raids here in the 1990s. Special Agent McDowell arranged it for us. Off the books, of course."

Marcel rolled his eyes. "Of course. But at least it will likely be a fortress and a damn good one."

"We'll spend the night at the Hotel Tequendama and then slip into the compound, but not before I scout out the

DEA digs. I don't want to go in blind. In the meantime, who's up first?"

Marcel had made a list on his cell phone. He glanced down and nodded. "Man by the name of John Blackletter who used to run Blackwater-Bogotá, making a million a year from the CIA. We worked together in Sarajevo until he took a bullet for a priest and got shipped back to the Bay Area. I talked to John, and he was a bit wishy-washy. He said he wanted to return to Oakland, Cali, for his wife and kids and wouldn't look back. I asked him to take one more for the team and told him we pay top dollar. He wants $25,000 a week, four weeks minimum. John is worth every dime."

"Sounds like a bargain to me. Let's grab him."

"I'm going to meet with him after check-in at the hotel."

"Right. Who else did we scrounge up?"

"Next up is a woman named of Elizabeth Janes. She's ex-DEA and a mapmaker extraordinaire with a degree in cartography from Stanford. Interpol has used her extensively, and they say she's so good she's even mapped the dark side of the moon."

"Who else?"

"A guy by the name of Lamont Wilkinson. This guy is Brooklyn born, hard-core joy killer who got kicked out of the DEA for taking scalps."

"So a bit of a ball-buster, eh?"

"No, I mean literally, he was scalping drug triggermen."

"Oh, God, that would make my wife so happy to hear," said Thaddeus. "All right, keep going."

"Pretty tough cookie by the name of Anna McKenzie. Anna is a college dropout who ran away from home when she was sixteen to join Isis. Of course, that didn't last, and she next surfaced working as a confidential informant for the DEA while in Afghanistan fighting the poppy wars. The DEA liked her enough to sign her up, and they moved her down here to Bogotá. She found there's more money to be made working freelance, and she's been on her own ever since. Interpol tells me she's the kind of woman you can dress up in glamour, send into a cocktail party, and she'll leave by the back door with the host's head in a paper bag without a spot of blood on her pretty white dress."

"Stone killer, then."

"Stone, yes. Interpol has a guy by the name of Muir Keystone. Keystone is a Brit on loan from MI6 who jumped ship in Bogotá. Now he's freelancing, too."

Thaddeus pursed his lips and turned to pick up his backpack. "What do we have in the way of air support?"

"Believe it or not, I found us a 70-year-old Vietnam chopper pilot who goes by the name of Huey. Anyway, Huey has a Huey, a Huey helicopter, I mean. He can help us get the hell out of the Monkey's Paw beaucoup fast if we're able to grab a kid or ten. He comes with a bird and a second bird with his son at the collective if we need it. Son's name is Matty, and they want ten grand a week—each— birds included."

Thaddeus nodded and slipped on his backpack. "I'd say ten grand a week is cheap at twice the price. I hope you signed on the dotted line."

"They'll be there tomorrow night. I just need an address."

"One-one-three Avenida de Leon. Right now, let's hit the hotel. I need to grab a couple of hours of sleep."

Marcel followed Thaddeus out of the private Gulfstream G550, the newest acquisition to the Murfee fleet. "And I need to pay a visit to John Blackletter."

Chapter 11

Whenever Marcel traveled to a new city, he followed the same routine when checking into his hotel. Before entering the room, he would don latex gloves, taking care not to touch the door handle with his bare hands. Once inside his room, he would place his bags in the bathtub and search the room for signs of surveillance: Webcams, phone wiretaps, vents leading to adjacent rooms. One could never be too careful—no matter where in the world he journeyed, someone was always trying to watch. It came with his job.

When he was satisfied that nobody was watching or listening, he would inspect the room for cleanliness, painstakingly combing over every inch. Starting in the bathroom, he would first check the drains, then the faucets and shower-heads. These were the areas that the maids were most likely to neglect and would tell him how meticulous they were in cleaning the room. After the bathroom, he would move to the sleeping area and look under the bed before peeling back the sheets and inspecting for bugs.

Finally, he would shake open the curtains and look closely for dust bunnies. If any part of the room did not pass muster, he would retrieve his bags, return to the front desk, and ask for another room to start the process all over again.

It was repetitious to the point of being neurotic, and he knew it sometimes cost him valuable time. But ever since he was a boy, he had been meticulous about staying clean. The filth and squalor of his childhood home had resulted in a type of OCD, and he had a hard time focusing when there was a mess. Although never diagnosed with the disorder, Marcel was aware of his neuroses and tried to work around them. He knew that a mess at the wrong time could cause him to lose his mental edge, and if it happened in bad company, it could have deadly consequences.

Marcel stepped out of the hotel lobby onto the busy downtown Bogotá sidewalk, moving quickly to blend into the crowd. He had left his luggage in the hotel room, but his check-in process had taken too long, and now he was running late. His pulse quickened as he stepped around slower walkers, threading his way along the busy sidewalk. After four blocks, he pulled open the heavy glass door and slipped into a noisy coffee shop. In a corner, he spied a familiar face and made a beeline for the table.

"Marcel!"

"John Blackletter! So sorry I'm late. Got checked into my hotel and got tied up with my usual nervous tics."

"Yes, I remember well. The man who doesn't sleep in hotels but instead spends the night with his ear to the door. A few wrinkles, a little gray around the temples, but we can work with that," he joked his old friend.

Marcel touched his hair. "Something like that. How long's it been now since Sarajevo?"

"Thirty years? I don't know, a lifetime. Anyway, it's really good to see you again."

Marcel took a seat at the table across from his old friend. "Good to see you again too, although I wish it were under different circumstances."

"So what's cooking this time?"

Marcel unbuttoned his jacket and looked around for the waitress. She saw him and nodded. Hopefully, she'd be over soon for his order. He could use a strong coffee, and there was nothing like Colombian coffee freshly roasted. He then turned back to his friend. "Different day, different people, same problems. Someone wants something someone else has and doesn't want to pay for it. It never ends, eh?"

The waitress arrived and took his order. Marcel's Spanish was rusty, but the longer he stayed here, the better it would get again. He ordered a café negro, and she returned shortly with a steaming mug. It smelled divine. "*Gracias, bella dama,*" he said with a smile.

He and John Blackletter had served together in Afghanistan in the early days of 9/11, working a security detail of General Abrams, and they had enjoyed the kinship that can be produced only by shared suffering as the world inside those Middle East borders was colorless, without laughter, ever, and a living hell for women. After their unit was sent home, Marcel began working private investigations, while John had moved into private security for corporate interests. They had kept in touch through secure email servers, often sharing secrets and motivational chain emails and dirty jokes. But it had been a long time since they had been eyeball to eyeball, and this was an unusual moment for them to be thrown back together.

"So I called the guys at Interpol, and they told me I might run into you here. Thanks for answering my email right away. So here's the deal. Interpol says I'm looking for a guy by the name of Franco Cárdenas. Ring a bell?"

John snorted. "A most unpopular gentleman around these parts. Rumor has it he's engaged in some large-scale child slavery. Last I heard, the bounty on his head was 500,000 U.S. dollars. Why, are you looking to make a quick 500K?"

"I'm looking to find the guy and find a child that I think he's taken away. This is strictly on the QT, but we're talking a four-year-old boy who was used to coerce his mother to give up Defense Department secrets in return for his safety."

"Why aren't the feds on this? Why you?"

"Ever since the Coke Wars, the Colombian government has made it very clear the CIA is no longer welcome down here, and the FBI has no jurisdiction across borders. The United States can't risk an international incident over a four-year-old boy. So here we are, instead, putting on a one-person show where there should've been at least a SEAL platoon. Whatever, we will eventually find him, and we will eventually get him the hell out of here. But in the meantime, I want to start with this Franco Cárdenas character. He has close ties to CSID, the company we believe was developing the secret Defense Department documents into war matériel of its own. My Intel makes him out to be maybe second or third in command at CSID. His last known location was Bogotá. I need him, and I need him bad. He's the link between CSID and the human trafficking. Can you help?"

"Heard that name—CSID." John slurped the last of his coffee and set down the empty mug. "More rumors are floating around about CSID than the Kardashians. It's the same old same old. Grow mushrooms in the dark, and sooner or later, everybody's gonna have a taste. Whatever

CSID has been up to, human trafficking, defense secrets, or whatever else, the news is on the streets, especially down here because of a certain location."

"What location would that be?"

"A place with a funny name. A place called the Monkey's Paw."

"Yep, that's what we heard from the feds—unofficially, of course. But they couldn't tell us anything else about it."

"That's all they got for you? A funny name? No coordinates, nothing?"

"Nope. No one knows where it is for sure, but my intel has it that's where CSID sends the little people, the kidnapped kids."

"And from there, they get trafficked into child slavery. Is that it?"

Marcel shrugged. "That's what we've come here to find out."

John Blackletter put his elbows on the table and leaned forward to speak in a hushed voice. "Jesus, what a sick bunch of rat turds. Glad I brought extra bullets for the pistola."

"I know," said Marcel. "The world would be a much nicer place without these two."

The waitress returned for their food order. Marcel wasn't hungry but asked for another coffee while John ordered a plate of *empanadas* and another coffee.

When she left, Marcel continued. "Here's the real deal, John. I'm working for an attorney now by the name of Thaddeus Murfee. Thaddeus has pretty much unlimited resources and is down here searching for his sister's kid, who we think is here. We're looking for a few hands to help us out. I told him about you, and he immediately told me to look you up and see if we could hire you away for a few weeks."

"How so, 'unlimited funds?'"

"In the early days, he sued the Chicago Mob and ended up owning one of its casinos in Vegas. Sold that at a huge profit and now is worth hundreds of millions. I'm guessing five- or six-hundred million by now. The kind of lawyer who doesn't take 'no' for an answer."

"Good on him, then. Impressive."

The waitress returned with another set of coffees and John's *empanadas*. Marcel hadn't been hungry after the long flight, but now his stomach rumbled. He leaned onto the table and clasped his hands in front of him. "So I'm asking —I'm begging, actually—that you'll give us a hand and run our troops for us while we exterminate this little problem down here. I know you're busy, I get that. But given the nature of this beast, I wonder if you might not have some free time coming and you could throw in with us for a while. Tell me I'm right about this, please."

John Blackletter set back from the table. He picked up his coffee spoon and began stirring the brackish brew almost absentmindedly. "Marcel, if it were anybody but you, I would dodge the bullet. But you and I go way back, and I know if the shoe were on the other foot and I needed you, you would set aside whatever you had going on and jump in with me. So I'm going to pay you that same respect. When do we start?"

Marcel took out his ink pen and scribbled an address on the back of their coffee tab. He slid it across the table to Blackletter and nodded. "If you could be at this address tomorrow night at seven o'clock, we begin then."

"Who else do we have?"

"A woman by the name of Elizabeth Janes, a mapmaker."

"Libby J, I know her well. She can get us in, and out of the darkest jungle they have down here. Who else?"

"Guy by the name of Lamont Wilkinson. It seems like he is a retired trigger man for the DEA who got too close to the fire."

"He's not a joke down here because what he did is no joking matter," said Blackletter. "He was scalping Colombian druggies. That's a no BS story. I'm glad he is working on our side."

"And then there's Anna Mackenzie. She's rumored to be everything that Wilkinson is, maybe even more. Comes from blue blood, but I can't hold that against her."

Blackletter shook his head. "The name doesn't ring a bell. I might recognize her when I see her. Who else?"

"Keystone. Muir Keystone. Keystone is a Brit who was on loan to the DEA from MI6. My information has it that he's still working out of the British Embassy here in Bogotá, still with MI6. I have yet to contact him." Marcel ticked the others off on his fingers. "I called Janes, and I've talked to Wilkinson, and I'm waiting for a call back from Mackenzie. So far, so good."

"What about air support? We don't do jungle warfare without helicopters, not down in this godforsaken jungle."

Marcel laughed. "I came across a guy named Huey who flies Huey's. He and his son have two Vietnam-era helicopters equipped with electric guns." John snorted, but before he could say anything, Marcel held up his hand. "I know, I'll believe it when I see it, but that's how Interpol gave it to me, and I trust those guys for the most part."

"I knew a Huey who was operating up around Rio, but I

think it got too hot for him up there. Last I heard, he was on his way back to Texas."

"Maybe so, but according to my intel, he's headed there by way of Bogotá, Colombia." Marcel leaned back from the table, his head cocked to one side. Blackletter waited, keeping eye contact, knowing there was more to come.

Marcel began speaking slowly again. "About this Franco Cárdenas guy… I'm going to have to find him. Any idea where he goes, where he drinks, where he eats?"

"There's a place called the Imperial Palace right downtown. I'm not sure of the street. A lot of these guys hang out down there where they trade trigger men around and do deals. If it were me, that's where I'd begin."

"Fair enough, then." Marcel stood up from the table and stretched. "You're the earner. You can buy. See you tomorrow night at seven."

"Haven't changed a bit. This time, you're good."

Chapter 12

Marcel wasted no time. How to find Cárdenas?
He rented a Range Rover and headed
downtown.

His mind raced while he eased the car out of the lot and
onto Avenida de General Jose Gutierrez, heading north
toward the heart of Bogotá. A plan was forming in his mind
as he merged onto the freeway. John Blackletter thought
Franco Cárdenas frequented the Imperial Restaurant on
Calle de Rosa across from the soccer stadium. Driving into
the area, Marcel's attention was drawn to a collection of
green tents, blue tarps, and silver shopping carts under
every bridge. He had read about the homeless problem in
Bogotá, but he was astonished by how many homeless
camps there were. After he passed what seemed like the
hundredth gaggle of tents, he came down off the freeway.
He pulled over beside a homeless encampment directly
across from the Imperial Restaurant and Hotel, and his
mind settled on a plan. He buttoned his jacket, hiding the

holstered pistol, and stepped out of the car on the side of the busy street. At the first tent closest to him stood a woman kicking dirt at a small propane stove in an attempt to snuff the fire within. He called to her in Spanish, "Hey, sweet lady, you doing okay over there?"

She stood up and eyed him. Then she replied in Spanish, "Sweet lady, your ass, Mister, and no, I ain't selling you a piece of me. I've already had my breakfast, thank you very much, and I don't need your goddamn money. So keep moving, keep your eyes straight ahead, and leave me the hell alone."

"Now that's what I like, a woman who talks sensibly and softly—definitely my type. I just saw this mess from the freeway, and my heart opened up. I just wanted to make sure that at least someone here had everything they needed. You say you're fixed?"

She shrugged. For the first time, she looked up and studied the man talking to her. "You the cops? I got no ID and no papers. Run me in if you think you have to, but the judge will just turn me loose in the morning after I've had a nice dry place to sleep and a decent breakfast." She held out her hands as if to receive handcuffs from a law enforcement officer.

He shook his head and gave a slight smile, "No, no, no, you don't understand. I really have stopped just to make sure you are okay and have everything you need. What about smokes? You fixed?"

She pursed her lips and nodded. "You got ciggies, I'm your gal. Can always use a smoke or two."

He walked back to his Range Rover, pulled open the door, reached inside his backpack, and returned to her with a pack of cigarettes. Emergency stash for just such an occasion. Then he remembered, went back to his bag, and came out with a bag of trail mix. He went to her and held out the cigarettes and the trail mix and indicated she should take them.

"A lot of people don't think about these things anymore, you know?" she said as she unwrapped the cellophane from the cigarette package. She stuck one of the white cylinders in her mouth and leaned toward Marcel, who produced a lighter from his jacket pocket and got her going. "I shit you not, Mister, every do-gooder in Bogotá wants to bring food to us, but it never occurs to any of them what we really need is a nice hot shower, two months of rent, enough food to get by, the haircut, clean clothes, and the Help Wanted pages from the Bogotá newspaper. You get my drift?"

"I do, I do get your drift. And maybe I've got something to offer you that might help that happen. Let me be blunt. I wanted to make sure you were okay when I saw you kicking the fire, but I had another motive, too."

She raised her eyebrows and pulled the cigarette away from her lips. "Listen, nice man, I don't know what you've heard about us down here, but you really don't want to get too close to anybody and put your you know what you know where. It might fall off a day later, and then you'd really be pissed and never come back with another pack of cigarettes." She giggled and took another drag off her cigarette.

"Oh, no." Marcel laughed. "Let me try again. I'm new here in town, and I need some help getting together some information."

She shook her head violently. "Nope, nope, we don't rat on each other either."

"We're standing across the street from the Imperial Restaurant."

"It might surprise you to know I'm following you so far," she said and took a deep drag.

"Well, good," he continued, "but let me tell you something true. The man I need to find is Franco Cárdenas. Crooked and dangerous—for all of us. I was homeless once a long time ago. And I know how quickly information can travel in the homeless community. I want to hire you to put out the word to your friends that I need information about Cárdenas, and I'm willing to pay good money for it."

She watched him then, suspicion written all over her face, as he reached into his pocket and pulled out five $100 bills. Her expression changed to one of shock as he handed one of the bills to her along with a business card with his cell phone number. "Help me spread the word until anyone who knows anything contacts me about Cárdenas. I need someone to text me the minute he shows up at the Imperial Restaurant. He likes to eat here."

"Sure, we've all seen him come and go. Much ado about nothing, you ask me." She spat on the ground.

He handed her another $100 bill, saying, "Let me make double sure you're on my side of the fence."

"Mister, you just bought yourself a set of eyes and ears. I got nothing else but time. If there is anyone within one mile of me who knows anything, you're going to know it, too. One problem. No phone."

Marcel handed her his cell phone. "Here's your phone. Text the number on my card. It's my other phone."

"How many cell phones you say you got?"

"Enough. Now, what's your name?"

"Miss Kitty."

"Tell you what, Miss Kitty, everything you tell me is another hundred bucks. There's plenty more where this came from, and you got a paying customer on your hands."

She tucked the bills away inside her blue work shirt. "You've got a friend. I'll text you myself."

"You'll be glad you did. I'll make sure you get that two month's rent, three hots, and a cot. How's that?"

"I'm on it."

Chapter 13

The text from Miss Kitty arrived the very next morning. *He's here, Cárdenas. Imperial Rest. Him and 4 men. Out.*

Marcel leaped into action, driving the Range Rover back downtown and parking in the tent city lot across from the Imperial Restaurant.

He backed up in the lot and parked between two tents facing the hotel across the street. He switched the ignition off and began waiting. Twenty minutes passed, and no Cárdenas. He studied the picture of the man he had pulled from the CSID files. He was an extraordinarily handsome person, long black hair down to his shoulders and a smile that would've made any woman swoon. But that was the end of any semblance of civility, for the man was a stone killer and would've sold his own mother for three pesos.

Ten minutes later yet, an entourage of four men and Cárdenas himself, wearing a Panama hat, came out onto the sidewalk in front of the Imperial Restaurant and paused.

Cárdenas rubbed his hands together, looked up and down the street, and then climbed into the back of the waiting limo. His men scattered for their cars and fell in behind him. They began pulling away, heading west on Rosa. Marcel waited for two cars to intervene and then pulled in behind them.

A block east, one of the cars, a black Impala, peeled off and headed south. On a hunch, Marcel decided to follow that one. They proceeded south for several blocks, then turned back east again and came back almost even with the tent city, which was now a good dozen blocks north. The man parked in front of an apartment complex, climbed out, hit his fob, and the brake lights flashed. Then he went inside a downstairs apartment beyond the stairwell. Marcel parked just outside the man's door and waited twenty minutes. Then he approached the door. He looked both ways, pulled the Sig Sauer .40 caliber from its holster, and kicked the door right beside the doorknob. It flew open, and he rushed inside.

The man, who was stretched out on his sofa, suddenly startled awake and reached for a gun. Marcel rushed to the man and put the muzzle of his gun against his forehead. "No no, señor."

The man saw his chance had passed and settled back onto the sofa. He asked in Spanish what Marcel wanted with him, and Marcel told him he was there to kill him. The man's eyes opened fearfully and his jaw dropped. "What for?" he asked.

"You are going to get one chance," Marcel said in Spanish. "You are going to tell me where Cárdenas hides the children. If you tell me, you live. If you don't tell me, you're going to die right here on this couch. Do you understand me?"

"I don't believe you," said the man. "You do not have the eyes of a killer."

Marcel placed the muzzle of the gun against the man's thigh and pulled the trigger in one sudden move. The gun erupted with a blast, and the bullet tore into the man's leg. The shock drew him upright on the couch in excruciating pain. He then flopped back down on the couch, cursing in Spanish and crying in pain.

"Now you tell me where Cárdenas hides the children. If you tell me, you live. If you refuse to tell me, the next bullet goes right into your head. Now do I have the eyes of a stone killer?"

The man cried out, "*¡La pata del mono! ¡La pata del mono!*"

They were on the right track. Marcel said out loud in English, "The Monkey's Paw."

"*¡Si, si!*"

"Now listen closely. You need to hear this. It's about values, how pragmatists make a value judgment, so you don't think I'm just making this up as I go. You're a human being, and that has value." He put the gun to the man's head and continued. "But our friend's nephew's a human being, too, and his life has more value."

The man was visibly sweating, his hands raised with palms out. "No, no, Señor," he kept repeating. The blood from his leg was seeping into the couch's cheap cloth material, staining it a dark wine red color.

"What is your name?" asked Marcel.

"Gordito Ibanez."

"All right, Gordito. This is what's going to happen. You're coming with me."

"Señor, my leg!"

Marcel motioned for the man to get up. "You'll live."

The man rose unsteadily onto his feet. Marcel grabbed

the man's arm and spun him toward the door. "You're going to walk out ahead of me to a black Range Rover just past the stairwell. You're going to get into the backseat where I'm going to handcuff both of your hands to the door. You with me so far?"

The man nodded. Beads of sweat rolled down the sides of his face. "Once you give us the information we need, we'll see to your leg. Okay, *amigo*?" Marcel smiled at him. "Now, get going. I'll have my gun in my pocket right behind you. *¡Vamonos!*"

The Monkey's Paw?

Now to make a way there.

Chapter 14

The old Bogotá DEA station was housed on Avenida de Leon in an old building that presented a steel door to the avenue. The door was graffitied with orange and yellow, and green pop art and fitted with a locking mechanism made accessible by a number pad.

Once inside, you passed into a large courtyard, a spraying fountain of four lions in the center, arranged haunch to haunch and facing the four points of the compass. Each lion seemed happy enough with having an endless spray of water issuing from its open mouth then dropping into the large pool below. Koi fish finned themselves lazily, fed by the caretakers at 9 a.m., which always created a show of burbling waters and some thrashing about on the surface as the food was devoured.

Arranged along the courtyard's perimeter were various station offices and a large conference room that also contained a wet bar that Thaddeus had filled for his guests, everything from the best Colombian coffee to iced tea to cold beers to U.S. bourbon and imported Scotch. He'd heard his vigilantes liked their drink, and if Thaddeus was going to ask them to put their lives on the line for his nephew, he was going to make sure they were comfortable doing it.

Thaddeus had a coffee in front of him at the conference table, and Marcel a Scotch neat. It was a 16-year-old Lagavulin, the smoky peat smell reaching Thaddeus's nose. Just before 7 p.m., the others started arriving. First was Muir Keystone. Punctual as any Englishman, Muir was the Brit on loan from MI6. Marcel introduced Muir to Thaddeus, who then offered for him to help himself to the bar where he grabbed a cold Aguila beer. He was a slight man with an aquiline nose and a briar pipe protruding from clenched teeth, a curl of smoke following along.

The next to arrive was Anna MacKenzie and, boy, was she a looker. Tall, leggy, with long dark hair and eyes. Thaddeus could see her dark skin tone and coloring would help her to blend here in Bogotá—if she so chose. But she was dressed to the nines in blue tailored pants and a white sleeveless blouse. Marcel was the first to react and stood to introduce himself and then Thaddeus. She grabbed a bottled vodka tonic and glass full of ice and sat to Marcel's left.

Next in was John Blackletter, followed closely by Elizabeth Janes. Elizabeth walked right up to Marcel and then Thaddeus and gave each a hearty handshake. She was used to the corporate world and had confidence in spades. She wore loose linen pants and a gypsy shirt with sandals. Her dishwater blond hair was kept in a bob to her chin. She chose to sit on the other side of Anna.

The helicopter pilot strolled in just after Anna. An older gentleman with white hair, his skin was weathered and dark brown. He had piercing blue eyes and a slight hunch to his posture, most likely all the hours sitting in the chopper.

The last to arrive, and ten minutes late, was Lamont Wilkinson. He looked like a combination of high school jock/mediocre golfer. He wore a Chicago Cubs baseball hat, cargo shorts, new Nike gym shoes, and a striped polo shirt, and in Bogotá, Colombia stuck out like a sore thumb. After grabbing a beer, he took a seat on the far side of the table by Keystone and Blackletter and removed the bottle cap using the edge of the table and his fist. Class.

Before he started the meeting, Thaddeus took a moment to refill his coffee and look at the group now all seated at the table. If Interpol and Marcel said this motley crew was the best of the best, Thaddeus would believe it.

Once everyone was seated and sipping, Thaddeus told the group, "I want the Monkey's Paw."

Muir Keystone raised a hand. "Heard of it. White gold."

"White gold?" asked Thaddeus. "Does that mean what I think it means?"

"Human trafficking."

John Blackletter stepped in. "How bad do you need this, Thaddeus?"

"Real bad. My nephew is there."

Marcel broke in, "We've 'acquired' a local who has information on the whereabouts of the compound, but we have yet to interrogate him."

Thaddeus told them, "We have him housed here in a spare room at the back. He's under lock and key and hand-cuffed to a bed-frame."

"Where did you get him?" asked Wilkinson.

"Not necessary information," said Marcel. "All you need to know is that he's one of Cárdenas' boys."

Wilkinson grunted. Thaddeus ignored him and instructed, "While the rest of the group goes over the logistics of the raid, Keystone, you and Janes go talk to the prisoner. See what he knows."

Marcel led Keystone and Janes straight to the back of the building and right down a hallway to the farthest southeast corner. They passed a men's and women's bathroom, and another door marked *cuarto de lavado*, laundry room. On the opposite wall, Marcel unlocked a door and handed the keys to Libby Janes. "Lock it back up when you're done."

And with that, he was gone.

"You ready?" she asked Keystone.

He removed his pipe with a nod, and they entered. The Colombian man, Gordito Ibanez, lay on the bed, his eyes closed and his hands clasped on his chest. His pants' right leg had been cut off at the thigh that was now wrapped from hip to knee in medical gauze.

Keystone walked over to the man and tapped him on the forehead with his pipe. "Wake up," he demanded in Spanish.

"I wasn't asleep."

"Good," said Janes. "We have some questions for you." She nodded at Keystone. "You can translate, right?"

Ibanez closed his eyes again and rolled his head toward the wall. At that, Keystone again knocked him on the forehead with his pipe.

"*Ay!*" he said and threw a nasty look at the Brit.

Janes was done with the games and began, "You told my colleague you know a place in the jungle. A place of a monkey."

In perfect South American Spanish, Keystone translated to Ibanez.

The man sighed as if resigned to his fate. "*La pata del mono*. It was a real monkey once. Now it's turned to stone."

"What's there?" asked Janes, and Keystone again translated.

"Oro blanca. Mucho oro blanca. I can show you if you get me out. There's little children there, too. Little children, I don't know why."

"White gold," he's saying, said Keystone. "Children."

Janes produced a book of maps. "Show me in here. What's the nearest town?"

Keystone asked him in Spanish, and he responded immediately with, "Ciudad de Jonas."

"Coming right up," said Janes as she turned pages. "How about here?" She opened the book and turned it upside down so he could study it. She waited as his dirty forefinger traced down the map.

"This jungle. Right here. The tip of the bull's horn."

"Where the river turns at the bull's horn?" Keystone asked.

"*Sí*. Is right there."

Keystone relayed the information to Janes, who then asked, "How far inside the jungle are we talking? Five feet? A kilometer? What?"

"Five feet."

"No, that was an example," Keystone said. "What, really?"

"No, it's just five feet. One second you're outside in the coca field, and you don't see nothing, next second you take two steps in jungle and it's right there."

Keystone tapped his chin. "So dense, you're saying. It can't be seen until you're right up on it."

"Si, si. Dense. Like *raíz de coca*."

Janes circled the spot on the map with a black pencil. "So, this place is known as the Monkey's Paw?"

After Keystone translated, Ibanez said, "This monkey is huge. It's a god to someone."

"A long time ago," Keystone noted.

"Si, si. But not my god." He was smiling now. "*Adoro el dinero, siento decirlo.*"

"He worships money?" Janes asked. She knew a little Spanish, enough to live in Bogotá, but not Keystone's expertise, and she didn't want to lose any specific information in translation. Thus, giving the Brit the reins on the interrogation.

"He is sorry to say he worships money. Not monkeys."

Janes nodded. "Tell him thanks."

"Gracias, señor," said Keystone. "We're leaving now."

Keystone opened the door for Janes, who passed through and waited for the Brit to exit. Then she locked the door and started back the way they'd come.

Janes told Keystone she thought the roads and trails would allow them to sneak up on the compound. "Take Rovers through the jungle. We can do a stealth infiltration and see what we have. I can find a way in on these maps. Assuming the roads haven't washed out and assuming we don't get kidnapped as we mosey on in."

"Assuming these things, I'm opting for the Hueys. We swoop in from the sky."

"Well, we'll need choppers in case there are kids. We can exfiltrate them the hell out of there."

"You're saying we go in on four wheels and call in the Hueys if the kids are found? Makes perfect sense."

"Otherwise, we'd be dropping in and maybe find ourselves outgunned. No, we'll do this on the backroads."

"Janes, it's all backroads."

"Well, you've got me there."

Chapter 15

Once they were all seated back in the conference room after a short break, Thaddeus stopped the chatter. It was time to firm up the infiltration of the Monkey's Paw.

Janes went first. "This prisoner, Gordito, has given me the exact location, a bigger operation than any he's ever seen." She spread a map open on the table. She turned it upside down toward Thaddeus so he could read it. She waited as he took it in. "Not only cocaine but trafficking. This man Cárdenas is operating big."

"Where are we talking? None of this looks familiar to anyone, I'm sure."

She answered, guiding his finger to the spot. "This jungle. Right here. The tip of the bull's horn."

"Where the river turns at the bull's horn? From my research, I've never heard of flat enough fields to grow in this area."

"I've got pictures." She pulled out a laptop from an oversize handbag and powered it up. "I took the liberty of going online for some schematics to prove or disprove Gordito. These are old DEA maps, but the elevations are accurate within twelve inches."

"How many days to this place by Range Rover?" Marcel asked.

"Two or three days, depending on flooding. It's springtime."

"How many boots on the ground?" Blackletter asked Thaddeus.

"The seven of us, plus I was thinking of hiring two truckloads of soldiers. Cárdenas' compound will likely be well-defended if it is what we think it is. We have the Hueys on call."

For the first time, Anna Mackenzie spoke up. "I just don't get why we haven't heard about this before. I mean, everyone knows Cárdenas, but children stashed in the middle of the jungle for trafficking? It sounds like a bad movie."

"We're just going on our intel," said Marcel. "We have to try. Thaddeus's nephew could be there, and that is more than enough reason for us. For each of you? That's your consideration."

"So this Cárdenas dude is somehow acquiring children to traffic around the world?" asked Wilkinson.

"Yes. But there could very well be other men working for him worldwide in the buying and selling of children. But if we shut down Cárdenas, he's the core, the key to it all. Then we save the kids." Thaddeus paused. "Especially my nephew, Simon."

There was quiet at the table, but Thaddeus didn't push it, didn't rush their thoughts. Even though the money was good, their lives were on the line, and there was no price tag on that. So to give his team a few minutes was nothing to

Thaddeus.

Finally, he said, "So...Operation Monkey's Paw. You all now have the information. Certainly, it's a risk to each of you, but you will be paid well, as you've already discussed with Marcel. Now I want to know for sure, who's in?"

Blackletter was the first to raise his hand.

Janes replied, "I'm in."

When Thaddeus looked at Keystone, he nodded.

Wilkinson rubbed a hand back through his hair. "I say it's a go."

"Anna?" Marcel asked.

The room was silent except for the clacking of her painted red nails on the table. She sighed audibly and then said, "Okay. I'll do it for the kids."

Thaddeus nodded slowly. "Thank you." The next he directed at Marcel. "I've spoken to this Gordito myself just now. If it turns out to be hot, we owe him medical expenses. Anything he needs for his leg, for his family. Anything. But explain to him we need silence."

"You mean threaten his kids."

Thaddeus smiled. "Whatever it takes to buy his silence, you do it."

"When are we leaving, boss?" Marcel asked.

"Day after tomorrow, first thing at dawn. That will give us time to stock and load. We'll be on the road for two days. Blackletter has the list of food and medical supplies. Wilkinson is going to arrange the Rovers and transport. MacKenzie will contact Huey and the Hueys and plans for extraction. Janes will be working her maps, and Keystone will research the territory and pinpoint any impediments we might have to work around regarding roads and flooding. Marcel and I will work on the soldiers for hire and all other incidentals. Pack lightly, only a backpack each, bring your favorite weaponry, and come prepared in jungle fatigues."

Thaddeus looked around the room at his Operation Monkey's Paw team. This was his hope right here. When there were no questions, he nodded. "We'll leave from here." Then he dismissed them.

Chapter 16

They took Highway 50 to Facatativa, then turned south. In the lead vehicle, Wilkinson drove until one p.m., then Thaddeus took over. Mackenzie rode with them. Marcel drove the second Range Rover, only handing off to Blackletter when they made it to Viani in the early afternoon. Janes and the Brit Keystone rode with them.

From Viani, they headed due west into the jungle to Libano. They made Chorro after nightfall, around nine p.m.. It had been sixteen hours without stopping except for two bathroom breaks and to swap drivers. Janes told the others the road conditions were the best she had ever seen, which said a lot because it had been a long and bumpy ride so far.

They made camp just off the road after the mercenaries hacked away a clearing for two Rovers and two ex-Army trucks. They ended up blocking the small road, but they'd only passed one other vehicle since the Libano turnoff. There would unlikely be any travelers overnight.

The next morning, they would be headed into the jungle on tertiary roads, some that would be covered with spring torrents and require detours. The travel would be much slower.

That night, Thaddeus pulled out his *CIA Rainforest Factbook* for they'd entered into that part of the jungle.

The region is home to about 2.5 million insect species, tens of thousands of plants, and some 2,000 birds and mammals. To date, at least 40,000 plant species, 2,200 fishes, 1,294 birds, 427 mammals, 428 amphibians, and 378 reptiles had been scientifically classified in the region. One in five of all bird species are found in the Amazon rainforest, and one in five of the fish species live in Amazonian rivers and streams. The biodiversity of plant species is the highest on Earth with one 2001 study finding a quarter square kilometer (62 acres) of rainforest supports more than 1,100 tree species. The rainforest contains several species that can pose a hazard. Among the largest predatory creatures are the black caiman, jaguar, cougar, and anaconda. In the river, electric eels can produce an electric shock that can stun or kill, while piranha are known to bite and injure humans. Various species of poison dart frogs secrete lipophilic alkaloid toxins through their flesh. There are also numerous parasites and disease vectors. Vampire bats dwell in the rainforest and can spread the rabies virus. Malaria, yellow fever, and dengue fever can also be contracted in the Amazon region.

He discussed the CIA book with mapmaker Janes before he retired to his tent. There he scoured the floor of the tent for scorpions and made doubly sure it was zipped up tight against the creepies and crawlies just outside. The paid soldiers built a sizable fire and kept that going all night, giving up a sense of some security to the campers. One of them pulled out a guitar, and the night was soothed over with the spellbinding riffs and chords of South American love songs. It took all that Thaddeus had to shut them out.

They were up and on the road at daybreak the next day, Wilkinson driving the lead vehicle again, but Keystone driving second, the army's deuce-and-a-half third, and the same vehicle fourth. The dawn was uneventful, though full of jungle sounds and the cries and moans of jungle cats, monkeys, and foraging wild pigs. Breakfast consisted of cold oatmeal with powdered milk and sugar, concocted as they rolled along.

Wilkinson was strangely quiet behind the wheel, so Thaddeus chatted with MacKenzie. Surprisingly, she wasn't shy and told him much of her childhood and how she ended up joining Isis. Her story was fascinating and one ready for a bestseller if she ever chose to put it down in words.

The sky suddenly broke wide open with pouring rain. Thunderclaps and lightning strikes nearby, then the sky shrouded over, and the travelers knew they were in a for a full day of jungle downpour. It was a slow, steady rain that neither sped nor slowed in its incessant deluge. A half-hour into it, they encountered water flowing across the dirt road and mud forming up over the tire treads.

At ten in the morning, they came to a wide spot in the road where a stream had jumped its boundaries. Through slagging windshield wipers, Thaddeus could see a stream that was deep enough to swallow a Range Rover, though the cars with their sealed engines and undercarriages were known for their ability to traverse such obstacles. Wilkinson pulled to the side and spoke by walkie-talkie to the other drivers. After a minute of back-and-forth, it was decided the army deuce-and-a-halves would proceed across the water first. The Rovers hugged the side of the road, allowing the army diesels to roll past and enter the stream.

The trucks provided a gauge of the stream's depth, which was beginning to resemble a river more than a stream. The water was over the trucks' wheels, almost reaching the tops of their wheel wells. Still, the truck drivers managed to make it across, accompanied by the cheers and catcalls of the soldiers inside, who were relieved they weren't going to be called on to unload and push the trucks out of the cold rushing waters.

Then it was Wilkinson's turn to take the lead Range Rover across. He slowly drove in lowest low gear up to the swirling outer waters and boldly raced on into the stream. The vehicle reached the midway point with the water topping the wheel wells, but Wilkinson refused to take his foot from the accelerator and kept pushing the vehicle even when it threatened to stall. Then they were climbing out on the other side, again to cheers and catcalls of the soldiers just ahead who watched all this from inside their canvas-shrouded caves.

Now it was Keystone's turn, driving the second Range Rover. Thaddeus could immediately tell that his driving was timid compared to Wilkinson's and that the upstream side of his vehicle was lifting and buffeted by the rushing waters. There was no doubt that he was losing traction on the upstream side as the oncoming water got purchase on the undercarriage of his Rover, threatening to wash it away downstream.

Wilkinson jumped from the lead vehicle and started waving with his jungle hat at the slow-moving Keystone vehicle. "Hit it!" he cried. "Hit it!" He implored Keystone to get heavy-footed with the gas. But Keystone's eyes were riveted to the swirling waters, and he slowed instead of speeding up. Now his vehicle was listing in the water in the downstream direction, and the others inside were crying out for help.

Then it happened—the engine died.

The vehicle sank slowly down into the mud at the bottom of the raging waters and settled there. The passengers were trapped inside. Elizabeth Janes could be seen trying to push open the passenger's door to get out, but the door wouldn't open on the downstream side, and her efforts failed. Wilkinson cupped his hands and called to Keystone, "You're going to have to wade your cable over." Meaning the cable from the winch on the front chassis of the Range Rover. Wilkinson meant to attach the cable to a solid point, maybe a truck bumper, and allow the Range Rover's winch to pull the vehicle out of the water for itself.

Keystone, never one to be overcome by circumstance, threw open his downstream door and bolted out the door—only to be swept off his feet. Luckily for him, he still had a hand on the door frame and managed to pull himself back to the vehicle and regain his footing. Holding the door frame, then the left front wheel well, he made his way around to the front bumper and disengaged the hook and cable from the winch. He looped it up over his shoulder and set out across the bludgeoning stream, keeping a death grip on the cable itself because, should he lose his footing again, the cable would act as his lifeline. He trudged from waist-deep to knee-deep, the cable unspooling behind him, then it was ankle-deep and he was shaking his head in relief. "Bollocks," he said when he stepped up onto the shore and kicked the mud off his feet.

Wilkinson clapped slowly for Keystone before reaching for the cable. He took it from Keystone and ran it over to the rear bumper of the closest diesel truck. By now,

Keystone was retracing his steps back to the stranded Range Rover. He swept around the door and hoisted himself back inside, ready to operate the winch. He took the controls, dropped the vehicle into low, and tromped the accelerator. The winch ground slowly around, pulling the vehicle from the front end as the four-wheel-drive caught and the vehicle sluggishly moved through the water, a giant metal fish that'd been caught and was giving up and allowing itself to be landed after all.

The SUV made the shore and roared across the mud shoreline as Keystone came off the accelerator and applied the brakes with a tap. Slowing to a sideways slip, the vehicle shuddered to a stop, and doors flew open. Keystone and Marcel stepped out first, followed by Blackletter, looking distressed, and then Anna Mackenzie, who was especially pale. Blackletter dropped to his knees and kissed the earth while the others around him smiled. "There's no shame in avoiding a certain death," Wilkinson said unexpectedly, the closet poet coming out at just the right moment.

Water bottles were opened and passed around. Then someone announced they had hot coffee in their thermos. Sandwiches were produced from someone's cooler, and those were inhaled as everyone flooded with relief at the crossing they'd just made. The soldiers passed out rations for additional sustenance.

When Thaddeus wondered aloud what new adventures awaited them as they continued, the others groaned. Marcel clapped him on the back and said, "I'm riding with you this time."

They loaded back into the vehicles, feeling blessed and happy as the lead vehicle, Thaddeus now driving, dropped into drive and circled around the diesel trucks to continue the convoy.

More streams were forded, and more thrills and excitement as the vehicles slipped and slid through the waters, momentarily stalling but pulling through again as only Range Rovers can do under such trying conditions. By late afternoon, they were so deep into the triple canopy jungle that it was dark, and headlights were switched on, even though above the uppermost branches and leaves, the sun still shone brightly. Anna, who now rode with Thaddeus and Marcel, remarked their convoy looked like a yellow caterpillar crawling through a garden.

At four-thirty, they paused and conferenced on the hood of Thaddeus's vehicle. The engine beneath the warm metal popped and snapped as it cooled after the uphill battle through the waters and mud and dense undergrowth along the plant-filled trail. They were now all but blazing along the overgrown road toward their target.

"My GPS tells me we're about here," said Janes, pointing to a spot on her map. Everyone clustered around and looked closer. Thaddeus snapped on a flashlight, and the entire trail surfaced through the dim light like a spider web swimming up through the gloom. "I'm going to guess we're about ten, maybe fifteen, miles from where we want to be."

"Still enough time today to start looking for the Monkey's Paw," said Thaddeus as he nodded in support of the position.

"We're definitely going to touch the Paw today," Marcel exclaimed in agreement. "Janes, why don't you come up front with me. Thaddeus, you climb into Keystone's Rover and keep him company. I don't want to miss our stopping point."

"Makes sense to me," Thaddeus said without hesitation. He was pierced that he would no longer be riding lead car, but he knew that Marcel, Blackletter, Janes, and Wilkinson were better trained and more qualified for the position. There, in the failed jungle light, amid the swarm of black gnats and sounds of water running someplace close by, he was stabbed by pangs of guilt as he remembered the home he left and his loved ones who worried for him. He knew they were wondering whether he was all right and whether he'd forgotten them, for it'd been over 24 hours since he'd managed to communicate even to say hello. He glanced at his satellite watch and considered calling Christine now, but they were pushing to get to the Paw. He shook his head, trying to clear the cobwebs.

It was time to get his head in the game.

Thirty minutes later, they stopped for the night. It had gotten too dark to see inside the thick jungle, and no one wanted to expose the troops before they were ready by over-running the target in the dark.

Camp was made, food was cooked, and early to bed for everyone.

Chapter 17

The next morning's trip lapsed into early afternoon when the lead vehicle suddenly flashed its taillights in a full stop. The agents gathered at Marcel's vehicle, where he'd already lit a smoke. He inhaled deeply and blew the smoke to the side.

"All right," said Marcel, spreading Janes' map, "the lady said we've arrived. Somewhere in this area is our Monkey's Paw. Let's pitch camp, form some search parties, and get busy finding the mother lode."

"Gordito mentioned a nearby coca field," said Thaddeus. "Do we know, is there one near?"

Janes shook her head. "Unknown. The frigging jungle is so dense there could be a field ten feet off the road, and we wouldn't know it."

"It is that," said Keystone, packing his pipe and patting his pockets for a lighter. "I say we go in groups of two. Two quick shots mean come running. The walkie-talkies, I don't think so. If there are coca fields nearby, the *narcotraficantes* will be monitoring those frequencies."

"For that reason, I say we keep the sidearms holstered, too," Anna said. She was checking her Glock's magazine as she said this. Since she was famous for being the first to draw and shoot, the others were surprised to hear her mention anything about staying holstered.

Thaddeus wrote it off to the fact they would be hugely outnumbered if a full-scale firefight broke out with the dozens of armed men and hand grenades and war materiel pressed into service by the cartels. He thought it wise what she was suggesting. "We key the mikes instead. We click at each other."

"Agree," Marcel said, "no gunshots. Why don't we meet back here in two hours and discuss then? We can update that way."

"I like that best," Wilkinson said. While he was ordinarily one of the first to display bravado, at that point, he was smart in not wanting to start World War Three in the jungle.

Marcel suggested, "Thaddeus, you go with Anna. Keystone, you take Janes. Wilkinson can come with me, and Blackletter can hang back and be in charge of the soldiers. All right, then?"

"What about the army?" asked Blackletter. "How do you want them?"

"Have them set up a tight perimeter. We don't know what's out there, and I don't want them wandering around shooting at us or each other. So, they'll stay put," Marcel said. The others nodded in agreement.

"Compass directions?" asked Keystone.

"All right," Marcel continued, "Wilkinson and I will take north-northeast. Thaddeus, you're north-northwest. Keys is south-southwest. That leaves a missing quadrant that we can hit later if need be. Take plenty of water, and everyone take a snakebite kit. Ready, then? Let's get after it, ladies and gentlemen. Daylight's a-burning." He said this last part in his best John Wayne impression.

Thaddeus and Anna exchanged a look and set out for their assigned quadrant. They decided to space themselves no more than ten yards apart. They'd have a hard time seeing each other even at that short distance since the growth was so dense and the light so dim inside the jungle gloom.

Thaddeus was thinking about nothing except branches and vines as he began hacking into the wild. His machete was immediately caught up in wiry bush and thick branches. It was going to be very slow going. Still, the notion of stumbling onto the Monkey's Paw drew him on, a magnet in its own right.

Thirty minutes later, Thaddeus and Anna were no more than thirty yards into the jungle. It was excruciatingly slow. Their hands and forearms were cut and oozing where they'd encountered sawtooth brush and thorny branches. They were parched and had already taken long pulls at their water jugs. Their clothes were sweat-stained through, and the sweat was running in streamlets into their eyes and mouths. There was no longer anything anywhere near exciting about the task at hand.

They paused for a break.

"Are you there?" he shouted.

"I'm here and ready for a rest," Anna yelled.

"Same here. Don't sit down; there are fire ants everywhere."

"Not to mention the snakes I've seen. Are you seeing lots of snakes?" she called.

"Just a few. I have no idea what they are, so I'm giving them a wide berth."

"You and me both," she called back to him. "And my hands are killing me. Blisters on blisters, even through my gloves."

"Yeah, I know," he said and pulled off his right glove to examine his palm. So far, so good there. Just a small water blister that'd soon pop.

They decided to cut their way in for another thirty minutes then return to the camp. It was beginning to cloud up for the afternoon downpour, and neither explorer was particularly fond of the idea of being caught out in that.

They cut and chopped and made their way another twenty yards before calling time and turning around. Now they walked single file back along the path. She was in the lead, Thaddeus behind her, when suddenly she stopped, holding up a hand for him to freeze. Sure enough, an anaconda snake large enough to swallow a barrel was making its way across their path. Its long, shiny body glistened in the grass against the dull background. It was simply ignoring them and taking its time, so they waited. Then, when the tail had disappeared into the tangle, they began moving again, albeit just a step or two more cautiously now. It was the first known man-killer they'd seen that day, and they weren't anxious to see whatever else was going to show up in second place.

The path back out was almost effortless, so they reached the camp in ten minutes and headed for the ice chests and cold drinks. Anna found a beer; Thaddeus found an iced tea in a can. They opened their drinks and sat out in the chairs provided by the soldiers. Tents were pitched as well, and a barbecue pit had been dug in hopes a wild pig wandered in. Blackletter had been busy with the soldiers, making a more permanent encampment, but Thaddeus doubted Marcel would allow much of a fire given they were so close to the

Paw and the coca fields. There was the possibility they were within shouting distance of a cocaine production facility and didn't know it. Caution was of the essence.

Soon, the others came straggling in. Wilkinson and Marcel arrived first. Said Wilkinson to Thaddeus and Anna, "I see you two had the same idea. Time for a break."

"Any luck?" Thaddeus asked Marcel.

"No, but Wilkinson had an idea. He wondered whether we might order the Huey to do a flyover and try to help us understand where we are. The problem with that is, if we actually are in the area of the Monkey's Paw, the Huey might discover it first. We can't have that, so my inclination is to nix the idea. Thaddeus?"

"Agree. Too risky. We don't want them to know we are here. The Huey would give them a heads-up."

"All right, then. We'll just cool our jets on that, Wilkinson."

"Whatever," he said. "For now, I just want to sit down and have a cold bottle of water. I don't much care who flies over or who doesn't. It was just a thought."

Keystone and Elizabeth Janes walked slowly into the camp. She looked bedraggled and heat frazzled. He didn't look much better. The others could tell the latest arrivals would prefer to call it a day. Thaddeus recognized the exhaustion and decided they'd done enough that first day themselves.

"I think I'll send out about six soldiers to continue cutting a path," he said and asked Blackletter to round up some reliable troops to do this bidding. Soon, the six soldiers were seen leaving the camp with machetes and water bottles. They wore bandannas of army camo tied around their heads, ready to catch the sweat. Just that fast, they disappeared into the dense overgrowth and were gone.

"I told them we're looking for anything unusual," Black-letter told the others. "No need to go into much detail with them. It also silenced them."

Food was retrieved from the cooler and passed around. The selection included either canned ham or canned ham spread on dry bread. But no one rejected the largesse, as stomachs were growling from the day's exertion.

Tents were soon furnished with backpacks and water bottles, and rain flies were in place when the heavens opened up and the afternoon deluge set in. When it came, everyone retreated to their tents and card decks. They shrugged out of wet clothing, changing into shorts and tees in the humid air. Thaddeus pegged the temperature and humidity at about 90 to 100 degrees. Inside Thaddeus's tent, Janes brought out maps and searched for landmarks with a square magnifying glass. As usual, she was all business with her maps and compass and protractor. Thaddeus was quite relieved she was along. At least someone had a clue where they were. Personally, Thaddeus had taken a liking to Janes. It was clear she would have anyone's back.

After a long nap, it was time for a supper of grilled steak —Marcel did allow an in-ground fire—and baked potatoes wrapped in foil. It was early to bed for the exhausted explorers as soon as even the dim jungle light failed. Tomorrow would be around fast; sleep was at a premium.

Then the camp lights flickered out, and soon there were snores and the sounds of hands slapping mosquitoes as a billion crickets drowned out all else.

Chapter 18

The second day onsite dawned with a brief, early rain shower that had the campers stuck inside their tents looking out, waiting for the sky to clear. It was a common enough occurrence, the early-dawn showers, so no one was put off since it would soon pass, and they could resume the hunt.

The soldiers who had gone out yesterday found nothing unusual, so Marcel decided on the same teams and tactics today.

The rain slowed to a mist. The campers drifted one by one to a small group collecting at Wilkinson's vehicle. Janes had drawn up maps of the cut-throughs made by the search parties. They were studied, and coffee was sipped.

Anna lit a cigarette and blew a plume of smoke across the thick air. She rubbed the moisture from her eyes and looked about, catching Thaddeus glancing sideways at her. Thaddeus looked back to the topmost map, paying attention now to what Wilkinson and Janes were proposing.

"We go in another fifty yards, then we meet back here

and reconsider," Marcel said. "At that point, Elizabeth has us about thirty yards from a large meadow, which may very well be coca plants. It would stack up with what Gordito told us about the area, that one minute you're in the coca fields and then five feet later you're at the paw of the monkey."

"Is there really going to be a monkey statue?" Anna wondered aloud. The others looked at her in silence. No one had an answer that made any sense out here in the total overgrowth. They had guesses and estimates but no real sense of closing in on any ruins. Even the mightiest structure would be overgrown by jungle in six months. Nothing could survive nature out here. So they had become dubious, all of them.

"Same teams as before," Marcel finished, then the maps were folded. Janes walked to Wilkinson's SUV to stow them in the console.

Anna sidled up to Thaddeus and paused, indicating her readiness to head back into the bush whenever he was. He noticed and sighed. "All right, then," he said, and together they headed for their quadrant.

It was slow-going at first. The vines and brush were particularly heavy as they neared the jungle's sunnier area, the closer they got to the field just beyond. Their machetes were slow and chopping and dodging through the brush drew more tiny punctures and scratches from the thorny branches intertwined with the thicker cane and wire brush. After an hour of this, they weren't that much closer to the clearing than when they'd started.

Just as they were about to break for water and a chat, however, Thaddeus's machete struck with a *chunk* sound. His blade had struck something solid. He swung it back and chopped again. *Chunk* sang the blade. He pushed forward, only to realize his path was blocked by a large gray-black obelisk rising from the jungle floor. He squeezed in beside it. It was solid but porous stone that was largely vine-covered and camouflaged by the jungle. The stone he was up against rose maybe thirty feet above his head. He began working along its flat surface, right to left, mindful that he might at any moment come to within just a meter or two of Cárdenas' people.

Running his hands along the stone and realizing he had probably found the Monkey's Paw, he called out to Anna. "Over here, Anna! I've found something!" She hurried through the brush separating them and came to his side.

"Holy crap," she muttered. "What in the world?"

"I know. It's enormous. Let's key our walkie talkies."

A voice came back. "Marcel," it whispered.

"Marcel," Thaddeus said into the walkie-talkie, "we've found what we came for. Trace my path and bring lights. We'll stand down until you get here."

"Roger that," came the return call. "Are there people?"

"We're behind the structure. Unknown. We'll stay put."

"Roger. Proceeding to your path now."

Anna arrived from her circuitous route around the rear of the stone carving and came up behind Thaddeus. "Oh, my God," she whispered, "a huge monkey?"

"So it appears. We found it at last. I've called Marcel and requested lights. They're on the way here."

"Yes, I need a minute to take this in. It's—it's enormous."

"I'm guessing thirty or forty feet to the top of the head and maybe that wide, paw to paw."

"It's amazing. Carved completely out of stone. What do we do now?"

"GPS it. Get ready for a raid with the Huey and soldiers."

They sat cross-legged on the stones underfoot. Thaddeus removed his water bottle and took several long pulls. He shut his eyes, thinking. Soon they heard the sound of others approaching.

Five minutes later, Marcel appeared, armed with two industrial torches. Wilkinson and Keystone, and Janes were there, too, bringing flashlights and more water. They wouldn't be there long. Just enough time for Janes to set her GPS coordinates.

The others studied the structure from corner to corner while Janes placed the statue on her maps. No one had ventured beyond the area of the paws. To do so would have given away their presence. So they backed off without divulging.

Then they were done and retreating.

Chapter 19

Marcel, along with advice from Blackletter, decided they would infiltrate Cárdenas' compound at night. Between their red lights and night-vision goggles, Blackletter felt that the element of surprise was more critical. Even though Keystone and Wilkinson argued that they weren't familiar with the area like Cárdenas' men, Marcel still insisted that they could rely on their soldiers to get them in and out of the compound, even in the dark.

Would it be safe at night for the children? Anna wondered. She had a good point. What if they lost one of the children to the darkness?

Marcel decided it was still their best bet. He arranged for Huey and his son Matty to be ready in the skies, too.

That night, at precisely 2 a.m., they retraced their steps back to the Monkey's Paw in single file. The majority of the paid soldiers went first, Thaddeus's mercenary team next, with more soldiers following, all in units of six. With their numbers, the brush and scrub was laid flat, and the going was easy. But the darkness was intense. Nothing could be seen beyond their headlamps. Only the first man or woman of each unit wore the night vision goggles.

Once to the statue, they followed the stone wall around to the main gate. The plan was to create a diversion and lure Cárdenas' men outside. At Marcel's signal, firecrackers were set off on either side of the main gate.

The first two guards to exit the main door—ten feet high and wide—of the sprawling Monkey's Paw were stitched across the chest and kicked aside by the soldiers as the structure was breached.

Thaddeus had been told to wait in the field of coca plants. He crouched there with Janes. Just beyond, Thaddeus's Army had set up a perimeter around the outer circle of the encampment. There would be no escapees to carry news back to Cárdenas's finca north of Bogotá that night.

The assault was fast—less than six minutes. Marcel exited the compound along with Blackletter and waved Thaddeus in. Altogether, they had killed half a dozen armed men, and another dozen more had been gathered together and were being held by the army at gunpoint along the wall.

Thaddeus left it in the hands of Marcel and went searching wildly for Simon, opening and closing doors, calling out his name. He dashed through the entire sprawl where he saw many children, most of them appearing in bedroom doorways, rubbing eyes, astonishment registering on their faces. Thaddeus completed his search of the main complex, but none of the children were Simon, none of them as young as Simon.

"Murfee," shouted Wilkinson, waving his arms. "Follow me!"

Thaddeus ran as fast as possible to keep up to him.

Then they were outside, running across a courtyard to another two-story building. Thaddeus was right on Wilkinson's heels, up a long mahogany staircase and then entering into sleeping quarters. It was an upstairs dormitory that covered the entire floor and held as many as thirty beds. Most were occupied by smaller children with mouths agape, looking fearfully into the searching torches until Blackletter, Keystone, and Mackenzie arrived. Blackletter flicked on the lights and bathed all of them in the incandescence.

Thaddeus hurried among them, bed after bed. No Simon. At the very end was a community bathroom. He dashed inside, clicked on the light, and then checked beneath each stall. Small legs—last stall on the left. He rushed over and yanked open the door.

"Hello, Uncle Thaddeus."

Thaddeus's heart exploded with joy. The boy was crouched on the floor, shivering. Thaddeus reached and lifted him into his arms. "Mama says hello, Simon," he whispered into the child's ear.

"Can we go home now?"

"We can. We're going to go see a nice doctor and have him look you over, and then we'll go home to see Mama and Daddy."

The boy was four feet tall, long hair past his ears in a bowl cut, wearing khaki shorts, blue tennies, and a white T-shirt with a pocket in which he had a small plastic truck with a rubber band holding the hood down. Unlike the image Nancy had shown him on her phone, the boy's eyes were open and appeared unsewn, undamaged. Thaddeus took all this in in a flash, and his heart broke. "Please, God," he muttered, "let this one—all of them—be okay. Hold them all in your palm." Tears washed from his eyes as he made his way downstairs, the boy in his arms and his face pressed into Thaddeus's shoulder, refusing to watch in case he was dreaming.

Then they were outside, running for the first Huey, which was filling with children. Suddenly, down from the sky swooped another Huey. Marcel rushed under the turning blades and pulled the door open. Mackenzie, Keystone, and Wilkinson herded more children into that one. Elizabeth Janes stepped up to him out of nowhere, holding out her arms to Simon. "Give him to me, Thaddeus."

Thaddeus allowed Janes to take Simon, turned to head back inside, but stopped. "This is my nephew, Simon. He's precious cargo. Please stay with him on the chopper, and I'll go back inside."

"Deal," said Janes. "Come on, Simon, we're going to ride in a helicopter."

Then they were gone, and Thaddeus was back inside.

Throughout the house, soldiers and Thaddeus's team were locating children, making certain no one was left behind.

Anna flew from room to room until, at the end, she spotted a door in the center of the wide hallway. She reached the door, pulled, and darted inside without first requisitioning a soldier to cover her. A Cárdenas guard had been trapped inside. A young girl was with him, maybe twelve.

"Oh!" cried Anna. Unable to restrain herself, she ran at the man.

Which was the exact moment he raised his Beretta 9mm and pulled the trigger twice. One missed, the other bullet taking her right ear and tearing it away. Suddenly her face and shoulder were covered in blood. She lunged one final time, reached the guard, and clawed at his face. In response, he brought his gun up against her chest and pulled the trigger a third time. She felt the bullet tear into her right lung, and she was out. She rolled to the side, a large bloody bubble issuing from her open mouth. And then she was still.

The guard stood and rushed for the door, where he was greeted by a three-round blast from one of the paid soldiers. The soldier began to pass by but then spotted Anna lying up against the wall, her back to him. He walked over and felt for a pulse. Then he nodded and ran to the next building to clear it.

It took longer than Thaddeus had hoped to get all the children clear of the compound. There were the bodies of coca workers everywhere, and in the darkness, there was chaos. Marcel ran up to him, and they conferred. Everyone had been accounted for except Anna MacKenzie. He said to Marcel, "Make sure every kid gets on those helos. I'm going back in to look for Anna."

Thaddeus then ran from room to room through the compound, looking for his teammate. No man, or woman, would be left behind. But everywhere was empty, and the only sound was the helicopter rotors in the distance.

Then, there she was, at the last doorway in the hallway. Anna! He dashed to her and knelt. Blood was everywhere. There was a weak pulse. He lifted her bodily and ran for the door. Then as he was moving down the hallway, she opened her eyes.

"Hurts!" she moaned, and he ran even faster. Outside, darkness. He realized the whir of blades he had been hearing were now overhead and retreating by the second. He looked wildly around, but the choppers and children were gone.

He carried her back inside the Monkey's Paw, where the team was supposed to reassemble. Except there was no one.

It was pitch black, but he had expected to see torches pushing back the night. "Help!" he cried out. "Muir, I have Anna here! She's badly hurt!" He felt his grip on the night fading in the confusion, the gunfire, the blood and killing, and now Anna. No teammates, no army. Then he realized he had to run back through the jungle to get back to their camp.

Every so gently, he carried Anna deeper into the Monkey's Paw to the righthand paw that opened into a great room. The floor was stone; the place was pitch black. He had a memory of a sphinx at the far wall, and he thought to hide her behind its vast body. Maybe—maybe Cárdenas' men, when they arrived tomorrow—and they would—wouldn't see her. Small chance of that, but maybe. At his wit's end, Thaddeus laid Anna on the floor against the wall, then arranged her into a sitting position. He removed his shirt and tore it into three long strips. The first of these, he wrapped around her chest, tearing a shorter piece and folding it into a 4x4 patch. This he inserted inside the band of the sweatshirt he had wrapped around her chest. With the remaining length of the shirt, he dressed her chest wound a second time.

Just then, her eyes fluttered open. "Thaddeus."

"Oh, my God," he breathed. "Oh, my God."

"I'm dying, aren't I?"

"Look, I'm going for help. Here's my cell phone. Use the flashlight in it sparingly. I will try calling you on my way back. You try calling me when you need."

"Okay. Hurry back. It's cold in here."

"Please don't die on me, Anna."

But she'd already closed her eyes. Thaddeus couldn't bear it if this woman lost her life helping to save Simon.

She'd had a hard enough youth, hard enough life fighting the drug wars. She didn't deserve to die like this.

Then he was outside in the night, bare-chested, blue jeans, and all-terrain hiking boots. He broke into his fastest run, retracing the tracks laid down by their group on the way in. He was almost back to camp when, in a moment of horror and terror, he heard helicopters dropping out of the sky back at the compound, and he knew. Cárdenas, the drug lord, the child trafficker, had returned to protect his investment.

Thaddeus knew it was only a matter of time before Cárdenas' people entered into the Monkey's Paw to clear it of invaders. They would find her, find her, and—who knew? Who knew what happened next?

He knew. She clearly didn't belong there. And she was wounded and probably wouldn't survive, so they would finish her.

Then he was breaking through the last of the jungle, and there, sure enough, there was the camp, men milling about, tending to injuries, eating rations, whispering amongst themselves under the safe cover of the jungle canopy.

"We have to go back!" he cried to the group. "Anna was shot! She's dying inside the Monkey's Paw! Let's go now!" He slumped down onto the ground and ran his bare arm across his face, dispersing the thick sweat from his exhausting run. Catching his breath, he called out again. "Marcel! We have to go back!"

Then Marcel was there, his hand on Thaddeus's shoulder. "We can't go back," he said quietly. "There will be Cárdenas' people everywhere. It's too late, Thaddeus. Simon is safely out. The rest of us are safe. Unfortunately, there are always casualties in war. Anna was a soldier, Thad. She knew what she was getting into. Like each one of us did. Like I said at the beginning of all this, it's their consideration. They were all in or not."

He realized just then that he was right. There was no returning; there was only fleeing for Bogotá and safety. Still, he was dying inside with anticipation for what Anna was facing. He couldn't stand it up. Up he jumped and began pacing fiercely back and forth.

He stopped and shrugged at Marcel. "Say something, dammit!" Marcel lit a cigarette. Then passed it to him, and Thaddeus took it. He didn't smoke, but he took it anyway and inhaled.

He shook his head and felt the tears of anger and frustration.

No, he didn't smoke.

But there was lots he didn't do. Like, leave a teammate behind. Now he did that, too.

He coughed and accepted a windbreaker someone had produced.

Then he sat back and folded his arms, watching the fire dance until it became dawn.

The next day they retreated, heading back to Bogotá. Oddly enough, they saw Cárdenas' men leaving, too. This wasn't surprising, given that the children were gone and the coca processing workers all dead.

Chapter 20

I n Viani, Thaddeus wasted no time. Anna needed him, and he wasn't going to quit.

He returned to the Monkey's Paw ten hours later, riding a motorcycle this time, a Yamaha on-road/off-road. He'd left the rest of the group camped just outside of Viani, where he'd acquired the bike. Each of the remaining team members, Blackletter, Keystone, and Wilkinson, had all fought him on returning for Anna. They'd all laid down valid arguments. There was little possibility she was still alive, especially after Cárdenas' men had arrived shortly after their Huey's lifted off with the children.

But Thaddeus was determined to go back on his own. He wouldn't risk another team member again. He could barely handle the guilt about Anna, let alone if something were to happen to another. So he told the team to idle for twenty-four hours at Viani until he returned. If she were still alive, he'd radio for one of the Huey's to return and leave with her that way.

Parking at their previous campsite, he hiked in, making

only the sound of wind passing through leaves, then he was there. He ran his field glasses across the burned-out fields—there was no one there, no one at all. Then he broke into a run for the Monkey's Paw, rushing inside through the broken door, back to the Sphinx, playing his light over where he had left her.

She was there. Her eyes were closed. She wasn't moving. He approached and reached down and took her arm. It was tight against her body, and his heart raced. She had stiffened in her death. Sure enough, he felt again and again for a pulse, all but digging the tips of his fingers into the wrist. But it was not there.

She was gone.

He sank beside her and placed his back against the wall. Despite her rigor mortis, he pulled her arm to him and held it there against his chest and wept. "I'm so sorry!" he cried to her.

When his thoughts returned to the moment, he found he was loading her onto the motorcycle and strapping her body against the bar with cargo straps he had brought along just in case. Her head lolled to the side. He placed the second helmet, covered in green glitter, on her head and fastened the chin strap. He fired up the Yamaha, and they were off for the nearest asphalt and the long drive to the western coast of Colombia. It was the only way he knew to go if he avoided Cárdenas' men, who would be scouring all roads leading back to Bogotá.

He tossed his head back and felt the wind slip under his helmet. It dried the tears from his cheeks, and he was better able to focus on the dirt road. When he got to the river, he diverted two kilometers north, crossed a bridge that Janes had found for him, and then proceeded northeasterly for thirty kilometers to the asphalt road. He then returned due north for half a day and then northwest, headed for the town of Buenaventura.

Thaddeus was exhausted, but still, he bent into the wind, keeping his head tucked low, his gaze never moving from the road ahead.

A waiting gun crew suddenly loomed into view at the end of an S-curve. The four men were Cárdenas' Colombians, frozen along the arroyo bank that skirted the road. Cárdenas had placed them everywhere.

Their eyes and gun muzzles peeped over the sand, waiting. Machine guns were aimed at the approaching headlights. When the Yamaha entered their field of view, the guns shattered the night. Bullets tore into flesh and rubber, puncturing the engine block and setting the cycle to spinning along the dark road, its headlight snapping around and around like a receding beacon as the gun crew watched. Then it flipped onto its side, and the driver and passenger skidded along the roadway, feet first, legs upraised, the nylon strap binding the passenger to the driver as they spun around and around. The driver's head missed the roadside reflector by one inch. When the sliding motorcycle caught up, it severed the strap holding them together, depositing the passenger on the road shoulder, but freeing the driver to tumble onto the edge of the steep embankment.

The gun crew waited until the night stilled. Crickets and sand frogs came back to life and sang out. Only then did the men climb up from the arroyo and onto the road. The leader of the group walked to the edge, shining his light down where he'd seen the driver disappear only moments before. Seeing nothing, he was satisfied that the problem had been handled, and he ordered the men to pack up and leave.

Chapter 21

Southwestern Colombia

Sheep swarmed over the hill and down onto the roadway. They parted at the man and the motorcycle, streaming around him on either side. There were several hundred animals still showing spring shear. Then came the dogs, circling and running ahead. Then came the shepherds. Horses brought up the rear, pulling a caravan holding supplies and food and water. Ordinarily, they didn't move at night, but the gunfire had spooked the flock, and they ran off. Only now were they being reassembled.

Crossing the road, the animals were getting dangerously close to the ocean cliffs where, in the dark, they might plunge 150 feet to the rocks below. The boys circled, getting ahead of the herd and throwing up their arms to turn them back. Likewise, the dogs refused passage to them. Now the sheep were stymied, gathering in the road where a current of confusion was building.

A boy ran between the sheep when he saw the man and the motorcycle. He knelt and hovered an ear above the man's bloody mouth and nose. He felt for a pulse. He stood and looked across the herd toward the wagon. "He's alive!" he cried.

The men came to him and loaded the man onto the wagon. The sheep turned back, then back up and over the road and down into an arroyo on the east side. They began grazing in a northerly direction. The woman's body, 200 meters south, was examined and left at the side of the road.

A sponge was produced, and the young shepherd dribbled water into the man's open mouth. He made no swallowing motions but choked instead. They turned him onto his side and pounded between his shoulder blades to bring the water back up. After he coughed and sputtered, they again turned him onto his back. The boy reached out and replaced the scalp flap that hung so precipitously atop one ear. Another boy fashioned a bandage of wool and tape to hold the flap in place.

Ignacio, the eldest of the shepherds, arrived with the wagon and produced a lantern to examine the man's face. Did they know him? The boy turned his face up so Ignacio could see. "Gringo," he said softly.

"He's not one of them," said one of the boys.

"They did this," said a third shepherd. "We should get help for him."

The flock came to a clearing between two hills where the grass grew. The shepherds halted the flow, and the dogs ranged to set the perimeter. Now all was still. The man's troubled breathing could be heard in the air. His chest rattled, and he coughed up more blood.

Ignacio pulled out his cell phone and tried to call Antonella's number. No service. The owner of the phone hiked onto higher ground and tried again. This time, she answered.

"Antonella, this is Ignacio. We have someone. He is badly injured."

"Where are you?"

"Kilometer fifty-nine. East side."

"I'm on my way."

Once Ignacio returned to the group, he had the boys fashion a litter, and they returned the man to the opposite roadside.

Twenty minutes passed without traffic. Then the whine of tires on the asphalt could be heard approaching.

Chapter 22

Thaddeus regained consciousness just as a car's brights came upon him. He heard the screech of brakes and the sound of a single truck door opening. The woman, Antonella, driving alone, had found the shepherds and their patient. She leaped out and ran forward.

She dropped to her knees. "Can you hear me?"

He looked up but then lost consciousness.

"Help me," she said to the shepherds standing there. "My truck."

They lifted and carried him to her tailgate, then laid the man crosswise in the bed. Antonella jumped into the bed of the truck with the man and moved his shoulders so his feet faced the tailgate. She tripped the cargo light, illuminating the man's head. Blood was everywhere. His eyes remained closed. He was unresponsive to anything she said. She removed her work shirt and wrapped his head to help staunch the bleeding. "I'm going to fix you," she said. "I'm a doctor. I've been to war zones. I see the bullet holes in your bike. We won't go into town because I know they'll be looking for you by morning when you're reported in the hospital. My name is Antonella."

The shepherds said their goodbyes and faded back into the night.

Antonella wasted no time climbing back into the cab and continuing on her way to the town of Buenaventura. On her left was the Pacific Ocean; on her right, the mountains grew taller and taller.

The driver's eyes opened then closed. He knew only that he was alive and being kicked in the back. Ever so slowly, he realized the kicking was actually the road surface he felt through the metal bed of a truck. He accepted the pain. At one point along the way, he opened his eyes again, but the moonlight was now so bright that he looked away. The movement of his head shot pain down his spine, into his legs and feet. That wouldn't happen again.

Twenty minutes later, Antonella turned off the road. When she passed a keycard in front of an electric eye, a gate rose. Antonella steered the truck across the cattle guard and nosed off the asphalt onto the gravel road that then turned right and sloped down a long hill before switching back and continuing down another quarter mile. She drove the gravel stretch and pulled into an open garage. The house was 150 feet from a cliff overlooking the breakers below. She honked the horn for help. Cavonna came running, a kitchen towel over one shoulder. "Médica?" he shouted.

"Back here. Help me with him."

Antonella and Cavonna lifted the man from the bed and carried him through the door into a large room with sliding doors overlooking the Pacific. Along one wall was a kitchenette with a stove and mini-refrigerator. On another wall was a painting, a Mexican pastoral in pink and tan hues.

The lighting cast the room in a somber light. After they placed the man atop a sturdy table, Antonella retrieved some scissors from a drawer and began snipping away the makeshift bandage she'd made from her shirt. Then she attacked the cotton and tape of the shepherds. Cavonna handed her a T-shirt from the closet to cover her nakedness.

She gently cleansed the open scalp flap and carefully sutured the area. It was swollen and looked like hell. A plastic surgeon would be sued for such a ragged closure. Then she cleaned and dressed the abrading wounds. Next, she cut away his clothes, looking for bullet holes. She was astonished to find there were none in light of all the hits on the motorcycle.

"No CT scan for you. If there is intracranial bleeding, you'll die. If there is internal bleeding, you will die. That's the chance you have to take rather than go to hospital where they have a scanner. You wouldn't make it until morning once the cartel knows about you."

"And they would learn of him," said Cavonna.

"Yes, they would."

Antonella sent Cavonna upstairs for coffee. She covered the man with a sheet. The night was warm, but his temperature was only slightly elevated. His heart sounded normal, and he was moving air.

She took a seat beside the table.

She had given all she had to offer at the moment. If he made it 'til morning, he might have a chance. But if the men got word he was missing, not dead, they would come looking.

All the medicine in Colombia wouldn't keep them away.

Chapter 23

Antonella looked up from the leashed Labrador. The waves roared 150 feet below. Seagulls wheeled in the sky and dove for fish. Two pelicans worked the breaker line. On the wind was the strong taste of salt and the caress of warm air. Her gaze traveled to the third floor, where they had moved the man. His window was open, and she wondered, was that a cry? The dog tugged politely at her hand. *I'm not finished*, said the Lab. *There's more walk yet.*

Feeling she might have heard her patient cry out, she returned to the house and unclipped the dog. He charged up the stairs. The walls were thick, three feet of concrete. They were painted white and dotted with framed art. At the first landing, she paused. Again, the sound; this time, she was sure it was a cry. Her step quickened. On the second landing, the air warmed on her arms. She was climbing ever nearer the tile roof and the blaze of the noonday sun.

At the third landing, the light shone brilliantly through the windows. She turned her face, and the pale skin of her hand and arm turned translucent until she moved beyond the glass. At the end of the hallway was his room. He was lying naked on the bed, the sheet kicked aside.

"Are we speaking?" she asked him.

He looked at her, following her without seeing her. As she neared, it was confirmed. He was looking through her, out the windows at her back, and into the sky where seagulls flitted past. It was very quiet. She heard a fly against the open glass. It was angry and insistent, furious at entrapment.

"Who are you?" she asked. "Do you have a name?"

As she spoke, she stood over him and inspected the wound on his crown. He sat propped up. Both hands were palm down on the mattress. She had stitched together the scalp, but it was white and swollen with fluids as only the head could produce. She spread the hair with two fingers. The stitches were holding. She wouldn't have expected otherwise since she'd trained four years in surgery at Universidad Nacional de Colombia. She could do wound closures with her eyes closed, but, in this case, her instruments were rudimentary at best, so the scar would be unsightly. But it was what was beneath the wound that left her troubled. The brain might be swollen. Or not.

Every three hours, she changed the dressings. She applied a saline solution to release the gauze then worked it loose. She dried it with compresses. She applied medicine and covered it again.

The next day she bathed him with a wet cloth. Working along his torso, she dipped the cloth in a basin of sudsy water. His ribcage was taut with muscle and sunburnt in an inverted triangle from throat to sternum, most likely from riding into the sun.

She turned him onto his stomach. The buttocks and

hips were perfect. She closed off her mind and cleaned him without thinking again. Then she turned him onto his back. His breathing was shallow and ragged, his eyes closed, and no movement of his limbs or fingers. "Don't die," she whispered to him, hoping her appraisal was wrong, hoping he wasn't dying even though everything medical told her he was.

His back and thighs were unmarked from the wreck. At the time, she'd been amazed there wasn't any loss of skin where he had slid along the highway. When she cut the leathers from his body, she found body armor in his jacket and pants. It had taken the friction. The leather had sanded away, but his clothes had done the job before the asphalt reached his skin.

When he arrived, she had searched through his pockets and found no identification or documents, only a battered wristphone locked with a passcode. She had put it in a drawer. She now tried to focus on the dying man in front of her.

Chapter 24

Señor Franco Cárdenas was a man of ice cream suits and riding crops. The suits were white and heavily starched, a new one for each day of the week. The riding crops—quirts—he carried under his left armpit, always within reach whenever an underling's misdeeds fell short of death by gunshot. Then the small whip was applied, often across the cheek in a sudden slapping motion. It wasn't unusual for the crop to leave a deep gash requiring stitches and a long white scar from the closure.

Today he waited in his lawn chair for Mirada Garcia to be brought before him. Garcia was the man who found Thaddeus; he also left Thaddeus alive on the roadway that night. The orders were to shoot to kill. Garcia had evaded Cárdenas long enough, but today, there was holy hell to pay.

He arrived in the back of a white van, handcuffed and looking terrified. Slowly, he was dragged across the lawn by two larger men, trusted bodyguards of Cárdenas, who did only his personal bidding on any given day. They were armed with pistols and machine guns hanging from webbing across their chests. Dragging Garcia by his elbows, they were not friendly and did not handle him carefully.

"Señor Garcia," said Cárdenas when the man was brought to face him. "What about my instructions were not clear to you?"

"You were clear, Señor Cárdenas. I failed you because I thought he was dead. It was a terrible crash and would have killed most men. And I saw him tumble over the edge of the cliff," he lied.

"You didn't want to climb down and verify that he was dead? Weren't my orders worth an hour of your time? You should have finished the job. That's my point. But you didn't. Why didn't you? Did you want to give him the chance to crawl away into the night?"

"No, señor. It was a terrible oversight by me. All I can say in my defense is that I thought he was dead."

"But he wasn't. And now we have reason to believe he survived. He knows about me, Señor Garcia. He knows everything about the trafficking. And he is an American. Can you even begin to imagine the risk you've exposed me to? The whole of the CIA after me and knowing where I am and how my business works? This is your legacy to me?"

His own words having angered him that much more, Cárdenas pulled out his pearl-handled revolver and fired a bullet into Garcia's forehead. The man's knees buckled. With a jerk of his head, Cárdenas told the bodyguards to remove Garcia's body. It was done.

But the problem still wasn't solved. He spoke to his closest. *confidante* even as Garcia's body was dragged away. "You must find the lawyer. If he is still in Colombia, he must remain here. He cannot be allowed to return to the States.

Now, while the scent is still on the air, search him down and finish him. The contract for death is on his head."

The *confidante*, Nico Lamontez, indicated he'd heard. "Your will, señor. It is done."

Lamontez moved away while Cárdenas took up his breakfast on the green, chuckling at his clever wordplay. "The contract lawyer."

Orders would flow, and men would scour the area where Thaddeus Murfee went down. From there, they would fan out, covering all of Colombia to the sea until the quarry was run to the ground.

Chapter 25

The calendar was marked with five red Xs. She had doctored him for five days. It was all but amazing he hadn't died, but there you were. He had opened his eyes on the second day and reached for the water glass. Alive, but he still didn't speak. He only watched. His eyes followed her every move. His mouth moved, but no words came out. Injuries to the brain were impossibly hard to understand here at her house, where there were no machines to scan and report back. Without testing, there was no telling. Yet she refused to take him into town to the clinic where he would receive preferred care. She refused because the traffickers would learn he survived and come for him. So, she hid him here in her rental house, where she came to spend her summer after four years of residency. It was to be her last hurrah before launching a full-time practice of general surgery.

His mouth gaped. She held up a glass of water. He looked at it. He reached and took the glass. To the lips and down, spilling none of it.

She broke off a bite of the morning banana. His eyes followed. She slipped it into his mouth. His jaw muscles worked up and down. He chewed. He had only swallowed whole bites minutes before, but now he chewed. He might survive. He'd passed the first test.

She bent again to the washbasin. As she wrung out the washcloth, he made a sound with his mouth.

"What?"

"More."

"More banana?"

"More."

She was thrilled. It was one word, but that meant another pathway in the brain had reopened. But she wouldn't get ahead of herself, for she knew trauma receded slowly. It might be the only word of the month.

Biting off a chunk, she placed the banana on his bedside table. She chewed, showing him to bite, then chew. His right hand lifted from the mattress, and he took the remaining banana. She guided his hand to his mouth. He bit down while looking at her. She nodded, and he chewed. She could jump up and down, but it would frighten him, so she resisted the celebration.

On day twelve, he added a few more words. "I am hungry."

She looked up from her washing. "You're always hungry."

"More."

She peeled chicken away from the wing bone. Pulling it apart, she sensed from the firm muscle the bird was full grown. He took the meat, opened his mouth, and popped in the morsel. He chewed. She was happy with his effort. He had learned to eat. There had been long nights of doubt in her mind, but now he swallowed and waited for another bite.

"What is your name?"

"I am hungry."

"Yes, you are one hungry *hombre*."

He lifted his hand again, waiting. She tugged at the chicken wing and passed the meat to him. He took it down in one chomp. Then he waited again, watching her separate flesh from bone. "Last piece. Don't want you getting sick. It's greasy."

Again, a chomp and a swallow. His eyes met her eyes. She sensed he might have more to say, but he didn't have the words. Not yet.

It had been three weeks, and there'd been perhaps 100 words. But no name.

"Who are you?"

"I'm right here."

"Should I read from a list of men's names?"

"Antonella."

"Antonella is my name. What's your name? It's a mystery we're waiting to solve, Cavonna and I. Name, please."

His face tightened. Cavonna had loaned him a purple Lakers shirt. It had *24* in big numbers on the front and *Bryant* across the back. The shirt was too large for him and hung loosely from his shoulders and gaped at the throat. "He was one of my heroes," she said of the deceased basketball player.

"What?"

"Let's do this. Where do you live?"

"LA."

"Los Angeles?"

"I'm right here."

"What do you do in Los Angeles?"

His eyes went blank. She had reached too far.

Cavonna brought a bench to the foot of the bed. A large mirror framed the patient. It was placed so that he might study himself. "Maybe you will see your name in the glass," she told him. "Or maybe a phone number, a wife, an address."

Antonella waited for the mirror to speak, but it didn't reply.

On day forty-one, he looked up from the mirror and asked, "Where is my motorcycle?"

"Your motorcycle was shot out from under you."

"Who shot my motorcycle?"

"I should ask you that."

He looked back into the mirror. "If I knew my name, I would know who to call."

At the mention of a call, she thought of the wristphone in the drawer behind her. She had heard it often buzzing in the first days but could never reach it before the call dropped, and the passcode once again stood guard. Now, it hadn't rung in several weeks. The battery was probably dead. Not wanting to disrupt the conversation, she pushed the thought from her mind.

"Be still," she said, examining his scalp with her expert fingers. "Don't try to force it."

"Will it come back?"

"I think so. I think you'll be reciting the Gettysburg Address before we are done."

"What is that?"

"Your president, Abraham Lincoln, spoke it at Gettysburg. I had it in American history, at school in Bogotá."

She rubbed her hands in the soapy water and then dried them on a hand towel.

"I once rode a motorcycle from Alaska to Rio."

"Remember that, do we?"

"Coming back up the Baja. That's where I learned to ride with a trailer. Was there a trailer?"

"There was no trailer." She'd read about the shooting in the newspaper and made clippings that she passed to him now. There were photographs of the shot-up bike and trailer. There was mention of a passenger, a woman, seen by witnesses but not located.

"Very bad men. They were making a statement. They were saying they couldn't be touched. And they are right."

"Was there really a girl? Who was she?"

"You tell me."

"Was she DEA? Have I said DEA? Should we call them?"

She paused and placed the towel back on its rod. She stood before him, thinking.

"I think we call no one until we know who's who. The DEA isn't safe either. At least not in Colombia."

Chapter 26

She delayed sending her résumé to medical practices she might join. Instead, she kept a journal. Maybe there would be a medical paper about the case later on. Or maybe she was kidding herself. Maybe there was something that kept her from giving him up and returning him to the world.

She tended her small garden in front. Stunted corn. Succulent carrots and peppers and tomatoes. The rabbits took the lettuce. Cavonna brought groceries twice a week and water in huge plastic jugs. The patient ate well. He was bathed, learned to talk, and sat outside with Antonella when Cavonna carried him to a bench overlooking the sea. But not much was said during their time on the beach. He just stared out at the waves and water while Antonella read out loud to him from a book by Gabriel García Márquez, *One Hundred Years of Solitude*.

One day, out of the blue, Thaddeus recalled. "This is the ocean."

"Yes, good for you. The big parts are called surf."

"I already knew that."

"That ship out there is taking oil to the refinery down the coast."

He turned and looked out to sea, shading his eyes. "There are children on board."

"You're fixated with children. Do you have kids?"

He ignored her. "I worked with the DEA before. I know it."

"It's time to get out. Time for your nap."

"Come here."

"Here, come, take your nap. I am your doctor."

"Give me a name."

"I have no name. Give me your name."

"Thaddeus is my name." He blinked. She could see the certainty on his face. Whether it was connected to a memory or not, she knew it was the truth.

"Well then, Thaddeus, it's nice to meet you officially. I'll get Cavonna to carry you inside. Time for a snack and a nap. Doctor's orders."

As she rose to fetch Cavonna, she felt his gaze on her back. She turned sharply to find him looking beyond her at the sea.

Chapter 27

Another day, another trauma. She began her night shift at six, clocking in with her pass card as she entered the hospital in Bogotá. Wearing green scrubs and a white T-shirt beneath, she was ready for her eighteen-hour shift that ended at noon the next day. Her Hispanic complexion was ruddy, for she had just spent the weekend with friends, surfing off the coast. One of the doctors had a plane and flew four of them to his favorite spot on the coast where they'd surfed by day and danced at night. Long, languorous nights in his beach house where there were actual servants—an astonishing fact in the life of a resident physician who was accustomed to waiting on everyone and everything. She'd been served butterfly shrimp cocktails in the morning with Bloody Marys and celery sticks while still in bed. She had to pinch herself to make sure she wasn't dreaming. But now, Monday evening, it was back to the sounds and rhythms of the hospital.

The nurses came and went to the nurses' station. There was the usual grab-ass and fooling around between the residents and some of the nurses adopted into their fold. Everyone was happy as they ate foods brought from home and pastries picked up on the way to work.

Then at 11:23, the ambulance call came in. Four ambulances were bearing down on the hospital since there'd been a shooting, and there were many wounded, most of them children. It was the worst call a hospital staff could receive.

Antonella rushed to the nurses' station and absently squirted hand sanitizer into her cupped hand. A supervisor told her she would attend to the first ambulance to hit the portal. The hair on her neck jumped, electric with anticipation. Gunshot wounds were a nightly occurrence. Gunshot wounds involving children were rare.

Then came the sirens, the wail from two blocks away, and her stomach flip-flopped. She was first up, no matter what the wounding, no matter how severe. She had trained for this and she was ready.

When the gurney came crashing through the double doors, she was immediately beside it, peering down, making her ABC assessment. An arm hung limply outside the sheet. It was impossibly small. Nothing that small—that youthful —should be arriving at a hospital on a gurney. She leaned forward and studied the face. It was a girl, possibly eight or nine years old, eyes closed, and she'd been intubated. A paramedic was breathing for her with a bag that he persisted to squeeze in a regular rhythm, no matter the irregularity of the run, the jarring, the chatter and chaos— no, this paramedic knew her stuff and was no quitter. She was going to bring this one through by her own iron will if necessary.

Antonella jumped past her ABC's and went from there.

They moved the child easily from the gurney to the examination table. The bag of Ringers came with her and was hung from a pole at the head of the bed. Oxygen replaced the bag as Antonella cut away the girl's shirt to access the GSW below. When she saw the girl's chest, Antonella shut her eyes, only to open them immediately. It was a mess, her chest partly shot away and massive bleeding.

It was unlikely she would make it—man could not replace with materials in ten minutes what God had so fastidiously developed from skin and bone over the years. Once the tissue and muscle and sinew and bone and cartilage and blood were gone, the body was gone. But Antonella wouldn't give up. She began cleaning and investigating to decide what, if anything, she might do to give the girl a fighting chance. There was very little she could do, but she was going to try.

She swabbed the area with antibiotics and tried to locate the bleeders through the blood pooling in the girl's chest cavity. She disregarded the suction hose as she stitched an artery and was encouraged when it was effective.

She delved deeper and deeper into the wound, tracing the course of the bullet and the damage it had done. She was totally immersed in her work and only sensed the nurses scissoring away her patient's pants and undergarments.

After thirty minutes of making every effort possible, Antonella came upright from the table and gulped a deep breath of air, then let it out. The unconscious girl was stabilized—so far. It would be touch and go all night after the patient went to surgery. Just as she was dispatching the patient to the surgical ward, another call for her help came across the PA. She was being paged for another patient. She arranged for the girl's transport and double-checked her lines and breathing before she ripped off her gloves and hurried away to the next challenge.

It was a long night that followed. All told, there were eight more patients, and Antonella's duties involved her in four of them. She was up to her elbows in blood when the last victim was wheeled off to surgery. She was exhausted, and the tears wouldn't stop coming. She went outside the ER doors and stood there in the pre-dawn with two other doctors. One of them produced a pack of cigarettes, and she accepted, even though she didn't smoke. She lit up and sucked the smoke deep into her lungs to suppress the emotion that was erupting and causing her to cry uncontrollably. They exchanged few words, the doctors, as they were all dealing with the same feelings.

An hour later, the whole team took to the cafeteria in a rare pre-dawn opening of the physicians' dining room. She and a dozen others from the ER gorged on *changua* and scrambled eggs and *tamales* and coffee, plenty of coffee. Feelings were soothed, and memories of the night were put into perspective. Said one doctor to the group, "Hey, it's our job."

"What happened?" asked a nurse beside Antonella. She had wondered the same, too. How did so many children get shot? Who did it?

A police officer who had joined them, along with several other police officers and ambulance attendants, answered from down the table, "The cartel had it wrong. They shot up the first school then figured out the drug kingpin's daughters weren't enrolled there after they'd already killed three children. So then they go to San Ramon School, steal into the dorm, and shoot up those kids, too. This time they got the girls. Six are dead, including the daughters of Miguel d' Llama, the man they wanted to terrorize."

"And we got the collateral damage," says Antonella.

The police officer studied her, then, "Pretty much. You got the children who just happened to be in the wrong place at the wrong time."

Antonella's grief turned to rage, which then turned back to tears and then rage again. She loathed the cartels, loathed what they stood for. Enraged, she cursed them all with profanity. Other staff and attendants, and police listened to her vent without missing a bite of their breakfast. Then another physician pursued the same kind of outburst, and so it went while they ate breakfast: feelings emerged and were roared away.

Chapter 28

Present day

Her memories looped, an endless cycle of violence to torment her. Antonella arose from her nightmares and snuck into the kitchen. While Thaddeus slept upstairs, Antonella opened a bottle of gin in the kitchen below and poured herself a glass of the clear liquid. Then she sat at the kitchen table alone and drank off half the glass. She coughed and gasped when the alcohol burned down her throat and then remembered why she came to sit down and drink.

As an intellectual matter, she knew the players were the same, that the cartel that attacked Thaddeus and his passenger consisted partly of the same men who had attacked those school children. It was never-ending, and she felt hopeless as she quaffed another inch of the glass of gin. Then the tears came again, and she sat there, shoulders shaking, weeping violently at her memories, her present feelings, and the lostness of her life, for she had forgotten what she had meant to do.

Just then, Cavonna padded into the kitchen, having been awoken by Antonella's cries of despair. He came up behind her, placed his hands on her shoulders, and began to massage. He was tender and strong and safe, and he told her to turn loose her grief and let it all out.

She and Cavonna stayed like that until the sun rose and the pale light filtered in through the kitchen window. Antonella had cried herself out once again. But just like every other time before, after she'd purged her body of all the excess emotion and stress, she gathered herself together and moved on. Life wouldn't stop. There was only moving forward.

"*Gracias, amigo*," she told Cavonna as she rose from the table. "I'm going to go get changed and start the day."

She needed food and medical supplies. There were groceries she would know only when she saw them, a whorl of labels and meal ideas that couldn't be passed to Cavonna so that he might make the trip into town. They would only be known to Antonella as she walked the aisles of the grocery store, and ideas sprung to mind. Besides, she needed to get out.

So, she left Cavonna in charge of Thaddeus, telling him what time he got his injection for pain, then she left the house and pulled her truck out of the garage where it had been since saving Thaddeus and bringing him home.

As she put it into drive and began the slow climb up out of the odd conglomeration of houses behind lock and key, houses arranged along a small hillside, so they all commanded a view of the sea, she had an idea. She would stop and see if Encia would like to ride along. Encia was her best friend and confidante about all things male and missing from her life. She drove up the first switchback, pulled over, put it into park, and left it running. She hurried to the steps of Encia's house trailer, took the three steps in two, and rapped her knuckles against the aluminum doorframe. "Encia, it's Antonella!"

The door creaked open on its loose hinges. "Come in, Antonella. But keep your voice down. San Lima is sleeping."

Antonella whispered, "I'm headed into town to the market. Come along with me, and we'll chit-chat and find something wonderful for dinner. Maybe we'll each cook enough to trade half."

"All right. He won't be awake for hours. Let me get my purse."

They snuck out so that the sleeping man was undisturbed and climbed into the truck. Antonella slipped it into drive, and off they went, taking the second switchback.

"A little bird tells me you've taken on a new patient?"

"How long has it been since we've spoken? He's been with me some time now."

"I've been busier than ever cleaning houses. It's probably been a month."

"Then this is long overdue. I've missed you."

"So, tell me about the new patient."

"He's very ill. A head injury, plus he cannot walk. There was a motorcycle accident."

Antonella was comfortable sharing the information with Encia, her trusted friend who wouldn't breathe a word of what she was told to anyone else. Secrets kept were never wasted words. So, she continued.

"I think he's in the police or the army. Something with guns. Very hush-hush, if you get me."

"My lips are sealed. How long will you keep him? I

144

thought when you came back, you weren't going to be here that long? I thought you were going to be looking for work?"

"That was the plan, certainly. But for now, those plans are on the back burner. If I turn him into the hospital, he dies because the people who hurt him are the cartel."

"Oh. Very hush-hush, then."

"Besides, he's my first real patient outside the hospital. I could do worse." She laughed, a laugh of irony and self-effacement. Antonella was particularly expert at both.

They drove on and, at the top of the hill, waited while the gate lifted and allowed them to pass on through. Then they were northbound, heading to Buenaventura, about fifteen kilometers north of their oceanside estate. The area they passed through was high plains, heavily treed in places and barren in others, with mountains surrounding the distance and foothills nearby. The women didn't see the glint of binoculars studying them as they drew near.

Two miles on, a gun cracked and echoed around the hills, like the sound of a branch splitting from a tree but really the sound of a high-powered Remington Model 783 30:06. The bullet shattered Encia's passenger window, passed into her jaw, and fragmented midway into her head. She slumped forward, then was thrown violently sideways in one slow-motion moment witnessed by Antonella, who looked from the road ahead to see her cream blouse suddenly covered in large blotches of blood and bone and skull fragments.

Antonella jerked the truck to a stop, opened the door, and crashed to the ground. She crawled beneath her truck, where she was found minutes later by a truckload of passing Federales in pursuit of the gunmen in the hills who were having target practice on the motoring population that morning. They talked Antonella out from under the truck and returned her home with her truck, a corporal driving while Antonella rode in the canvas-covered rear, held by two soldiers who tried to calm her hysteria.

She ran inside her house and collapsed in Cavonna's arms. He poured a shot of tequila into the lukewarm coffee from the stove and made her drink it down. Then another. She was crying and raging and lashing out at whoever did this to her friend. "I hate the narcos!" she cried. "I absolutely hate those bastards! I am never leaving Thaddeus to them!"

Cavonna walked her into the living room and had her lie down on the leather couch perpendicular to the sea. He removed her hiking boots and socks. Then he went into the kitchen and returned with a damp cloth, which he laid across her forehead. He knelt on the floor beside her and held her hand until the crying subsided. Finally, she turned onto her side and half-smiled, saying to her friend, "I'm okay now. You go out and tend to the truck in case we need to use it right away. I'll lie here and try to nap."

"All right," he said, "whistle if you need me."

"Will do."

Cavonna hosed skull and jaw and flesh out of the truck cab. He used the garden hose with its brass nozzle that twisted into a strong stream, strong enough to dislodge bony fragments from the truck's seats and floor mats.

Cavonna left the doors of the truck open to dry in the baking sun for two hours. A rough-cut oval of cardboard was taped up where the passenger window was. Then Cavonna went back inside to check on Antonella. He heard her voice upstairs, speaking brightly to her patient as if none of this had happened. He smiled and shook his head, his look one of admiration for Antonella. Back outside, he went and climbed into the yet-damp truck and drove into town. He shopped the market, purchasing only enough food and groceries for that night's meal. He returned home without incident.

Antonella tended to Thaddeus and tried to push the morning from her mind. She had seen death hundreds of times before, but never from violence committed right beside her. She struggled with her feelings, but, for once, the needs of Thaddeus helped calm her nerves, diverting her attention just enough that the inner wound in her soul could begin to close.

Later that night, she went downstairs to the empty downstairs apartment and went straight to the mini-refrigerator's freezer, where a bottle of vodka was stored. She had put it there a month before as a housewarming gift for the tenant who never materialized. She stole back upstairs with the iced bottle into the kitchen, where she removed the seal and poured out a tumbler. She sat down at the kitchen table and, moments later, cradled her head in her arms as she cried, weeping violently and pounding the table in rage.

She drank another tumbler and climbed into the bed in the room next door to Thaddeus's. He heard her cry herself to sleep, and then all was still.

At midnight, she jerked awake, and the crying resumed, but only for a very few minutes until she slept again after drinking off another mouthful of the vodka.

She slept through the rest of the night until five a.m., when she awoke to bedpan Thaddeus, take his temperature, listen to his heart, and ask how he felt.

A new day was upon them. They didn't speak that day of the Encia incident, nor the next or the next.

On the third day, Thaddeus asked, "What was it?"

"Nothing. A friend died."

"Oh. I'm sorry."

"She wasn't a close friend. But it upset me. It was very sudden and unexpected."

"Those are the worst," he said.

"Are they?" she replied. "I thought they were all the worst."

"True," he said, watching her wipe down his chest. "Very true."

Chapter 29

S he was running the vacuum in the room. When he spoke Marcel Rainford's name, Antonella noticed. She shouted above the unholy roar of the machine. "You remembered a man's name," she said. "There's progress."

He shrugged, accepting her compliment sideways. "But I don't know who it is." His face told her he was despondent now, so she shut off the vacuum.

"Trust me," she said to him, "every little bit is encouraging."

She moved a six-foot picture into his room and leaned it against the wall beside him. It was a photographic blowup from the large-format printer in the basement of the house she rented. A wheat field swayed in the breeze beneath an enormous setting sun. Thaddeus studied the rendering and looked at Antonella. "It reminds me of the fields adjacent to some areas of the Colombian jungle. I have been there when it's high noon in the wheat field and midnight just inside the triple canopy jungle. Fantastic places."

"Did you track the coca workers inside the jungles?"

"I think so, but I'm not sure. There were children there, too."

"How dangerous."

"We had great people. Including people like Marcel Rainford."

"Do any other names come to you?"

His dark eyes narrowed. "There was a woman…" His voice trailed off.

"Any names?"

He turned his head away from the picture, so it was out of his field of view. "No names."

"Was this woman—?"

"She was no one."

Chapter 30

The microfiche was smothered in dust, looking like it hadn't been used in years. The glass lens was so heavily smeared with fingerprints he could make out nothing until he returned with damp paper towels and cleaned it.

Nico Lamontez sat down at the table and examined the picture closely. Damn his eye! He could barely see. He used the knob to zoom in closer to see the images. There were images of the accident itself--broken glass, metal shards, and disarray all over the road where the bike had collided with the heavy guard rail.

There were two pictures of the livestock that had been present, along with their shepherds. Nico moved on to the next image and made out a few facial features of the men. He didn't recognize anything yet. The scenery was blurry on the last few slides and could be anywhere in the region.

He moved the glass to see the last few pictures. The first one was a closer shot of the crash scene, but what was that in the background? From this second angle, a road sign was visible behind the remnants of the crash. What did it say? Which highway was that?

The last photo was of the reporter who had documented the article, Antonio Valencia. A name was something.

Reporters in South America were desperate. They would do anything for a story to sell, anything to make some extra pesos. This would be like taking candy from a baby. He swiped the microfiche and stuffed it in his satchel and was off.

There was work to be done. Antonio Valencia.

Chapter 31

The army arrived in front of Antonella's house several days later, just after lunchtime. There were three truckloads of soldiers and a jeep leading the procession. Two soldiers came to the door and hammered with their fists. Antonella answered.

The youngest soldier, a husky man of maybe twenty, wearing the stripes of a corporal, said, "Our lieutenant wants you to leave here today. He says it is too dangerous for you." His eyes and voice were gruff and empty.

"I'm sorry, but tell your lieutenant that is impossible. This is my home, and I have nowhere else to go," replied Antonella.

"My lieutenant will be displeased. He is out in the hills even now, searching for the shooters. We are on our way to join him. He will tell me to return here and insist if I show up without you."

"In that case, come back and insist," said Antonella. She cleared her throat before she added sternly, "I'm unwilling to leave my home."

"They say a man got away after that motorcycle wreck a few months back. They say you saw him?"

"I'm sure I don't know anything of the sort," she said and shut the door on the soldier. He and his cohort were left staring at an imposing oak door. They stepped back and looked at the upstairs window. A breeze moved the curtain. Then all was placid.

The soldiers gave up and rejoined their caravan. The trucks could be heard grinding their gears as they chugged back up the switchbacks.

"You're unsafe here," Thaddeus told Antonella. He had heard the exchange through his window overlooking the yard and porch below.

"You're unsafe anyplace else," Antonella replied. "For now, this is the best we can do with you. When you can travel, after you remember your life, we will send you back. But for now, who do you trust?"

"I think I'm very cautious of that answer," Thaddeus said, choosing his words carefully. He had given this no small thought. Unsure who shot up his motorcycle and killed his passenger, he, too, was wary, though he felt less valuable in the grand scheme than perhaps Antonella viewed him. "I have done things," he said. "Dreams come to me. Or maybe they are memories. I'm not proud. Maybe I deserve to be found."

"Nonsense." Antonella could tell Thaddeus had thought about this more than he let on. "No one deserves to be found by the cartel. You're not in your right mind. I'll do your thinking for you until you're able. So far, that hasn't been so bad, am I right?"

He studied her as she changed his sheets beneath him. Her hair needed a professional cut, but he knew she wouldn't go for any such thing until he was gone. She was committed to outwitting the cartel. Her eyes were tired but determined. For just a moment, he was relieved to be in her care even more than usual. He was grateful, but he was also sad because he felt that she wouldn't be so keen to like him if she knew his whole story. If he knew his whole story, would he even like himself?

Thaddeus decided to share a little more. "There was a woman," he said. "She was beautiful and strong, brave. I remember her, but I'm not sure why."

"Did you love her?" asked Antonella, startling him with her insight.

He turned away. "Yes, I did."

She returned an hour later, bearing a handful of wild-flowers from the hillside. She had cut their bottoms with scissors and placed them into a vase of purple glass. The petals were purple. He inhaled but got no scent. She placed them on the table at his bedside and closed the book he had been napping with as it rose and fell with his deep breathing.

"You may give these to the woman," said Antonella. "In your dreams, in your memories, whatever you decide."

He reached and brushed his hand across the bouquet. He smiled at the touch. "I've never had flowers before."

"You've never lost your memory before, either."

"So, this is what it's like."

She smiled. "Something like that."

She saw an opening and took it. "What does this girl in your dreams look like?"

He smiled up at her. "Dark brown hair. Beautiful eyes. A kind smile. A lot like you, actually."

Thaddeus saw the color rise in her cheeks.

"What do you and your dream girl do, then? Ride bicycles? Have a picnic?"

155

"We do whatever we set our minds to." Thaddeus closed his eyes and lay his head back on the pillow as if to return to his dream woman. Before she could stop him, he was out.

She stepped out of the room and noted his care on her small makeshift chart. *Breathe, Antonella,* she told herself. She couldn't help but stop and smile at the most recent interaction with her patient. Which was the moment she first realized, trying to squirm free of the thought with all her strength, that she was falling for a man who didn't even remember his own mother's name, didn't even remember his life from just a short while ago.

She sagged cross-legged to the floor, her breath catching in her throat. Did she allow herself to think she liked this patient, that she might be falling for a patient? *Physician*, she cried in her mind, *heal thyself!* She drove the thought from her mind, strong in her commitment to avoiding those thoughts again.

She needed to distract herself and get out of her head. Making dinner was a good distraction, but she couldn't help but think of what Thaddeus would like best for supper.

This was going to be more challenging than she thought.

Chapter 32

An old man driving an ancient yellow Toyota pickup stopped at Antonella's front door. He knocked and waited. She answered.

"My name is Matias, and I'm here to run the Internet wire," he said.

"I'd almost forgotten my order," she replied. "It's been months since I contacted ColombiaTel."

"I don't know. I'm here to run the wire. That's all I know."

"Make yourself at home. Do you need to come inside?"

"I would need to measure, yes. Show me on the wall where you want the outlet, please."

She turned, and he followed her upstairs into the office. She showed him the dead Internet outlet. He pulled a tape measure from his belt and began measuring from the wall down the hallway, then down the stairs to the house's front door.

"The connection is up at the road," stated Matias.

"And you're running the wire down the hillside? Is there a trench already dug? Are there telephone poles?"

"I have my shovel. I will dig the trench."

"That's fifty yards. You're digging a trench with one shovel?"

"Yes, one shovel. Three inches deep."

Antonella blew out a sigh of relief. "Oh, we're not talking about a major excavation then."

The man realized she was suspicious of him, and maybe she wasn't comfortable with strangers. He considered showing her some ID, but she hadn't asked. So, he returned to his truck and pulled back up the hillside to the Internet connection at the top. He wondered at her surprise that he planned to dig a trench all in one day. He realized she was maybe expecting more. From her accent, she wasn't from the area where all installations and repairs are accomplished with duct tape and baling wire. Then he turned to his work.

"Who was that?" asked Thaddeus, attuned to all sounds and comings and goings at the front door.

"Oh, just the Internet man."

"Did he show ID?"

"He's a little old man. I didn't ask."

Thaddeus stared hard at her. "I would've asked."

"So far, you're safe. I won't allow unnecessary risk to come knocking. You can trust me, friend." She returned his look. "Well?"

"Well, I don't know. I feel helpless here, confined to this bed."

"Yes, that's really what it is. And I don't blame you one bit."

"Can you get me a firearm?" he asked, eyes piercing. "I'd feel less helpless with some cold steel under my pillow."

She pursed her lips, thinking. She usually would reject

such an idea out of hand, but since watching Encia die, she had wondered the same thing. Would a loaded gun in the house make her feel safer or less safe? She nodded slowly, thinking, and changed the subject to buy more time.

"How is your pain this morning?"

"Middling."

She prepared a syringe and injected him in the hip. "Sleep now. I've got this."

"Promise me you'll consider it."

"Sleep, please. You need it."

"I do. Thank you for everything you're doing for me."

"You're most welcome."

She pressed the back of her hand against his forehead when he slept. Warm, but not too warm. She touched her finger to his lips, then crept out of the room. "Night," she whispered from the stairs. "Sweet dreams."

Chapter 33

He fought his way to wakefulness from a deep sleep. Dreams—the colorful, pursuing kind of dreams, of being chased. He awakened in a sweat, his arms thrashing wildly, his frozen legs unmoving. When his arms flailed, he felt flesh. His eyes popped open because the flesh was not his own. In the dim light from the hallway, he saw her there on his bed, stretched out alongside him, asleep and becalmed. Antonella had dropped off to sleep with a damp washcloth in her hand. His shirt was raised where she'd been washing him down. He pulled down the front of his shirt and removed the washcloth from her hand.

He listened. Her breathing was regular and peaceful. He remembered the face of a woman, a woman with no name. He remembered others, farther-back people asleep beside him, trusting him, fully at peace to be at his side without fear or worry. His eyes fluttered and closed. He found her still-damp hand with his dry one and placed his hand over hers, wishing her gentle sleep.

When he awakened in the morning, she was gone. He heard her outside, singing in her garden as she tended to her corn and squash. He imagined her tomatoes, full and lush, as she had described them to him. He could all but taste their heavy, red flesh and made a swallowing contraction with his mouth and throat.

Then he heard her voice speaking and a voice in reply. It was the dream woman, and she, too, took up the song. Now they were singing together. Thaddeus waited, listening, wishing against wish that it was him in the garden, singing and smelling the vegetables, turning the sandy soil with his blade, tilling and caressing the earth that was so good it favored them with life-sustaining food. Of course, they were singing! Who wouldn't?

Out the other window of his bedroom, he could hear the sweet coos of the doves on the wires running up the hill. They were sweetly calling and making their music of peace without any expectation. *How blessed am I?* he thought. *How blessed am I to be here, to be alive!*

He didn't dwell on his useless legs. His hope was that he would walk again, that the paralysis was temporary, just as Antonella had helped him to hope it would be. He moved his hand to the table, turning a book lying there so he might see its spine. It was a book by Salinger, titled *Nine Stories*. He picked it up and opened to the first story. He read about a woman talking to her mother on the phone. She was on her honeymoon, and her new husband was up to hijinks of some kind. He took a young girl into the sea on an air mattress. He convinced the child they were looking for banana fish. Thaddeus read on, then rested his eyes.

He looked carefully around the room. Was there a gun? Of course not. Antonella would never own a gun. But was there one in the house? Would Cavonna have a gun in the garage or his room attached to the garage?

In the story Thaddeus had just read, the man left the girl on the beach after finishing their hunt for banana fish. Then he went back into his room and shot himself in the head.

There it was, sudden and without any warning, his life ended by his own hand.

Thaddeus wondered if the man's mental illness made him do it or if it was the man's predicament. And what about his own predicament? Would he be able to continue if he knew he would never walk again? If he did, he would be incontinent and have to wear a diaper and a bag. Would he end his own life? Or would he find the courage to go on, to be willing to listen for songs from some unknown garden, for calls from as yet unborn doves? Would those things be enough to sustain him?

And if they were not, would he have a gun? Would she allow him to own a gun in his own house in America?

And what of it? What of a gun that could silence song and call? That could treat, in the most extreme way, his paralysis.

He thought it might be time to leave Antonella's house.

Now, if he only knew where he was going. Maybe that would return. Maybe his paralyzed brain would recover its memory and take him home.

He slumped back against his pillow and replaced the Salinger book on the nightstand. He appreciated what he had read. He appreciated finding the book and realized, with a start, Antonella might have meant for him to find it. That she might have meant for him to address whether he would shoot himself after his metaphorical days at the beach. It would be just like her to sidle up to him and speak of these things through a story in a book.

That's just how gentle she was. The book was a damp washcloth in its own way, a rinse for his mind. He realized she was speaking to him and tending to his mind even while it was asleep.

She would be so easy to love. If he didn't care for her so much, he might just love her, too. But as it is, he respected her too much to inflict his damaged life upon her innocence. She had the entire world ahead of her, the whole world to visit, while his world was brutal and fearsome. He would not touch her with his world for anything. No, she deserved far better.

So, he shut his eyes and thought about banana fish and young girls who had gone to sea with strange men pushing air mattresses.

And he prayed he was not that man and she was not that girl.

Chapter 34

Franco Cárdenas stood on his front porch, waiting for the call from Felix. Did these amateurs think he didn't control every step of this game? There was a reason people shook when his name was mentioned. He checked his watch. It should be anytime soon.

His pocket vibrated. He slid to answer the call but remained silent until the caller spoke first.

"Jefe, I have eyes."

"Were they suspicious?"

"*Más o menos*. A little. I can make her trust me, though. The man was upstairs in another room. I can make this job take days. Weeks."

"Very good, Felix. I want an update tomorrow at noon."

"Si, señor. Adios."

Cárdenas paced back and forth. If Thaddeus were Colombian, he would already be dead. He was too connected to Americans, though. The queen would become the pawn, no doubt. No one stepped foot in his territory without permission. No one breathed. And he would be suffocated.

But what to play next? He had eyes. He had ears. How would it be made an accident?

"Alana!" he demanded to the air.

A petite woman, about 20 years old, with long wavy hair, entered his room.

"A cigar. Now!"

Alana retrieved the Cubans from their shelf, walked over to the porch, and opened the box to allow him to choose. After he did, she clipped the end and ignited it for him as he drew until it was lit. She stood there, waiting to be dismissed.

"You may leave."

As she walked away, he called her attention one more time. "Alana?"

"Si, señor?"

"I will need your company later."

Alana could only nod in complicity. She bowed out of the room and closed the door behind her.

The next day, Cárdenas awoke and shooed Alana out of the room.

She returned with a plate of *huevos rancheros* for his breakfast, more like lunch, and quickly left again.

Just as Cárdenas took a few bites of his food, he was interrupted by a call. Felix.

"Speak. What do you have?"

"There are two men and one woman. One of the men left to go to market this morning, leaving your guy and the woman alone. Very quiet. They have kept the doors locked and windows shut. The woman offered me coffee this morning. I accepted and sat on the doorstep with her. She is very kind, jefe."

"I don't care if she is Madre María, Felix! She has positioned herself against me. She will not be spared."

"Si, señor. You are right. I am wrong."

"Very good. Now, call me immediately if anything changes. You will watch when cars come, when cars go, when they sleep and when they wake. I will know all of it."

"Si, señor. I'll be in conta—"

"Felix? Felix! *Estás ahí?* Are you there?"

All Cárdenas could hear was a woman's voice on the other end. She was asking who Felix was talking to.

Dammit! Cárdenas hung up the phone and cursed under his breath. He grabbed his tequila bottle off the table next to his bed and drank straight from the bottle.

Felix was done. Any mistake was unacceptable. He would need to be dealt with.

Chapter 35

"Who shot you?" she asked. They had played this game a hundred times, but she kept playing, hoping against hope to spark some memory. She had little faith in his answers. Each time they played the game, his responses were different.

"The cartel."

"Are they looking for you?"

"They are looking for Thaddeus."

"They know your real name?"

"Nobody knows anybody's real name. Thaddeus is my work name."

"What is your real name, then?"

"Isn't Thaddeus real enough? Wait, I think Thaddeus is my real name."

"Who was the girl?"

"Someone. Maybe a hitchhiker. I don't know any more than that."

"What is your last name?"

"Seriously? I don't know."

"Where do you live?"

"I don't know."

"Are you married?"

"I don't know that either."

"Do you have kids?"

"I don't know."

"Who is your boss?"

"I don't know."

"Where is your office?"

"I don't know."

"You're not yet ready."

"But it's coming back."

He told her about human trafficking deep in the jungle. Sometimes she believed him. Sometimes she thought he was backfilling. She made notes at night, long after he was asleep. Cavonna brought drugs from the *farmacia*. Her name was well-known there. Thaddeus took what she gave him without question.

Chapter 36

"I think I need to see her," he said deliriously from flat on his back.

Antonella, sitting in the corner, shook her head. "You have a fever. You don't need to see anyone."

He looked wildly around the room. "I don't remember being here before."

"Hush, it's the fever talking. You've been here for months."

He shook his head wildly, eyes rolling back. She stood and moved closer to place a hand on his chest, and his thrashing subsided. "Easy now, Thaddeus. You need to rest."

He moved to sit up but was unable to manage it alone. She held him by the shoulders as his feeble squirming slowed. His breathing resumed its regular rhythm, and his eyes opened to focus on Antonella.

"I saw her in Bogotá at Punto Denales, you know."

"Who, Thaddeus? You saw who?"

"Anna. You know who I mean." Thaddeus's voice was filled with disgust. His doctor wasn't keeping up.

"The girl on the bike?"

"Where is she now?"

"I showed you the clipping. She was never found after the crash."

"That would be impossible."

Antonella watched him, concerned. The fever had raged for forty-eight hours and surely must break soon. Now it was making him delusional.

"Is there wine?"

She went to the medical cart and opened a bottle of burgundy. She poured two fingers in a plastic cup and took it to him. He greedily gulped it down. "More."

"That's all for now. Maybe this afternoon."

"Who appointed you Mother Superior?"

"You did. When you landed on my doorstep. you appointed me."

He tried to roll over onto his side. Sweat dripped down his brow. "Help me, please."

"We're doing everything we can. You need rest and recuperation."

"Is there medicine?"

"For what ails you? I think not. Pain shots, and I'm trying anti-inflammatories. If we try to move you to the hospital, we lose you to the cartel. You've told me Cárdenas has men scouring the countryside for you. You're stuck with me for now."

"I think Bogotá doesn't know. I need to contact Bogotá."

"It's the fever talking, I told you. I will tell you later, and you will thank me again. No phones, no computers, no contact." As she said it, she thought of the wristphone in the drawer. Was that who had been trying to contact him before the battery died? Was it an agent in Bogotá? Was it a wife or friend, worried sick about him?

As his eyes fluttered and he drifted off to sleep, her mind raced through dozens of scenarios. If the phone was linked to the cartel, they could use it to find her hideout. But if the phone was linked to his life in the States, it could be the key to his rescue.

She busied herself with her injection preparations, deep in thought. Then she injected him in the hip, and he moaned in his sleep with relief.

"Cavonna," she called as she walked toward the door, "would you run to the store for me to buy a cell phone charger?"

Chapter 37

Thaddeus blinked awake. It was dark outside. Antonella sat beside him in her overstuffed chair. Her chin was on her chest. She was asleep.

The dream. Or was it a memory as he came awake? A woman in a home. So long ago. The same woman, same face, as he was becoming accustomed to. Always the same. What happened to her? He thought back to the motorcycle accident. Was that her on the bike? No. That woman had died, and it was Thaddeus's fault. What had he done? What terrible thing had he done?

"Antonella," he said softly. "Antonella, I'm scared."

Her eyes opened. "Scared of what, dear man?"

Now he was plugged in. "I've done something terrible, but I don't know what."

"What does it feel like?"

He struggled with his answer but had to smile. The woman went straight to the feelings. That much he had learned by now.

"It feels like I hurt someone."

"There was a passenger on your motorcycle. You know about it. Was that her? Do you have a name yet?"

Tears formed in his eyes. "I think it was. It's making me insane because I don't know. I can almost see it. I can feel it all around, but there's no face I can put to it. Do you know what I mean? A memory without form?"

"We all have memories. Some are in our heads. Some are in our bodies. Some are both places. Maybe yours is just outside your head, just outside your body. Maybe you're catching up to it is all. But for right now, right here, you're safe. There's no reason to be scared. We have Cavonna sleeping downstairs. He is very strong, and he hates the cartels. He is good."

A look of alarm crossed his face. "What's his name?"

"Cavonna."

"That doesn't ring a bell."

"I'm sure it doesn't, but you know him well."

"Is he a very dark man, wide-spaced eyes, black hair he wears back in a ponytail?"

"Why, yes."

"Does he drive a truck?"

"Yes, he lives above the garage."

"I can see his face. There's a memory. Why are my memories so random? Why would I know this man but not my passenger?"

"Because you see him every day? But I don't know why you remember some things and not others, and some days but not others. I'm not that kind of doctor. I'm trying, but I'm limited."

"I know, I know. You're right. Cavonna is a good man."

"So, you *do* know him."

"Like I know my own palm."

"Cavonna heard something while he was in town this

173

morning. A top drug lord was shot to death in a restaurant. They said a man on a motorcycle shot him through the window. Thaddeus, did you ever deal with Cárdenas's cartel?"

"I don't know. Have I said something in my sleep?"

"No, no, you haven't. I only know they're looking for you. I just wonder that's all."

"I don't remember. I'm sorry. Did I just move my foot?"

"Try it again because I wasn't watching."

He grimaced in concentration and effort. He looked from his feet to Antonella. "Well?"

"I don't think I saw movement. Do you feel something?"

"Like something crawling inside my foot. Like nerves tingling."

"That can only be a good sign. Feelings are a good sign."

"Yes, I do know about feelings. You have lots of them, Antonella. We should talk sometime."

"I'm sure we will. Are you ready to try to sleep again?"

"I'm ready. Sorry I woke you."

"That's what I'm here for."

"Why isn't Cavonna here?"

"It's only eleven. He has another hour before his shift begins."

"I'm glad it was you here."

"Good. I'm glad, too."

"I'm going to dream her name now, Antonella. I'm closing my eyes."

"I'm holding you to that. In the morning, I want a name."

"Say no more."

"Till the morning, then."

He was asleep. The pain medication had caught up. She

crossed her hands in her lap and watched him settle back into his bed. When he was sleeping, she stood and kissed him on the forehead ever so gently. Then she turned off his light and tiptoed from the room.

"Help him remember," she said to the ocean as she passed the window.

Chapter 38

She stood in her garden on the shady side of the house and cupped her hand over her eyes. A tall, slender man limped down the path directly toward the house. Antonella stepped out of the shade to make her presence known, but the man continued to come closer. When he reached the front of the house he stopped, looking up from his feet to see Antonella.

"I'm afraid you're on private property, sir. Is there something I can do for you?"

"Yes, ma'am. I heard word around town that you have a problem you may need help with."

She didn't respond, only looked him slowly up and down. She could tell at first sight of his pale skin that he wasn't from around here. His Spanish had a thick accent, and his jowls were covered in a thick brown beard, a black eye patch resting over his right eye.

"I don't need help here. I don't know where you got that idea."

"You're a doctor?"

"I am. Why do you ask?"

"I'm a nurse," he said after a moment, cracking a charming smile. "We could open a clinic to attend to surfing injuries. There's a fantastic break off these cliffs."

"Funny man. I'm only here for a short time more, then I'm off to take up my practice in the city."

"What practice is that?"

"The practice I'll be—I'll be joining. I don't actually know yet. But my residency was a smash hit. I'm sure I'll be hired with my first resume."

"I'm sure you will."

She looked back up the long path and noticed a dark sedan parked next to Cavonna's truck outside the gate. The gate was still closed and latched. Looking back toward the bearded stranger, she found him peering closely at her house, trying to see in the windows. She stepped in front of him, not sure whether to be unnerved or amused by his boldness.

"I hope it's not rude to ask—how did you get in through the gates?"

"Really? I squeezed through. Just turned sideways and walked through. I'm no Houdini. Do you have patients here now?"

"No, no patients."

"Word around town is that there's one patient. A man with memory loss."

Antonella stiffened.

"That's why I came all this way. I heard you were caring for a patient, and I figured you would need help with him. Surely, you must be exhausted."

Her mind raced. She had been so careful. How could

people know? Had Cavonna let something slip at the *farmacia*? She could feel the man's one eye on her, could feel the seconds slipping by as she tried to determine if this man was friend or foe.

"Listen, miss, I can tell you're nervous here," he said, sincerity written across his face. "The truth is, I really need work. I've had to sleep in my car for the last week, and I can't keep doing that. The narcos have targeted me, and they've scared away any possible employment for me. I hear you're not afraid of them."

The idea of a full night's sleep without waking three times to check on her patient suddenly stole into her head. There was Cavonna, but he had no medical skills. He would wake her if necessary. But someone with training. She found it hugely inviting. But she resisted. "I can't pay for a nurse. This man isn't a paying patient. He has no money."

"Just let me have the use of your kitchen and bathroom. Maybe a couch to sleep on? I can sleep anywhere. Maybe down on the beach?"

"There's an old rickety stairway down to a tiny slice of sand. Some might call it a beach, though I certainly would not. A beach is one you can walk on, sit on when the tide's in. This one goes under with the tide. No beach."

"That's good enough. Is there a landing on the stairs?"

"I don't know. You'll need to look." She decided to jump off her safe perch. "I could use help on the midnight shift."

"The midnight shift is perfect. I don't sleep at night. Midnights have always been my best shift."

"Then let's try it tonight."

"Can I come inside and shower this morning?"

"Certainly. The water is probably still hot. You're welcome to bathe here."

"What's your name?"

"Antonella."

"Doctor something?"

"Just Antonella will do. And what's your name?"

"I go by many names, but my friends call me Nico."

Chapter 39

The sun had just set when Antonella was alarmed by a clamor at the front door. It sounded like someone kicking it. She hurried downstairs and peered through the security hole. There stood Nico, his arms full of tinfoil and paper sacks, and he kicked the heavy door with his huarache. He called her name. His eyepatch was askew with his efforts, and she found herself looking directly into the socket where there was once an eyeball. It wasn't pretty, but she was a doctor. She'd seen much worse. She unlocked the door and pulled it open.

Nico all but fell through the doorway. His reeking breath was an immediate tipoff—he had been drinking heavily. He tripped on a Mexican rug, and the tinfoil parcels surged up and almost out of his arms, but he collected himself just in time to keep them from scattering like logs across the floor.

"Barbecued swordfish," he said in a hoarse voice. "All you can eat, forty-one thousand pesos. The price of a good red wine. Cheap."

He staggered into the kitchen and plopped his gifts

down on the counter. The room filled with the seductive aroma of barbecue. She hurried to the cabinet for plates, and he rummaged through drawers for flatware. "I waited to get home before eating."

"Where were you, up at the highway?"

"Club Forty-Nine," he said, meaning the club at 49 kilometers. "Yes, highway." Their enclave consisted of a fenced quarter mile of houses and buildings, fronted by a nightclub called Club Forty-Nine just inside the top gate. The club could be entered from the highway without passing through the gate or the gated interior could be accessed from the club's southern entrance and exit.

"Cavonna is working on the Range Rover in the garage. Let me go call him."

"No problem, I'll get him. We need four plates, including one for the narc upstairs. Thaddeus Murfee is, I believe, the name he goes by." He was drunk but joking around, so she wasn't worried about him.

She made up four plates of the fish and slaw and French fries and put two of the plates on a tray. She would serve him upstairs and eat with him. Nico and Cavonna could join them or not.

As she was serving a sleepy, just-awakened, Thaddeus, she heard Cavonna and Nico follow her into the room. When she turned, they were seating themselves side-by-side in the window seat on the ocean side of the house. Cavonna tore apart a filet and stuffed a large piece into his mouth. He chewed earnestly and noisily. Nico had brought along a beer from the fridge and took a large sip before picking at his fish with two fingers. Antonella placed a plate on the serving tray on the swing-away table and slid it in front of Thaddeus. She handed him a fork.

"Thank you," he said sleepily. He yawned and stared at his plate. "Food. Good stuff," he said and took a bite.

"I met a man tonight who says he knows you," Nico said, indicating Thaddeus with his fork. "He knows you from Bogotá."

Antonella's head snapped up. "You told someone he was here?" she said in alarm. "How could you!"

"Relax, he doesn't know where I stay. He doesn't care, anyway. He's not army and he's not *narcotraficante*."

But she was worried. "What were you thinking? What I do here is nobody's business," she snapped at Nico. "You are never to mention a word of him again. Do you understand me?"

"Well—"

"Do you understand me?" she cried.

"I understand," Nico said in a toneless voice. He was meek when he spoke, like a chastened schoolboy. "I didn't know he was a secret."

"Do you wish he was found by the men who are looking for him?"

Nico grunted and looked out the window.

"Nico," said Antonella, "you're on at midnight. Do you plan to be sober by then?" Her voice was filled with disgust as she watched him drink his beer.

"I am having one final beer. Relax, this is nothing. You will shoot him full of morphine at midnight, and I'll watch him sleep for five hours. I'll be as sharp as I need to be."

She set aside her plate then shook her head. "This isn't working. I cannot have you going around and telling strangers about my patient. I cannot have you coming to work intoxicated. This is my patient, and he is going to have a good result under my care. If you don't want to be part of that, then I want you to take your things and leave immediately because I cannot afford to have you here. This is unacceptable."

Nico set aside his beer bottle. He took his napkin and scrubbed his hands with it. Long barbecue smudges streaked the paper. "I'm sorry. I truly did not know about your secret. Yes, I will be sober at midnight. That's four hours, and I was planning coffee next. I'll be fine for him."

Nico stood and collected his plate and flatware and beer bottle. He held them carefully before him and made his way from the room and down the stairs. Antonella was relieved to hear he didn't fall and require medical attention himself. She sat beside Thaddeus's bed, a look of disgust contorting her face.

"There is more to him than he's telling," she said at last, speaking to no one in particular. She stood while Cavonna and Thaddeus watched her begin to load up the tray she had brought. "He has brought anger into my house, and I won't have it. We were better before he came. I will tell him that when he sobers up. But not tonight. Tonight, I will get a good night's rest and then I'll tell him. He cannot bring his anger in here. He'll have to check it at the door or leave and go somewhere else."

"He knows about Thaddeus," says Cavonna, unsure of what he meant when he said it exactly, because he didn't really know what information Nico had picked up at the club. "He's dangerous, I'm thinking. Maybe I should go down to his camp and shoot him."

Antonella and Thaddeus both stiffened. Cavonna was a quiet, peaceful, unassuming man. Had he actually just offered to kill the man?

"Nonsense," Antonella said, "nobody is shooting anybody. It's just something we might have to deal with. No more talk of shooting. Get back to my truck's brakes and fix that squeal, Cavonna."

"Yes," said Cavonna sheepishly. "Maybe I didn't mean actually *shoot* shoot."

"And maybe you did," said Antonella. "Always my trusted friend, my dear, sweet Cavonna."

"But if there's shooting to be done…" His voice trailed off.

Chapter 40

Antonella scrubbed down the medical supply table and cabinets with bleach and water. The smell of disinfectant permeated the room. She turned in time to see Nico enter with a slight knock on the doorframe before he continued walking on in. Thaddeus turned his head to see.

"Our new attendant," says Thaddeus. "That's quite a shiner you've got there, friend," he said about the eyepatch worn by the nurse.

"A little gift from a fiasco in Bogotá," Nico replied, a strange look on his face. After a moment's hesitation, he continued. "I believe you were present, were you not?"

"Me?" Thaddeus shook his head. "I think not. You have me confused with someone else."

"Ahh, I don't think so. I'd know your face anywhere."

"Wrong man. Antonella, could you crack a window, please? I'm dizzy from the bleach."

"Of course," she said and stood. She went to the window and pushed it fully open. "An ocean breeze will take it right out." She crossed the room and opened those windows, too. A draft blustered in, blowing the sheer curtains away from the ocean window. Thaddeus thanked her, and she left the room.

Nico circled the bed, his lone good eye raking over Thaddeus's withered body.

"How fortunate you are here now with a full-time doctor, recovering from your wounds. What was it, a motorcycle, I think Antonella told me?"

"A motorcycle. I remember none of it."

"Not at all? No recall of where you were coming from?"

"No."

"Or where you were going?"

"Not that, either."

"She showed me the clippings last night. Was there a girl with you?"

"I read that in the newspaper clippings. I have no idea who she was or what happened to her."

"I think I do. And I think you do, too. I think you might just be keeping it at bay. I'm here because I need to know the truth to be certain."

Thaddeus squinted up at Nico, unable to shake the feeling of uncertainty with this man.

"What do you remember?" Nico asked.

"The woman? I have no memory of her. Enlighten me."

"You're lying! Where is she? The other American vigilante."

"A vigilante?" Thaddeus said, mostly to himself. "I was right. I did have a gun."

"What, you don't remember what you were doing in Bogotá either?"

"Very little. I remember a name. Marcel Rainsford. Something about that."

Nico dropped his gaze and busied himself with cleaning the countertop.

"Antonella, could I bother you for that light blanket?" Thaddeus asked. "That air is chill."

Antonella smiled, and from the bottom drawer, she retrieved a brown army blanket. She shook it out and spread it over her patient. "Better?"

"Much better, thank you."

Nico cleared his throat noisily, but Thaddeus ignored him. He was finished with Nico. He watched as Cavonna opened a new cell phone charger, plugged it into the wall, and connected it to the watchphone in the drawer.

"Could you cover for me now, Nico?" asked Antonella, turning. "I have a phone interview today for a job."

"Certainly, just let me use the restroom first."

"Thank you."

"Thaddeus and I will have that much more time to talk, right old man?"

Thaddeus appeared to be asleep now. Voices lowered as Antonella and Nico crept from the room.

Chapter 41

"Do you remember the jungle?" Nico asked Thaddeus when Antonella was downstairs one afternoon.

She prepared a late lunch for Thaddeus since she'd donned a disguise and ventured into the city. Returning with meats and medicines, she was now preparing to ply her patient with both. The pharmacist thought the non-narcotic pain killer she purchased would remove him from the pain cycle while allowing him to remain awake for longer stretches.

Antonella's theory was that only wakeful consciousness could work a full restoration of memory and lying in bed in a narcoleptic state did no one any good. Part of her thinking was that she would like to see a recovery such that she would begin her new life. But paramount to that was her dedication to her patient. She wouldn't even allow herself to think of rejoining the world as long as Thaddeus needed her.

She returned upstairs with a plate of meats and finger

foods in time to hear from the hallway Nico saying to Thaddeus, "You don't remember the Monkey's Paw? How you invaded Cárdenas' property and privacy? I heard down at the club, you're the man."

"Do what you will, then. I can't fight back."

"There is only acknowledgment first. Of course, I could always slip and double your morphine injection by mistake. There's always that possibility."

"Which is why I always make the injections," said Antonella, entering the room and interrupting the interrogation and accusations. "I'm sure poor Thaddeus did whatever you claim he did for good reason. At least that's my position. And if this ever happens again, you will be fired on the spot, Nico. Do I make myself clear, sir?"

"Very clear. Forgive me for losing it. Sometimes I get overwhelmed by the rumors. Please accept my apologies, Thaddeus."

Thaddeus was on edge. It had been three hours since his last injection. "Apology accepted. It's just that you're becoming boring, Nico. I much preferred you when you read to me out of Antonella's library. Much preferred you then."

"I can get back to that," Nico said. "Consider it done."

"Well," Antonella said, considering her next words, "I don't much care for you and your intrusive behavior with Thaddeus, but having a nurse onboard has restored my sleep and changed my life. Just remember you're not the only nurse in town. You can be replaced, and I will replace you if you can't let go of this crap. Enough. Now run along. Be back at midnight, ready to take on your duties in a reformed frame of mind. Do you read me?"

"Loud and clear. I'm leaving now," he said with a smirk.

Nico hurried from the room. Antonella served Thaddeus his plate and then went to the seaside windows. She looked below and watched Wilkinson as he disappeared over the edge of the cliff on the stairway heading down to his landing tent. She was glad to see him go.

"That's it. I'm looking for a replacement," she said from her thoughtful place. She hadn't meant for Thaddeus to hear this thought but spoke absently without thinking.

"I don't understand Nico," said Thaddeus. "Why is he so interested in who I am?"

She turned. "He's wearing on my patient. I've had it with him. Psst!" She made the sound and motion of swatting a bothersome fly.

"Whatever. Thanks for this great food. I don't know how I'm ever going to repay you."

"Nonsense. You're my first patient post-residency. Repay me by getting well and away from the cartel's assault. That's repayment enough to defeat the cartel in its desire to finish you. Get well, my friend."

"I'm trying. The memory is the worst. I can accept the paralysis—somewhat. But the lost memories are making me crazy. I don't know how to live with ninety-percent of my life missing in action."

"It must be horrible, dear man. But I believe it will return. It's just a matter of time to recover from your trauma. Every peer journal and article seem to tell me that. TBI is the slowest recovery of all."

"I'm trying. I spend hours every day trying to recall specific things. My real name, my family, if there is any. My home is a big problem. Every man needs to be from somewhere. I can't even remember that, or I would already be back there."

"Yes, home is a big one. When we can get your home,

the rest of it will fall into place quite easily, I'm thinking. Well, let's work toward that, shall we?"

"Yes. We'll work toward getting me home. For better or worse." He was referring to his paralysis then. He knew he'd be a burden on someone out there.

"For better then," she said. "For better."

"I can only hope. Do you expect that one day I will stand and walk out of here?"

"I have dreams about that. Expectations, not so much, if I'm being honest with you. Spinal injuries are tricky. Once the swelling is gone, who knows?" Tears came to her eyes. "Who knows anything?"

"Now, I know. I've never seen your tears. I knew they were there when you weren't around me."

She was softly crying now. She turned away. "For better or worse, I'm here to the end. Count on it."

"I do. I do count on it. Blessings, Antonella."

"Accepted. Thank you."

He returned to his plate of food, unable to watch her any longer.

But it didn't matter. She had quickly collected herself and cursed her lapse. "That won't happen again."

"I know. This roast beef is wonderful."

"Fresh Colombian beef. The best."

"Yes." He laughed. "Your bribe is accepted. I will use the nourishment well in my recovery. Thank you."

"Godspeed."

Chapter 42

Nico had pitched his tent on the cliff wall that ran from Antonella's house 100 feet down to the ocean. The first stairway landing was 25 feet below the top. It was on this landing that Nico had set up his temporary home.

"Yes," he told Antonella, "I am there because it is safe and out of the way. Nobody sees me there. Nobody is going to come snooping around asking me questions."

"When will you be leaving here? It isn't safe after you talked to the man from Bogotá at the club?"

"He was drunk. I'm safe here."

"And what about Thaddeus? Is he safe here?"

"I didn't give names. I just said there was a man."

"And who was this man? Was he army?"

"He was just some man having two drinks after work. He has no interest in checking into Thaddeus."

"But you said the man knew him in Bogotá."

"No, no, he said if it's the man he was thinking of, then

he knew him from Bogotá. He's never seen Thaddeus, and he won't be snooping around for him."

"And we know that how?"

"Because it was just two acquaintances over drinks. Lots of things get said over drinks. Things nobody thinks about once they leave the bar."

"Thank heavens for that," she said. "Your cavalier attitude is all wrong for me. I'm going to ask you to leave if this happens again."

"Like I said the other night, I didn't know he was a secret. I'll be more circumspect."

"Please do."

When someone knocked on the front door that afternoon, Antonella cringed. She was feeding Thaddeus as he sat up in bed, chewing and nodding off from the recent injection. She was wiping his chin repeatedly since he didn't seem to keep his bites entirely in his mouth today. She set aside the hand towel she was using to clean him up and went to the ocean-facing window. She looked down at the porch below. It was a man wearing a hat, but she couldn't see his face. What to do?

She wiped her hands on her jeans as she made the trip downstairs to the front door. Looking through the peephole, it was no one she recognized, so she pulled it open just a crack and looked out.

"Hello?"

He smiled a friendly, even smile and tipped his hat. "Miss, my name is Muir Keystone," he said in perfect Spanish, although there was no way he was Colombian. He was dressed in jeans and an expensive anorak. "I'm looking for a man who disappeared in this area. His name is Thaddeus Murfee. We used to work together in Bogotá."

"I'm afraid you're knocking on the wrong door. I've

never heard of any such man," she said. Her affect was quite flat, her face expressionless as well.

The man shuffled his feet on the mat. "You see, I was talking to a Mr. Nico Lamontez the other night, and he told me there might be a man answering my friend's description staying here. He said he thought he knew the man from Bogotá himself."

She edged the door all but closed. "No one here like that. I think your friend is mistaken."

"Mr. Lamontez also told me he was staying in the area. Can you perhaps direct me to him? Do you know him?"

"I'm afraid I don't know any of the men you're looking for, Mister—Mister—"

"Keystone. Muir Keystone. Look, I won't waste your time. I am a British citizen but work legally in South America." He stopped and produced identification. He held it up to the light for her to examine.

"I see."

"This Thaddeus fellow is—was—on my team. We think outlaws may've attacked him in this area. We're anxious about him and would like to get him returned."

"Returned? Returned where?"

Keystone's eyes narrow. "You do know?"

"No. I'm only curious. It sounds like quite a tale."

"We'll return him to Bogotá if we get the chance. We're afraid he's in great danger. That is if he's even still alive."

"Afraid I don't know, and I cannot help. Goodbye, now."

He seized the door. "One more thing, please. If you see him, would you please tell him I am looking for her grave and will see that arrangements are made? He'll know who."

She closed the door and immediately put her ear against

the wood. She listened for receding footsteps but heard none. She retreated upstairs, double-time.

"A man came to the door. He says he worked with you, and you're in great danger. He wants to return you to Bogotá."

When his eyes flickered open, she was reminded of sluggish butterflies settling on gauze. The wings were blue.

"Is that a good thing?" he asked.

"I'm sure I don't know. It turns out Nico mentioned you a night or two ago at the club. Now half the country knows you're around. I've half a mind to try and move you."

"What did you tell him?"

"I lied for you. I told him I knew of no such man as a Thaddeus Murfee. What else could I say?"

"Good, good. What was his name again?"

"Muir Keystone."

"Keystone...Keystone. I'm sure I don't know any such name."

"Might it be that you've just forgotten?"

"Antonella," he said with a wide smile, "anything's possible along those lines. Don't we know?"

"Yes, we know. Now I'm perplexed. The man might have an answer for you."

"Well, we don't know, good or bad. I say you did the right thing. Let's leave it alone, then."

"Fair enough. We'll just deny everything if he returns. But what if he returns with the police? What will I do then?"

"Tell them to go away. And if they do come up here, I'll tell them another name. I have no ID, no badge, nothing they can trace me with. I'll tell them I was robbed and my name's James Adams. No, John Adams. I think he was a president. Can you remember John Adams?"

"John Adams. Yes, I can remember," she said evenly. She was very used to meeting new patients and committing their names to memory day after day as the faces changed in the hospital. "John Adams, it is."

"Did he say anything else?"

"He said he's looking for the girl's grave. He will make arrangements."

"Now that's random. I'm sure I don't know who he means."

Chapter 43

Cavonna entered the room as Antonella finished reading for the day. He held out a paper sack to Antonella. The name of the *farmacia* was stamped on the side. She opened it and examined the contents. "It's all here?"

"I told them everything," said Cavonna. He said to Thaddeus, "When are you going to leave that bed and walk again?"

Thaddeus only shrugged.

"Do you want I should help you up and hold you to try?"

Again, a shrug. Then, "Ask the doctor when I'm ready to try."

Antonella closed the paper bag and set it on the medication table. "That might not be a bad idea. Even sitting up alone with your feet on the floor. That is good for you."

Thaddeus studied the two of them. "Is there a real belief here that I might walk again? Or is this some dutiful performance that's just done in all cases, even the hopeless ones?"

"That's the thing about paralysis," she said. "We never know until we know. You could be walking by Friday, and no one would be surprised. Or you might never walk again, and that would surprise no one, either. We don't know until we know."

"Sure," said Thaddeus. "Come here and help me sit up, Cavonna."

Cavonna walked to the bed and sat down. He held out two hands to Thaddeus, who reached out to him. Cavonna assisted him in turning his legs and torso to the side.

"Do you feel your feet on the floor?" asks Antonella.

The patient looked up at the ceiling as if concentrating. "Nope. I feel nothing. Are my toes moving? My brain says my toes are moving on the floor."

"Your toes are doing nothing," Cavonna offered. "Try lifting your right foot."

Thaddeus shut his eyes, and his forehead wrinkled. He was making a great effort.

"Well?"

"Well, nothing," Cavonna said. "Should I help you stand?"

"Yes, please. Let's see if I can stand."

Cavonna wrapped an arm around Thaddeus's waist and stood, pulling the patient upright with him. Thaddeus stood briefly before toppling back onto the bed.

"Damn," says Thaddeus. "Just that movement alone was exhausting."

"It's been months," says Antonella. "One step at a time."

"Let me try again."

Cavonna seized Thaddeus around the waist and stood back up again.

When Thaddeus felt stable enough, he said, "Okay, let me go."

Cavonna did and stepped away. Thaddeus stood on his own briefly before his legs gave out and, his arms flailing wildly, fell into Cavonna's arms.

Thaddeus growled in frustration.

"It's okay," said Antonella. "We'll make sure to massage your legs every day and move them to get the muscles stimulated again. You can do this."

"We're just starting," Cavonna said. "I've seen worse than you come back."

"Seriously?"

"Antonella works miracles. I've seen them."

"Where?"

"Here. Everywhere."

"I'll take your word on that. Pain, Antonella."

She turned to prepare the injection. She was fast, and the injection flowed into the hip. Thaddeus sighed with relief.

Cavonna pulled Antonella over to the far side of the room, away from Thaddeus. "Should we try again every day?" whispered Cavonna.

"Yes, and like I said, let's continue therapy on his legs. With his body's movement, with him walking, it may very well stimulate other parts of his brain to remember. You know how they say about muscle memory and your body attaching itself to certain thoughts and actions?"

"I don't know much about that," said Cavonna, "but I trust that you do. Let's try for him."

Just as they were about to leave the room, a loud buzzing sound broke the silence. Antonella startled, but

Cavonna moved swiftly past her, opened the drawer, and retrieved the wristphone that she had found in Thaddeus's pocket so many months before.

Of course, she thought. The phone was ringing.

Cavonna looked at her, then over at Thaddeus. He pushed the green button and raised the watch to his ear. "Hello?"

Chapter 44

Christine's heart nearly stopped. There was no noise, no sound whatsoever, in her La Jolla home. She felt her pulse then made herself speak.

"Hello?" she whispered into the phone.

There was no response. She had heard a man's voice answer, though. Was that Thaddeus's voice? She didn't think so.

How many times had she tried to call his phone over the last months? It had always gone straight to Thaddeus's voicemail. But this time, someone had answered.

"Hello," she said again, but again there was no response. She could hear breathing on the other end.

"Please, Thaddeus, is that you? It's me, Christine. Talk to me."

Again, the only response was the rhythmic breathing on the other end. Desperation rose in her throat, and tears began to spill down her cheeks. "Thaddeus, I miss you. Come home!"

Another moment of silence, and then she heard the male voice speaking, although not to her.

"It's Christine. I don't know her."

"Thaddeus, do you know someone named Christine?" a female voice said in the background.

She listened, her heart beating out of her chest. For a moment, she expected to hear his voice come over the line, reassuring her that he was fine, he was coming home. She had longed to hear his voice for months now.

The silence stretched on. Something was happening on the other end of the line, but she couldn't make out what it was. She strained to hear.

Click.

The call went dead.

————

"TURQUOISE, IT'S ME," she shouted into the phone as the car hit 80 mph on the Southern California interstate. "I'm coming to pick you up."

"What are you talking about?" came the sleepy voice of her step-daughter.

"I found Thaddeus."

A moment of silence on the other side of the call, then Turquoise's voice, fully awake this time, "I'm listening."

"I tried calling his phone again tonight, and someone picked up. They wouldn't let me talk to Thad, but I was able to log the location data on the call."

"Wow, really? Chris, that's amazing! I was starting to give up hope!"

"Me too, honey, me too," Christine said, eyes watering. Shaking her head, she wiped away the tears. There would be time for tears later. Now there was only one thing to do. "Grab a change of clothes and your passport. I'll be there in ten."

Chapter 45

Then he was walking. It returned in the afternoon when he felt compelled suddenly to stand. He had climbed from his bed, placed his feet on the floor, and stood upright. Just as easily, he had walked off across the room. Slowly, at first, but then more powerfully as muscle memory responded. He had fallen back into bed, exhausted, then slept.

Thaddeus opened his eyes to the first rays of the morning light filtering through windows. How late did he stay up? The previous night was a fog, a nightmare that he didn't wish to remember.

But he did remember.

He remembered Christine.

And walking! Now, he was asleep in a strange room. He must be downstairs in Antonella's house. He sat up and looked around.

He remembered.

Christine. He remembered the smell of her hair. He remembered the way the whole world stopped spinning when she smiled at him. He remembered the way his heart sped up at the sound of her voice.

Through the fog, he remembered the phone ringing, Cavonna answering, someone asking for him, but it didn't matter.

In the instant that his memories of Christine had returned, so too had his memories of Operation Monkey's Paw. Cárdenas and the cartel, the drugs, the children.

If Cárdenas found Thaddeus, he would tear him limb from limb. Not only had Thaddeus's team taken away all the children he was to traffic, most likely worth millions, but the fighting and explosions destroyed parts of his coca fields, more money lost by Cárdenas.

Thaddeus shook his head, suddenly overcome. He should get up and leave before Cárdenas came for him. And he surely would. Maybe then Antonella and Cavonna would be spared.

As he considered the best way to face his personal gallows, a shadow passed outside the window, and then there was a loud knock on the door. He crawled from the couch and stood. They were downstairs in the living room. He had walked downstairs!

At the sound, Antonella and Cavonna stirred behind him. They'd both fallen asleep after dinner last night. She opened one eye, looking toward the door. Cavonna silently rose and stepped toward the door. Motioning to Thaddeus, he grabbed a kitchen knife and positioned himself next to the closed door.

Thaddeus stood and approached the door, wiping his hands on his jeans. He briefly peeked through the window, then pulled the door open just a crack and looked out.

"Hello?"

The man at the door broke into a broad smile. "Thaddeus! I hoped I'd find you here!" he said, his voice cracking with genuine joy.

Confused, Thaddeus only looked at the man, then turned toward Antonella. She nodded at the gentleman as if she'd met him before.

"Who are you?" Thaddeus asked.

"Seriously, Thad? It's me, Muir," the man said as he shuffled his feet on the mat. "I ran into a man by the name of Lamontez at the bar the other night, and he told me that you were staying here. He says you had an accident and are having trouble with your memory. That's why we couldn't find you."

Antonella stepped in front of Thaddeus and edged the door all but closed. "I'm sorry, Mr…

"Keystone."

"Mr. Keystone, you can't be here." She glanced past him up the lane, but nothing else moved outside.

"Did Cárdenas already do something? We've all been worried about you," Muir said, and Thaddeus could see the truth written on his face. "I knew as soon as I saw Lamontez that if he was talking about you, you would need my help."

Antonella and Thaddeus looked out at him through the crack in the door. Cavonna hid only inches away, knife in hand.

"Truth is, I'm surprised to see Thaddeus alive," Muir continued. "After everything fell apart at the Monkey's Paw…" His voice trailed off.

"So, you were part of that secret mission?" Antonella asked, her curiosity outweighing her caution.

"Yes, ma'am. I used to work with MI6 but recently have been doing some contract work for the Colombian government. But before that, I was part of Mr. Murfee's team." He stopped and produced an identification card. He held it up in the light for her to examine. Thaddeus watched, curious.

"Now, tell me the truth, has Cárdenas found you? When Lamontez left the bar the other night, half the people in the club knew you lived here."

Antonella turned to look at Thaddeus, and he could feel her concern for him. She'd always cared for him.

Cavonna stepped out from his hiding place as they held eye contact and grabbed the door with his large hand. Muir stepped back in surprise as Cavonna pulled the door open and gestured for Muir to come inside. "If you're not with Cárdenas, you're with us. Why don't you come in, and we can get to the bottom of this?"

Chapter 46

M uir stepped through the door, his blue shirt accenting the light blue of his eyes.

"Why are you here?" Thaddeus asked, his mind racing to put the pieces together. "If you were part of my team, as you claim, how did you end up here?"

"I've been embedded in Colombia for three years," Muir responded, "and cover all of the territories of Cárdenas from coast to jungle. I know his lieutenants have been active around Buenaventura lately, and I'm here keeping my ear to the ground. We've been looking for you, Thaddeus. Don't think we forgot about you or ever gave up."

"How do we know you're not working with Cárdenas?" asks Cavonna as they sit down around the table.

Diego leaned forward on his elbows, eyes flashing. "Cárdenas is not a man but a monster. He is evil incarnate. And the only reason I left the MI6 and working to eliminate Cárdenas and his cartel was that acting in a freelance capacity gave me more freedom to act swiftly. If you know what I mean."

"I do," said Thaddeus softly, looking at Muir. "I remember the children. I remember what this man Cárdenas had done to them."

"Boy, the memory thing is no joke," said Muir in wonder. "You really can't remember anything, can you?"

"Not really. Not anything important."

Muir took a deep breath. "You are a millionaire. You are American. You are a lawyer in California. You came to Colombia to locate a kid, your nephew, held hostage at the Monkey's Paw by Cárdenas' cartel."

"Nephew?"

"Yes, his name is Simon, and he is safe."

At the name, Thaddeus was overcome with a rush of vivid memories. He remembered the folder full of information on Cárdenas with stationary marked *Marcel Rainford*. He remembered opening a bathroom stall door to see a little boy huddled on the floor: his nephew, Simon.

"Earth to Thaddeus."

Thaddeus blinked and shook his head. "Are all the children safe?"

"There were so many of them, and Cárdenas's men were back so quickly, but that we know, we have evacuated them all," Muir replied. "A fellow agent by the name of Janes personally put your nephew on a chopper headed to Bogotá. Rainford and the team would have arranged transport back to the U.S.. It's been months. I'm sure he's safe at home by now."

Thaddeus walked over to the sink and splashed water on his face. He couldn't unravel his emotions; the relief that he felt about his nephew, the confusion at all the new information, the wonderment of all the rest of the story that was sure to come.

Muir filled in Antonella and Thaddeus as Cavonna made a pot of coffee. "You're taking a huge risk by protecting him from the cartel and Cárdenas," Muir said to Antonella.

"I would guard him with my life."

"And so would I."

"Would you ever consider taking him back to the States?" asked Antonella.

"I don't know that I could. I'm not an American citizen, but British. Not that it would matter too much. But right now, I'm only here by motorcycle. The Ducati monster parked outside is mine."

"I see. If I ever made a truck available to you, might you consider driving him?"

"Perhaps, but that would be a long road to freedom with many dangers along the way. It would be better if we had a full team to evacuate him. Cárdenas will be waiting around every corner."

They talked another thirty minutes. He had been up for days, though, searching for Thaddeus and looked ready to fall asleep on the chair as they sipped coffee and talked. Antonella arranged a room for him and told him to bring in his stuff. He had no luggage, so she provided him with the barest essentials borrowed from Cavonna. He was exhausted and flung himself down on the bed as she was closing his door. He was immediately asleep, his snoring loud enough to be heard through the door.

That night, Antonella and Cavonna sent Nico packing. He had shown up for his midnight shift, but he had been drinking. His timing couldn't have been worse because she was in a rage when he had shared about her patient in a barroom conversation anyway. Cavonna stuck a finger in the man's face and turned him around. Then he followed him to the stairway landing and made him retrieve his things and leave. Up to the locked gate Cavonna led, then unlocked the gate and pushed Nico through.

"Where do I go? It's the middle of the night?"

"You should have thought of that long ago. If you return, I will shoot you. Don't test me on this."

Cavonna then spun around and returned to the house, where Antonella and Thaddeus were. He watched over Thaddeus until the sun rose.

Chapter 47

Antonella had been upon the hillside, collecting
wildflowers and watching the highway. She had
plucked two dozen flowers to create a bouquet,
which she proudly held before her as she slid and skittered
back down to the beach below. She sat on the sand and
removed her boots, then tied the laces together so she could
drape them over her shoulder. The far end of the beach
beckoned, and she headed in that direction. Suddenly, the
sound of a motorcycle firing up cracked apart the morning
peace, and she stopped. The sound, the rup-rup-rup-rup-
rup, was emanating from her garage. Ever so tentatively, she
turned and waited. There, the engine sped up again and
then fell away, making the same rup-rup as before. She
abandoned her walk toward the far end of the beach and
turned back to the stairs, then upstairs and toward her
garage.

Two doors were open. She peered inside. There was
Muir on his knees, working at the front end of the bike. He

reached up and twisted the throttle again as she watched. Rup-rup-rup-rup-rup!

He felt her eyes upon him, so he cut the engine. He rose to his feet. "Is it disturbing you?" he asked.

"Not at all. I thought it was probably you and came to see."

"You have hill flowers. They are beautiful, like their owner."

She blushed and allowed the bouquet to fall to her side. "You'll find me spending lots of time among the wildflowers. They know all is well."

"Despite what we sometimes think."

"Despite what we sometimes think, yes."

"Hey, come here a moment."

She advanced and stood beside the bike. He took the wildflowers from her hand and placed them on the workbench. "Just for a moment," he promised.

She allowed herself to be lifted—effortlessly—and placed on the motorcycle's passenger seat.

"What is it?"

"Ducati. Italian bike."

"How fast can it go?"

"I've had it up to two-hundred. It had more, but I backed off."

"Two-hundred kilometers per hour? Where was that?"

"In Bogotá. Along the freeway."

"Were you being pursued?"

"Let's put it this way. I was making sure I wasn't pursued. Not many cars can split and weave through traffic. I was long gone, and they were still thinking about catching me. It wasn't fair."

"Who was this who was after you, if I may be so bold as to ask?"

"Cartel. They don't like me very much."

"Because of Thaddeus?"

"Oh, no. My relationship with Cárdenas started well before Thaddeus and Operation Monkey's Paw."

They stood there in silence a moment before Muir asked her, "Would you like to go for a ride?"

"I can't today. We have no idea what Cárdenas is capable of. We don't want to become easy targets. Thaddeus needs us here to protect him."

He nodded appreciatively. "There is one lucky man. He has your full attention, even your adoration, if I may say so."

"Something like that. It's the physician in me, nothing more. I cannot stand to see suffering. I've been that way since I was a child and helped dying birds with broken wings. Assisted my cat as she gave birth. Comforted a neighbor who'd had a stroke. Went to her house every day for six months, taking soup and watching it run down the corner of her mouth. That's been me, always there for the wounded and dying. We'll go riding some other time."

"Indeed."

"So, what are you doing on your bike?"

"Adjusting the throttle cable, adjusting the front suspension. It's gotten sluggish. I want my suspension tight. Just like my—" He broke off.

"Women," she dared to say, finishing what might have been his thought.

"Women," he agreed. "Now we can change that subject."

"Like I said, we'll take that ride another day."

She dismounted and retrieved her flowers. Studying them, her face fell. "Look. It's hot in this air. They've started to wilt already. I must get them inside, into water."

"You do that. Can I go get anything to add to dinner?"

"Really? That would be lovely."

"I'll ride into town to the farmers' market. I'll pick up greens and vegetables and fish. I'll cook you a nice meal for tending to our Thaddeus so well."

Chapter 48

The second Antonella stepped inside she knew something was wrong.

Thaddeus lay sprawled out on the couch, sleeping, but his breathing was rapid and shallow, and his skin was soaked with sweat. Antonella dropped the flowers on the counter and rushed to kneel next to the couch. Thaddeus's eyes were rolled in the back of his head, and he didn't wake when she tries to shake him.

"Cavonna! Muir!"

Muir ran in behind her, and Cavonna raced up the stairs, both dialed in on Thaddeus.

"What happened?" Muir asked.

"I don't know! He's crashing. Some kind of infection maybe? Cavonna, get me a syringe of epi and a drip bag of saline."

Cavonna jumped away while Antonella and Muir exchanged worried looks. What could have gone wrong so quickly?

Cavonna was back in seconds with bad news. "We're

out of epinephrine. Used it all up last week and haven't had a chance to refill."

Antonella took a steadying breath to get her hands to stop trembling, then turned to Muir. "Is that offer for a motorcycle ride still on the table? We need to get medicine fast, and if I come to the *farmacia* in person, we can get what we need right away."

He nodded.

She wrapped herself in a wide scarf and a helmet. She wore no jewelry, no rings, and no makeup. She must look very plain and hard to describe once she left the *farmacia*.

She mounted the back of the Ducati and held Muir tightly while they raced toward town. Five kilometers outside of town, an Army road blockade stopped her, and a soldier carrying an automatic gun approached the motorcycle. "Visors up, please," he called and gestured. They both complied.

"Where are you going?"

"Buenaventura."

"What is the purpose of your trip?"

"I'm going to the *farmacia*. I need medicine."

"What kind of medicine?"

"Medicine for a patient. I am a doctor."

"Papers, please."

She reached into a pocket and pulled out her medical license—the copy she was required to carry. She presented it to the soldier and then stared straight ahead.

"Well, Antonella," he said, handing back her papers, "have a good day in the city. Avoid Santa Fe. There was a killing there this morning."

She had seen the news coverage of a cartel death that morning but had not asked Muir about it. She felt him tense up on the seat in front of her. They had no intention of going that far into town, or anywhere near, anyway.

"We'll avoid it, certainly."

He lifted a hand and waved her through. "Please proceed."

Muir drove on into the western outskirts to an area known as Marta, a safe, middle-class neighborhood with strip malls and small medical buildings and abogado offices. At Farmacia Marta, they pull into the lot and park.

The pharmacist, a small bald man with a bulbous nose that indicated to Antonella a compromised liver function from alcoholism, stood behind the cash register. "*Buenas dias*," he called to her as they entered. Muir ducked down an aisle, pretending to shop.

"*Buenas dias*," she replied. "How are you?"

"I'm very good."

Closer to him, her initial appraisal was confirmed. The nose was red and swollen where it was storing alcohol the liver was unable to process. The pharmacist was in the process of poisoning himself with his disease. She would say something to him, but that's not why she had come there to diagnose and prescribe withdrawal.

"I have prescribed epinephrine for my patient." She passed the brown plastic bottle across the counter. "That's my name on the bottom of the label." She repeated, "I am the doctor. I'm afraid it's rather urgent."

The pharmacist examined the bottle and handed it back. "Do you have a prescription pad with you?"

"I do." She rummaged inside another side zipper on her backpack and pulled out her pad. She wrote another prescription for Thaddeus, this one doubling the dosage.

"I will put this together right away," the pharmacist said as he turned to fill the prescription. "Give me ten minutes?"

"I'll wait outside," she said, anxious. "I'll come back at twelve-twenty."

"Twelve-twenty-five, to be sure."

"All right, then. Try to hurry."

She tried to spot Muir, but he had disappeared in the maze of aisles. She turned and left the store.

Next to the sidewalk, a group of six men wearing black T-shirts, leather vests with silver disks, and black denim jeans appeared to be waiting for her. Six motorcycles were parked in a row behind them. Two other bikers sat astride their bikes at the end of the sidewalk.

"You told the soldier you're a doctor?" said the biker nearest her truck. "At the checkpoint."

"How did you know that?" she asked. "I am a doctor."

The biker smiled, displaying black holes where his canines should be. *Meth head.*

"How do I know?" he said, smiling even broader and touching the side of his head. "Little bird told me."

"Little bird…" she repeated, then. "Excuse me, I'm in a bit of a hurry."

"You're leaving? Not yet, if you please. I need a prescription."

"For what?"

"Oxy. I need one-hundred pills."

"That's ridiculous. You're not my patient, and I would never prescribe over thirty pills even if you were."

"Thirty, then. I can be your patient starting right now."

She moved to step past him on the sidewalk, but he extended his arm and placed it against the facade of the building, cutting her off. "Not so fast. What about your patient's Oxycontin first?"

"No way. You're not my patient. Now, please, excuse me, I'm tired of this."

"I'm not your patient yet? Doctor, my back is hurting. I can't feel my legs. I need pain pills."

"You need to move out of my way!"

The man stepped toward her. One of his thugs cracked his knuckles. The two seated bikers dismounted as well.

Just at that moment, the door dinged behind her, and Muir came out of the *farmacia*. He looked angry.

"What are these men saying?" he asked Antonella.

"They are demanding a prescription for drugs."

The biker in charge turned and faced Keystone. "Listen, you would be smart to take a hike. Run along now. There are six of us and one of you. This is a bad idea you have."

Muir slowly reached into a jacket pocket and produced his Sig Sauer pistol. He held it up for all to see. The blue steel caught the golden evening light. "Fourteen bullets. I've got you outnumbered. Now climb back on your putt-putts and leave. Do not return here, or I will not hesitate to shoot you."

The biker was startled. Only cartels and cops had guns. Ordinary citizens were afraid to keep guns where it was a felony in the entire country to have one. The biker stepped back and threw a leg over his bike. He pressed the starter, the cycle caught, and he moved backward with his feet. Once he was clear of a truck, he turned the handlebars and roared off, his friends following.

"They'll be back with guns of their own," Muir stated. "Are we ready to leave?"

"My medicine isn't ready yet."

"Then I'll wait with you. They won't return that fast. These are dangerous times, Antonella. It isn't safe for people to travel alone anymore."

"I'm glad you were here."

Her cell phone rang. She checked the screen: Cavonna. She held up a finger to Muir, then answered the call.

"Cavonna? Is Thaddeus OK?"

A long pause.

"Antonella. He's here."

"Who?"

Silence.

"Do you mean Cárdenas is there?"

From the other end of the call, she heard a whistle and a thud, followed by a sickening crunch.

"Cavonna!" she screamed.

There was silence for a moment, then an unmistakable voice, a thick, broken Spanish accent. Nico. "You should hurry home. I'd hate for you to miss all the fun."

Chapter 49

Thaddeus could hardly see straight, his vision blurred and discolored. He tried to turn on his side, but the pain in his chest was too great, and he let out a groan. Cavonna lay on the floor only steps away, unconscious after being pistol-whipped in the back of the head, but Thaddeus couldn't move any closer to him.

Nico was crouched between them, grinning like a tomcat playing with a mouse. In one hand, he held Cavonna's cell phone. In the other, he held a Smith and Wesson 9mm handgun. How he got it, Thaddeus had not the energy to guess.

"I told you I would be back," Nico said, watching Thaddeus writhe in pain. "I assumed I'd have to work harder to separate you from your caregiver."

Thaddeus only grunted, his gaze focusing past Nico to Cavonna, who still did not move.

"All for the best, I suppose," Nico continued. "When she gets back, I'm going to make you watch as I kill her. And then, only then, will you have my permission to die."

Thaddeus believed him. Why wouldn't he? Of course, this was the end; he knew it.

Nico looked down at the pistol in his hand, and with his thumb, drew back the hammer. Then he switched off the safety.

The sound of a motorcycle engine approaching, and Thaddeus heard it turn off up at the end of the cobbled lane. A deranged smile spread across Nico's face.

"Playtime."

A shadow passed in front of the window. Thaddeus heard Antonella's light footsteps approach then watched the door handle turn. She stood for a moment, framed in the dying sunset, alone.

Nico turned toward her, gun still at his side, the psychotic smile distorting his features. "Antonella, nice of you to join us. Come in, won't you?"

Antonella stood still, too scared to move.

"I said, come in." Nico raised his voice and turned his shoulders fully toward her. He raised the pistol and gestured in her direction, waving her inside.

As soon as his shoulders were turned, there was a flash of activity from behind Thaddeus. All at once, he felt a breeze from an open door, heard rapid footsteps, and saw a large blur of black and blue fly over the couch on which he lay, slamming into Nico with tremendous force.

Through bleary eyes, he could just see Muir wrapping his arms around Nico, trying to wrestle him into submission. The force of his tackle knocked Nico to his knees, but Nico fought back. The two highly trained operatives wrestled in the living room, each straining for the upper hand in a life or death struggle.

Nico still held the handgun, and as Muir grabbed his forearm, the gun went off. Antonella ducked into the room, covering her head, and moved toward where Cavonna lay prone on the floor.

Another shot rang out, and Thaddeus struggled to understand what was happening. Nico had worked around to Muir's back and quickly got one arm wrapped around Muir's neck. Muir held Nico's gun hand tightly, but Nico squeezed around Muir's neck with all his might, cutting off his air. For a few hopeful seconds, it looked as though Muir would be able to roll out of Nico's grasp, but then his face started to go blue, and his eyes bugged out.

Antonella whimpered in the corner as she tried to rouse Cavonna.

Thaddeus groaned, unable to move, barely clinging to consciousness.

Nico squeezed even harder, and Muir went limp.

Heavy breathing filled the air as Nico freed himself from the tangle of Muir's lifeless arms and legs. He stood, struggling for breath, still holding the 9mm pistol.

Thaddeus closed his eyes.

This was the end.

"Oh, no, you don't," Nico shouted at Thaddeus. "Open your eyes. I want you to watch while I kill her."

Thaddeus opened his eyes to see Nico pointing the gun at Antonella, still huddled on the floor with Cavonna.

"This is your fault, Thaddeus." He smiled again, bloody teeth visible. He looked at his target, and his finger tightened on the trigger.

A deafening blast rang out.

Thaddeus watched Antonella, but she didn't move. For a long moment, nothing moved.

She did not scream or stagger or fall. Finally, she looked up at Nico, confusion on her face. They both watched as

Nico looked down at his chest, where a red stain was quickly growing larger and darker.

He looked at Thaddeus and back at Antonella, then finally toward the still-open door behind him. There, silhouetted against the sunset, Thaddeus saw a slim, dark-haired woman holding a smoking handgun.

At first sight, Thaddeus's heart leaped in recognition.

Christine.

Chapter 50

Bogota Airport, 3 Days Later

The SUV pulled across the tarmac toward the private hangar. Cavonna drove, making small talk with Turquoise, who rode in the front seat. Thaddeus sat in the middle seat between Christine and Antonella, and he nervously rubbed his eyelid with his thumb.

"What if I can't remember?"

Antonella peered into his eyes. "It seems to me the greater question is, what sort of life can you make with the memories you have?"

He looked from her over to Christine.

Antonella continued as he stared at his wife. "Thaddeus, when you get back to the States, you're going to have to learn how to reach out and get help from the people around you. My role with you is finished. I am a medical doctor, not a head doctor. But I think your head will be just fine if you give it time to heal naturally."

Christine reached over and held his hand. She had been his rock the last three days, ever since the showdown with Nico Lamontez, Cárdenas' hired assassin. It had been a challenging 72 hours, but she had not left his side even once. Not when Antonella had to give him shots of epinephrine to fight off the infection growing in his kidney. Not when the coroner had come to collect the bodies of Muir and Nico or when the police had come to ask hundreds of questions. She had not left his side as he slept, ate, or cried.

Seeing her face was like the key to unlocking his memories. As soon as she walked into the room, he was flooded with memories from his life in the States. Not everything; there was much that still eluded him. But as he looked at her, he remembered the first time he'd laid eyes on her and smiled at the memory.

"I love you more than ever," she said. "We're going to take this one day at a time."

"I know, Chris," he said. "I'm worried about the work that's waiting for me at home. Nancy's still waiting for me to get her acquitted. But I can't remember any of that law stuff. I don't even know any law. If I was once a lawyer, then I think I must've been brimming with law stuff. But the truth is, I can't think of any law that I know. I can't think of even one law."

Christine gave him a reassuring look and squeezed his hand. "That's all right. We can have law classes every night and all day if we want to."

Cavonna pulled the car into the hangar, and they all get out. On instinct, Thaddeus followed out Antonella's door and let her help him stand.

"All right then, thank you," Christine said as she moved around the SUV next to Antonella and put her arm around the younger woman. She whispered into Antonella's ear, "I cannot tell you how grateful I am to you for taking care of my husband. He means everything in the world to me, and I would've died if anything had happened to him to take him away forever. I know that his guardian angels were sitting on his shoulder when you came into his life and rescued him off the roadway."

Tears washed into Antonella's eyes. She was both touched and saddened that she was about to lose someone she loved, and she couldn't even tell him that. Nor could she tell Christine that, but for a moment, just for a split second, she recognized a look in the older woman's eye, and she believed there was a connection, that Christine knew how she felt.

Despite her resolve, Antonella suddenly found she wasn't quite ready to let Thaddeus go. Moreover, there were things she needed to know to get closure in her own life. She made a slight frown, thinking about how she would ask the next question. Then she plunged ahead. "There is so much that I've struggled to understand. It's hard to separate what's true from what's not. Whatever on earth was Thaddeus doing down in Bogotá with guns?"

"It's a long story, but what it amounted to was that his sister's four-year-old boy was kidnapped and taken to Bogotá. Thaddeus wanted to come there and bring the boy home. That's the short version."

Antonella shook her head. "I don't think he remembers any of that stuff. I have asked and asked, but none of it seems to be at the top of his mind where he can access it."

"For his sake, I am so sorry to hear that. But let me also say that he did save his nephew Simon and that the four-year-old, now five, is back with his mother in Pacific Beach. I saw them two days ago and watched the little boy on the beach with his sand bucket, surrounded by seagulls, which he couldn't get enough of chasing. He seemed quite happy and well-adjusted, considering what he's been through. But Nancy, the sister, is also going to begin taking the boy to therapy in hopes of helping him get in touch with any bad feelings and working through those things before he gets much older."

"And then all this time, you haven't known what happened to Thaddeus. Where does this story leave off for you? Maybe I can help fill in some of those spaces."

"To be honest, all I know is that he went to Bogotá. Whatever came after that, I'm going to have to try to piece together through Marcel, his PI, and our good friend, his teammates on the operation, or from his memory as it returns. It will return at some point, won't it, doctor?"

"It might and it might not. Only time will tell. I know that's a half-assed answer and that everyone wants more certainty than that, but with the damaged mind, medicine becomes less of science and more of art at that jumping-off point. If you regularly take him to a psychiatrist to do memory work—and I hope you do—you're probably going to hear a lot more about his time in South America. On the other hand, there may be parts of it that you wish you had never known, and there may be parts of it that he's better off not recalling. I don't know about these things because he and I, at this point, are still pretty much new at learning how to remember things again. How far he goes in this is a total unknown."

"Dumbest question of the day, but is he going to remember what lawyers do and his life as a lawyer?"

"That is extremely difficult to say. Like all professions, the practice of law requires a very finely tuned sense of right and wrong and the ability to size up people in an instant and make life-altering decisions even faster. Right now, Thaddeus has none of that. Again, what the future may hold for him will depend a lot on what kind of help he gets and how severe his injury was. One of these you can control; the other one nobody but God can control."

Christine grabbed Antonella's hand and held it firmly. "Thank you." She then checked her wristwatch and moved back toward Thaddeus. She said to Antonella, "Is there anything else you need to tell Thaddeus in private before I leave with him?"

Antonella recognized what was being said. She knew that now was her turn with the man they both loved. She had no further right of any more time with him. It was time for her to step back and let life take its course, as it always must. She folded her arms and looked down at the ground. "You know, I think I've shared with Thaddeus everything I had to share. It's probably best right now if you take him, turn away, and leave, and I never give him another thought."

Christine's look changed as she immediately caught on. She took Thaddeus's backpack and draped it over her free shoulder. With her other hand, she took Thaddeus by the hand and turned away from Antonella. She said loud enough for Antonella to hear, "Are you ready to go back to California?"

"I hope so."

Antonella watched as they climbed the stairs into the private plane. It was over. She had done what she came to do, and the person she had nursed back to health was leaving the nest. As a physician, she realized that her life would repeat this scenario hundreds, maybe thousands, more times. It was the way of the healer, but in this one case, she had learned the most important lesson she would ever learn: *do not fall in love with your patient.*

She and Cavonna turned and walked together back to the SUV. As the car pulled away, she felt she was moving away from him in a physical sense, but it was much easier than the emotional leaving she must now face.

Chapter 51

San Diego and Home

U pon arriving home from the airport, Christine watched as the kids threw themselves upon Thaddeus. They guided him to his chair, chattering, hugging him, each trying to tell him their latest accomplishment. He was wholly overcome, but he was calm about their affections and attempted to return the same. She saw him trying to force it, the feelings, and she knew that it was nothing more than a facade.

However, the kids knew no such thing, and their joy at having Daddy home seemed endless. In turn, he sized up someone's frog, inspected the progress of a knitted sweater, looked at someone's photographs on their iPad, and watched as yet another solved equations for X. He uttered the right notes of appreciation at the right moments. She could tell by the look on his face that he was surprising even himself at how quickly he was falling back into the role of father and lover of the swarm of children. With tears in her eyes, she took his few things upstairs to their bedroom and went to his bag. Most of what he had could be thrown out, but she wouldn't dare get rid of anything without talking it over with him first.

Later that day, he helped her prepare a dinner of spaghetti and meatballs when he said out of the blue, "Will we be having sex together?"

She almost staggered where she stood. "Much of that will depend on you, Thaddeus. It will depend on how you feel and how you make me feel. We will know when the time is right by these things. Why, are you anxious about this or anxious to get it underway?"

"Both. I feel like at one time, I was a great lover. I can feel that coming back."

She was laughing and laughing, hands on the sink top, unable to control herself. "You fancy yourself a great lover, do you? Well, let me just say I hope you're right. We could use a great lover around here."

"Oh, yes, I think you're going to be completely satisfied to have me home." He said this last part with no small mystery, which made her very happy because it was the first time he had said words that might have more than one meaning. She knew this was a significant progress point. To be able to speak the English language and mean two different things at once. It was significantly grown up to be able to do that, and she was ecstatic to see that it had returned so fast.

Another time that first week, Christine took him out for an afternoon of shopping and helped him select all the right kind of underwear, shorts, T-shirts, sandals, and sneakers, all the items of casual wear that he'd always preferred. They also replaced his toilette, including the medium-hard toothbrush and the Brut aftershave he splashed on every morning after his shower.

Shopping completed, she drove him to their law office and parked out front. "Do you recognize anything?"

"Why? Should I?"

"Well, let me just tell you. The two doors on this building are the front doors of the offices where you and I practice law and have for some time now. You have staff waiting inside that's anxious to see you and say hello. Are you ready to do something like that?"

"I don't think so. "

"Then we won't do that. Not yet."

On their fifth night together, the Murfees entertained Marcel and Turquoise. It couldn't have gone worse. Marcel became rankled at Thaddeus when he refused to discuss Operation Monkey's Paw, Cárdenas, the cartel, their fallen colleagues.

"I searched for you for months!" Marcel cried out. "And I failed! Miserably. But I wouldn't leave. Christine called my cell and said she had you. And you won't talk about it?"

"I'm sorry. I just don't remember. And I don't remember you. I'm sorry."

Marcel became angry and stomped out to his truck and drove away, Turquoise at his side.

When they were gone, Thaddeus shrugged and slowly shook his head. "To be honest, I don't see why Marcel insisted on emphasizing the name and goings-on of a person I don't think I ever met."

"It wasn't about that. It was more about you acknowledging everything your team has been through, how two of them died for our cause, to get back Simon. It's frustrating to him since what happened in Colombia was so profound for so many people. And that happens. People can't understand another's indifference about something they are so passionate about. Not that you are indifferent. You just don't remember. That's what is frustrating for Marcel. Please try to understand. We were all so worried about you. Bogotá, Colombia, the jungle—it changed everyone that was part of Operation Monkey's Paw."

Thaddeus was holding the channel changer. "Can we watch something before we fall asleep?"

"Of course, honey, get up here on the bed beside me, and we can watch whatever you want. I have briefs I need to read for tomorrow's court, so I won't bother you, and you will be able to watch whatever tickles your fancy."

"Good, because I have started liking soccer. I don't know where that comes from, but I have the feeling that I watched a lot of soccer in my previous life. Would that be possible?"

Christine patted the bed beside her and put her arm around him as he lay down in his underwear and socks. "Yes, that would be possible. You might just have become a great adherent to the sport of soccer. I wouldn't put it past you."

Chapter 52

On the tenth day, the day of the acid test arrived.

Christine drove them to the law office, and they went inside. The staff was warned ahead of time that Thaddeus remembered none of them and remembered nothing about his work. It was a very awkward half hour, including the moments when he was ushered into his own office and confronted with the memorabilia: wall hangings, certificates, and plaques and awards on his ego wall. They left after thirty minutes. Christine was feeling very sad, though she knew the time had come and that this would have to take place at some point.

For his part, Thaddeus just rode along and stared out the passenger window as they came up through La Jolla on Beach Drive. At the second stoplight, across the street from the salon, where Christine had her hair done by the woman who spent her winters in Paris, he turned a troubled face to his wife. She saw, then, the tears in his eyes and heard the pain in his voice as he spoke to her.

"I'm afraid this isn't working for me. I didn't know any

of the people you just had me talk to. And I don't recognize that office. I don't recognize my bedroom. I don't recognize the children, and I don't recognize my kitchen. Worst of all, I don't know who you are, and I don't recognize you, and I'm afraid of the entire situation."

"What do you want to do about all that?"

"I want to go home, back to Antonella."

Christine suddenly felt like she was going to be sick in the car. She had known this time might come, but all along, she had told herself they were doing so much better. This moment could be held off, held at bay, never allowed inside the circle of family and work. "Honey, this is home. Antonella is not home. It's just going to take time before you recognize that."

Tears streamed down his face as he said, "Would you call her for me and ask if I can come home?"

"Of course, I will. I don't want you doing something you don't want to do."

"I don't know if I ever want to do this. But right now, I know I'm not ready. I need to feel safe again in my own home, and I don't here. Are you mad at me?"

She held back her tears. It seemed like a dream just then, what he was saying, and she tried to rise above it and see the whole situation as an adult, as a married woman with an injured husband who wanted to relapse. Still, she would do anything for him, so she proceeded to do just that.

"Of course, I will call her for you. And, of course, you can go back there if she has room for you. It would be best if you were where you feel safe now, whether with Antonella or me. It would hurt me very much if you left your home, but it also might hurt you much more if you stay. So I'm not going to stand between you and what you need. I will call her as soon as we get home."

"It just feels right to me to be with Antonella right now. I'm very sorry, but I'm not comfortable here, and it doesn't feel like home."

"You don't need ever to tell me that again. I understand."

"Thank you for understanding. I need someone like you. And I'm sure I will want to come back here when I'm well. After all, every man should be with his wife and children. Or at least I'm told that."

"Yes, every man does need to be with his wife and children. And I am sure you have been told that. All right now, would you like to stop at 31 Flavors and get some more ice cream?"

It was something he loved doing, 31 Flavors. He thought about it just for a moment and then said, "I don't think so. I think I would rather get home and call Antonella before she moves, and I don't know where she is."

"All right, the ice cream will have to wait. But when you're ready, think of your wife and 31 flavors. We're both right there for you, mister."

"Yes, let's wait on the ice cream. At least for now."

Chapter 53

They couldn't connect with Antonella, not at first, as there was no answer on her phone. Thaddeus went out on the patio and looked longingly at the ocean. Christine decided to try another approach with him.

She drove Thaddeus from their home in La Jolla down to Pacific Beach to see Nancy. He was nervous on the way and wondered out loud how she would take it that he no longer knew her, Simon, or Jeff. As they drove down the freeway, Thaddeus found himself retreating inside his mind and putting up barriers to what he already knew would happen when he first saw his sister.

"It's just your sister," said Christine. "She's already been told about the head injury, and she knows there has been a certain difficulty with facial recognition."

"That's not even half of it. It's not only facial recognition, but there's no memory of any time we spent together, any inside jokes, any brotherly-sisterly things shared from childhood, none of that. She has lost one half of the carrier of that information."

They took the Pacific Beach turn-off and began wending their way to Nancy's house, a three-bedroom, two-bath about two miles from the beach in a neighborhood of similar homes. When they parked in front of one of the houses, Thaddeus's heart fell. He knew he didn't remember it even though he had been told he had been here dozens of times in the past. He looked for the inside man in his mind who might have that information and be holding out on him. But no one answered to that description; no one came forward. "Oh my God," he breezed. "Is someone looking out at us from the window. Is that her, Chris?"

"Please, just relax. We're going to walk up to the door, ring the doorbell, and wait to be invited inside. I don't plan to make any introductions because you already know her. We'll just let the conversation flow, and when the moment arises when she asks you something you would have known in your prior life, you can jump in and explain about the head injury and your loss of those memories. If you do this one time, all will be well after that. Or maybe it will take twice; I don't know. Now, the little boy you're going to see is your nephew Simon. He's the little one you saved from the Monkey's Paw. He will remember you and may shower you with love, affection, and attention. Don't be afraid to proceed with him as if you know him already because he's not going to know the difference. No need to try to explain yourself to a five-year-old."

Thaddeus drew a deep breath and felt around the waist of his khaki trousers, making sure that his blue oxford cloth shirt was properly tucked in. This was one thing he had noticed about himself: he did like to dress well and with class. So far, he was not given over to wearing T-shirts and shorts as Christine had told him he once preferred. All of which mattered to him, not one bit.

Christine had no more rung the bell when the door flew open, and there stood Simon and his mother, Nancy, Thaddeus's sister. She invited them to come inside and make themselves comfortable. He chose a white wingback chair, and Chris selected its twin, right beside him. She reached over, took his hand in hers, and lightly held on. His instinct was to pull away, the manly thing to do—behavior he was making up as he went along—but his fear in that moment greatly outweighed his instinct, and he found himself hanging onto her for her support.

Nancy approached Thaddeus, bent down, and threw her arms around him. "Oh, my God, you saved Simon's life, and that means you saved me!" The tears began flowing, making Thaddeus uncomfortable since he did not know this woman who was bestowing love and gratitude upon him. He shuffled his feet and leaned back from her.

"I'm glad I could help," he said. "But let me be honest, Nancy. Much of that is a blank in my mind at the moment. My head got hurt after I helped Simon escape, and I don't remember so much."

She blinked hard and stepped away, lowering herself onto her floral couch underneath the front window. "Don't you worry about that for a second," she said. "I know that science and prayer will bring your memory back. In the meantime, I'm in no hurry. Now tell me what you remember about saving Simon, please."

Thaddeus looked at Christine, who shrugged back and indicated he should tell what he remembered.

"To be very honest, I remember none of that. I don't remember saving Simon, but I do have a mental image of putting him on a helicopter or protecting him before or after our raid. This is what I'm afraid of, that you're going to hate me because I can't help you. Please give me some space, and let's see if some of this naturally comes back to me."

"Oh, my God, yes!" she cried. "I don't want you to worry about this for even a second. When the time comes, you'll talk about it. Okay? Let's leave it right there. You guys want something to drink?"

Christine shook her head, and Thaddeus joined her. "Not me. We're good."

"One thing I do wonder about is my case. Is Thaddeus going to be able to help with my case, or should I consider getting a new lawyer?"

Christine spoke up. "Let's talk about that for a minute. While Thaddeus was away, I went to the court and filed a joint affidavit with the FBI agents to the effect that Thaddeus was away on business relating to the case. Judge Franklin kindly extended all time periods and deadlines and said they would begin running again once Thaddeus was back. So, we're at the point where Thaddeus is back, and trial preparations need to begin. We are going to prepare to do some interviews, take some statements, and file several motions. This is even before we step into the court."

Nancy shook her head. "Please don't think I'm mean, but who is going to handle my case, you or Thaddeus?"

Christine again spoke up. "Thaddeus will handle your case with me there to back him up at every step. If you get stuck, or if something comes up that he doesn't remember, I will jump in and take over momentarily, get a recess, take him out in the hallway, and update him on what he needs to know. The fact that your brother has suffered a head injury is not going to imperil your case. They say that two heads are better than one, and we're about to prove that."

"How are you going to defend me when they have me

on video doing hand-to-hand transactions nine times previous to the FBI?"

"That's an excellent question. But let me explain that your defense will be the defense called 'duress.' This defense means that you were forced against your will to turn over Lockheed Martin documents to CSID. You were put in a position where no reasonable person could resist their demands."

Just then, Simon came into the room carrying a soft drink. He approached his uncle, held out the bottle, and said, "Want some?"

Thaddeus took the orange drink from the boy and pretended to drink from the bottle. He then handed it back to the child and told him thank you. The boy then sidled up closer and put his chest against Thaddeus's knees before turning around backward as if he were about to participate in the conversation. Thaddeus reached out his arm and dropped it around the little boy's chest very lightly. They stayed like that for a good 15 seconds until Simon ducked away and went to his mom with the same proffer of orange soda.

"So, duress is all that's standing between me and life in the penitentiary, is that it?"

"Pretty much," said Christine. "I don't mean to alarm you, but duress is an affirmative defense, and that means that if it can be proven, it will definitely work inside a federal court to set you free."

Out of nowhere, Thaddeus added, "Duress is said to excuse criminal conduct where the actor was under an unlawful threat of imminent death or serious bodily injury. But I'm wondering whether duress is our best defense. I'm thinking that a defense based on defense of others, which is an affirmative defense for murder, voluntary manslaughter, and assault, might not be the better defense. Of course, there isn't any murder, voluntary manslaughter, or assault. But the prospect of the same happening to the kidnapped child should be enough to meet the requirements for the defense."

Christine's mouth fell open as she listened to her husband recite a portion of the law that could get quite esoteric. "Well, well, buddy, where in the world is all this coming from? What you just said amounts to an excellent point, and I might have missed it had you not spoken up just this moment. What is going on with you?"

A sheepish look came over Thaddeus's face, and he shook his head. "I have no explanation for that. I have no explanation for where it came from. I wasn't trying to access those thoughts in my mind. It just suddenly came out. Anyway, how close am I to being right?"

"You're spot on, mister. Welcome back to the team," said Christine, a cautious smile spreading across her face. Thaddeus could tell she didn't want to put too much weight on what he'd just said as something he might be able to duplicate. But he was glad he'd spoken up and astonished by what he had said. He wondered if he would ever say something like that again.

Thaddeus was feeling much better about the whole visit. He told his sister that he would appreciate a cup of coffee before leaving. Nancy made the coffee and served, and guards were let down, and a free flow of information and fears and thoughts and worries ensued.

It was a good half hour that followed, and by the time they were finished, Thaddeus was beginning to think that maybe Nancy was his sister after all.

Chapter 54

At 4 p.m. that day, they made contact with Antonella by telephone. She was very unsure of the conversation, very worried why Thaddeus and Christine had called her. All three were on different lines to talk, and, as Thaddeus had requested, they were unable to see each other.

Christine started. "Antonella, we have reached somewhat of an impasse here. Thaddeus has seen the younger kids, his sister, and his older child, Turquoise, has even seen his workmates, including his closest friend Marcel, and it has gone pretty much as you might expect from a man who remembers nothing from before. Thaddeus and I have spent time together, we have talked, and we have done some things we used to do that we enjoyed together, including riding horses and swimming at the beach. We have even been intimate more than once. But a strange thing has happened, at least strange to me, maybe commonplace to those in the medical profession, I don't know."

Antonella's voice was soft and sincere from the other

end as she replied, "You may tell me about this new thing. Maybe I will be surprised, and maybe I won't be. But let's talk."

Christine choked back a cry, but neither Thaddeus nor Antonella knew this when Christine said, "Thaddeus says he's not ready to be here with us yet. He wants to go back to you. What are your feelings about this?"

There was a long silence. Then Antonella could be heard, clearing her throat to speak. "That would be acceptable on one condition. Thaddeus, I would first expect you to see an excellent counselor at least three times before any decision about this is made. Are you willing to do that?"

"I will see someone," he said. "Just don't expect me to change my mind. I don't change my mind all that often anymore. I'm like a man of one mind. Tell me who to see, and I will go."

"I think that's fair, and I understand the need," said Christine. "Would you like to make the referral for us up here, Antonella, or should I take care of that?"

"You go right ahead and take care of that, Christine, please. I don't know anyone up there, and I trust your judgment in this. I will be in and out for the next few weeks, as I plan to return to the small town on the ocean where I grew up. I have taken a job with a medical practice doing general surgery."

"Can I ask you something personal?" asked Christine.

"Why, sure."

"Would you even want to take him back?"

Antonella didn't hesitate. "Thaddeus, please hang up now." She waited until she repeated his name, and there was no response. Then she said, "I would love nothing better than to have Thaddeus back. He is everything to me. And I know he is everything to you. Just let me say that I think it's a process where he will finally end up. And though he might come back to me at this time, I am not sure it's going to be his final move. And you should not be sure either."

"Wow," said Christine. "That's laying it on the line. For my part, just let me say that I will never stop loving him, and I will never stop waiting for him. I won't remarry, and I won't leave our relationship. He means that much to me. If he wants to come back here, please don't ever call me and ask. Just send him instead."

Christine could take it no longer, and she hung up the call.

Chapter 55

Christine drove Thaddeus to their law office in La Jolla. They went inside, smiling and saying hello to the staff, and made their way back to the first conference room on the left. It was meant to hold sixteen people as there were eight chairs on each side of the massive conference table. That morning, seated at the near end on the far side of the table, was Marcel, Thaddeus's investigator. And to his left was seated Turquoise, Thaddeus's oldest daughter.

The last time he'd seen Marcel, their time together had been awkward, uncomfortable for both of them. Marcel stood when he came into the conference room, and they awkwardly shook hands as if they were just meeting each other. Thaddeus felt no connection whatsoever to his dearest friend, and he had no idea what Marcel felt. But this much was true: they had no option except to plow ahead and establish and reestablish what they'd done before because it was necessary.

Marcel spoke up first. "How are you feeling, boss? I

hope this hasn't all been too much for you coming back here."

"Physically, I'm feeling excellent. Mentally, I'm a wreck. Let me just be really upfront with you guys. I don't remember anybody, I don't remember our relationships, and I don't remember working together with any of you. It's all going to have to be rebuilt, and I'm going to be counting on you quite a bit to teach me what we had, where we trusted each other, and where we were a little recalcitrant about that trust. So, please step right in if, at any time, you feel like I'm missing the point about something. If we can all agree to that, then we at least have a place to begin. Without that, I'm lost. What I'm saying is I'm lost without your help."

Christine took a seat and grabbed a legal pad from the table's center, her pen poised above the yellow paper. "First, let's talk about what needs to be done on Nancy's case. As you guys know, the case was put on the inactive calendar just at the point of her initial hearing and release on bail. Nothing's happened on the case since then from our end. I'm sure the FBI has been all over it in the background and by now has every last i dotted and t crossed. This means we will have to do formal discovery on what they have and don't have. Thaddeus, I'm going to assign all discovery to you. I want you to obtain a list of all of the government's witnesses and all their documents. I also want you to obtain a list of all of their exhibits. Taking the exhibits first, please review them, handle them, make your notes, make a file memo, and insert that into our case file. Especially, we will be looking for the video of the ten sales Nancy made. The FBI said it would turn that over; all we had to do was call them. We will also need a copy of the documents Nancy allegedly turned over so that we can have those reviewed by our expert to establish whether or not they were, in fact, secret. If they were not secret, the government has no case. So, we need to know that."

"Unless I miss my guess, that's going to be quite an undertaking and is going to require a court battle," said Marcel. "Thaddeus, what do you say I help you with these things and give you some support?"

"Definitely," said Thaddeus. "I need your help and will be relying on you to keep me headed in the right direction and obtaining what we need to know."

Christine spoke up. "Well, I'm going to tell you it is going to be worse than pulling teeth from an angry cage fighter to get the government's documents. Assuming they're secret documents, the court will not require them to turn them over, but I think it will allow the supervised review of the documents by our expert. So that's the route I would suggest we take on those."

Thaddeus shifted in his seat. "Next, she says she wants me to interview all witnesses. Folks, I have no clue how to interview witnesses, so I am going to need backup. Who will be my backup for these interviews?"

Christine immediately responded, "I will be right there with you at the interview table every step of the way. If you get in trouble or miss things, I will be right there to conference with you so that we don't walk away without obtaining key information. Now, as far as interviewing the government's witnesses, they have no obligation to speak to us and can tell us to go jump in the lake. That's federal law, Thaddeus. In another life, you got around this by filing a lawsuit against someone and then taking the witness's depositions in that lawsuit and using those statements in the criminal trial."

"Let me get this straight," Thaddeus said. "I would file a

civil lawsuit, okay. In this case, then, I will file a lawsuit against CSID--"

"Already done," Christine broke in. "And several depositions have been taken."

He continued. "All right. I now need to take government witness depositions, and I will then use them in the criminal trial to impeach those witnesses as necessary. In this manner, we know exactly what they are going to say at trial, and we can prepare our responses accordingly."

"Exactly." Christine then leaned forward and punched a button on the intercom system. She requested that Gina come to the conference room and join them. Gina appeared within minutes, complete with her notepad and a worried look. She stood, not having been asked to take a seat, and anxiously tried not to stare at Thaddeus, but it was no use. She locked eyes with him several times until he said, "I used to work with you, didn't I?"

Tears washed into her eyes. "Mr. Murfee, I've been your chief paralegal for over five years now. We know each other extremely well, and I'm having a lot of trouble right now. Please forgive me."

Thaddeus gave her his best smile and said, "Never mind. Why don't you take a seat right there next to Christine, and she will tell you why she paged."

Christine began, saying, "All right, Gina, we are going to need you to prepare a second lawsuit against CSID Corporation. There will be numerous counts in the case. And you will create those counts out of the factual memo that I'm going to prepare and send to you. You will have counts for civil kidnapping, what they did to Simon, and all the rest of the people we've been sorting through that were saved from the Monkey's Paw. When you are done with your first draft, let Thaddeus see it and shoot me a copy. We will need you to work closely with Thaddeus and just assume that he has been away and has forgotten quite a bit of what he used to know. I've noticed that some of it is coming back to him in bits and pieces, but we're all going to have to pitch in and keep an eye on him. Can I count on you to do that?"

By now, Gina was dabbing her eyes with a tissue and managed a smile. "Oh, my God, yes. Mr. Murfee, I'm just so glad you're home safe and sound. We've all been so worried about you around here. Thank God you made it back. I'll get this lawsuit typed up and get copies to both of you before the close of business today. I'm standing by to do anything I can."

"Good timing," said Christine. "The faster we can get these things down and out, the better. Now, Gina, I'm going to tell you what we need second. Please create and file with the court, after Thaddeus reviews it, a motion to accelerate discovery so that we can begin taking the depositions of the FBI agents involved in the sales by Nancy Bergholzer. Just FYI, these FBI agents will also be testifying in the criminal trial, and that is why we are taking their depositions in the civil trial, just to pin them down."

"Just like you always did, Mr. Murfee, just like you always did."

Christine turned to page two and began a new page of notes. "All right, next, Marcel has attempted to infiltrate the CSID company. Marcel, let's hear from you about your efforts and how far you got."

Marcel leaned back. "I made contact with a high-up accounting professional by the name of Devonna Mertz. She and I became friends. We even dated—with my fiancée Turquoise's knowledge and permission, of course. One thing led to another, and money was exchanged for copies of files from the company's financial database. I've located money coming in—disguised—and money going out—also disguised—but all having to do with the theft of government documents and the resale of systems created from those documents. We're talking in the billions of dollars. It's going to take a tall building full of CPA's to ever plow through all of it. At least we have enough to take this case to trial, so you can prove who the bad guys are."

Thaddeus looked at Christine. "Doesn't that exonerate Nancy?"

Christine met his eyes. "Well, it's a start, for sure."

"I thought it would be a start,' Thaddeus said, "I did."

No one replied.

Chapter 56

The process of discovery began with depositions. Thaddeus and his team set up the testimonies of Damon McDowell, the senior FBI agent in charge at San Diego; Jim Smithers, the agent who provided backup with his guns at the time of the sale in the Avion Kite Store; and Ronnie Martinez, the FBI agent who made the buy of the Lockheed Martin information contained on the thumb drive that Nancy brought to the exchange. The three agents were brought into Thaddeus's office complex, and each one ensconced in a room separate from the others so there would be no discussion of testimony beforehand. The agents were then called one at a time into their depositions. Thaddeus began with SAIC Damon McDowell.

SAIC McDowell entered the deposition room casually, took the seat where Thaddeus directed him, laid one arm across the back of the chair next to him, and laid his notepad on the table in front of him, unopened.

The deposition then began. Thaddeus went through the rules of depositions, including the rules applicable to the deponents themselves, then he began with the who, what, when, where questions he had written out in advance.

"Were you aware at the time of the arrest of Nancy Bergholzer that her four-year-old son had been kidnapped by the people she thought she was selling the documents to?"

Agent McDowell did not hesitate, saying, "No, at the time of the sale and transfer of the secrets to the FBI, we were not aware that her son had been kidnapped."

Thaddeus went right along. He had no recall of their prior conversations.

"Had you known that would it have changed how you handled this case?"

"As the SAIC, I can tell you that, had we had this information beforehand, we would have contacted Nancy Bergholzer in secret, confirmed that her son was indeed kidnapped, and then sought to help her."

Thaddeus felt he was about to win the case altogether when he said, "So instead of arresting her, you would have tried to help her as a citizen being blackmailed by a corporate agency?"

"No, that's not what I'm saying at all. Don't forget that, in total, she made nine sales of secret information to a company that sold to a foreign adversary. That's still treason, no matter why she did it. She still has to answer for her crimes."

"What if our defense was of duress? We're thinking—"

Christine quickly broke in. He was about to reveal, not a defense, but an internal theory. A colossal no-no to give away an attorney's thoughts and impressions. She quickly said, "Thaddeus, let me rephrase that, please. Agent, would knowing that Nancy's son had been kidnapped have suggested any defenses she might use in her case?"

The FBI agent wrinkled his brow. His face said he couldn't understand her asking him what defenses Nancy's kidnapped son would suggest. She might as well be asking what defenses were going to be used at trial. Nevertheless, he gamely plunged on, stating, "I can't think of any defenses that would legitimately arise. My true opinion is your client is guilty, and she is going to have to pay by being incarcerated."

Christine smiled. "Yes, yes, of course."

After another thirty minutes of questions in the area of affirmative defenses, Christine decided to dismiss the witness and move on to the next. She decided she would call Ronnie Martinez, the FBI agent who had made the buy.

Chapter 57

Before calling FBI agent Ronnie Martinez into the deposition room, they excused agent Damon McDowell, and he was free to leave the building. Christine then had a heart-to-heart with Thaddeus.

"Honey, I'm not sure I entirely trust you right now because I think your injury has maybe impaired your ability as a lawyer more than I knew. But I'm going to go ahead and let you begin questioning Ronnie Martinez, the FBI agent who made the buy from Nancy and put the 5000 dollars cash in her pocket. Do you feel like this is something you can do?"

"There's only one way to find out," he said. He closed his eyes at the table for just a moment, thinking. Then he opened them and said, "Yes, I think I can do this. I would appreciate another chance."

FBI agent Ronnie Martinez was summoned into the deposition room, sworn by the court reporter, and told to take a seat. They then got into his time with the FBI, his regular duties with the agency, and confirmed he was with the other officers on the day Nancy was finally arrested.

"Tell us what you saw happen that day," Thaddeus said.

"We parked, went up to the building and confirmed that Nancy Bergholzer was inside. I then went up to within three or four feet of her and waited while she placed the thumb drive on the top righthand side. She then moved down to the shelves' left-hand side and stood there as if considering buying a kite. I reached my hand up to the top right shelf, located the thumb drive, retrieved it, and put it into my coat pocket. I then came up behind her. Her coat pocket was slightly open, so I slipped to her $5000 in cash as agreed. As she exited the store, she was seized and arrested by the other members of my team. Pretty much, that's what I saw and observed that day."

"Were you aware at the time of the transaction that Nancy Bergholzer's son had been kidnapped and was being held to force her to sell those secrets on the thumb drive?"

"Was I aware? How would I have been aware?"

Thaddeus appeared thoughtful. "Well, did your team leader Damon McDowell make you aware that her son had been kidnapped?"

"Sir, I don't get what you're driving at. You must know by now that none of us knew her son had been kidnapped. So, let me ask you, how would SAIC McDowell have made me aware of the kidnapping before she told us about it?"

"I—I—"

Christine rustled her papers on the table and then spoke up. "Agent Martinez, I'm going to ask you a few questions now, and I would appreciate your true and complete answers."

"True and complete answers? That's all I've been giving. Are you people trying to trick me or something? To any jury that hears this deposition, it's gonna look like you either don't know what you're talking about or you were trying to trick me up about her kidnapped son and suggest I knew about it before she had even told us about it. Which is it? Don't know Jack? Or trying to trick me?"

"I appreciate your thinking on that, but I can assure you neither one is true. Please just let me continue, and we'll get you right out of here. In line with what you're saying, would you please state for the record when you did first become aware that Nancy Bergholzer's son had been kidnapped?"

"I'm going to say that she told us about her son's kidnapping within the first ten minutes after her arrest. It wouldn't have been any longer than that. And no, none of us knew about it beforehand. We debriefed back at the office, and nobody had this information."

"What happened to Nancy after she was arrested at the kite store?"

"She was taken to the correctional center by Jimmy Smithers and me. We turned her over to the jailers who, I can only assume, processed her in. Pretty much you've covered everything I know about this case."

"Had anyone from the FBI taken any steps to locate the missing child?"

"I think that SAIC McDowell spoke with Mr. Murfee at some point. I wasn't privy to that conversation and didn't know what was said."

"Is there anything else I should ask you that I haven't asked regarding what you know?"

"No, ma'am, not a thing. Am I free to go?"

"Thaddeus, you have any further questions for the witness?"

"No."

The witness was then excused, and Christine sat for

several moments staring at the tabletop. Thaddeus riffled through the paper spread before him, his jaw clenched. He ever so slightly shook his head as if upset.

Christine began softly speaking. "Honey, you blew it again, implying that the agent knew before the arrest that Nancy's son had been kidnapped. I think I'm going to go ahead and do the rest of the depositions myself. But I still want you to sit in so that you are up to speed when we go to trial. Is that fair?"

"Yes, I think that is more than fair. I did blow it, and right now, I'm feeling a lot of shame. I'm going to go back to my office and close the door and have a cup of coffee. Just give me ten minutes to collect myself, and then I'll come back in here. Is that okay?"

"That will be just fine. Do what you need, and then we'll take it up from there."

Chapter 58

The next deposition that day began at 11 a.m.. Vijay Singh, the project manager at Lockheed Martin under whom Nancy Bergholzer had worked, appeared on time. He came into the deposition room with his attorney, a woman named Alice King. They were dressed in pinstripes, sported sunglasses in their coats' breast pockets, and carried black binders embossed on the front with *Lockheed Martin* and a jet screaming past. They were asked to sit across from Christine and Thaddeus after Vijay Singh had been sworn and promised to tell the truth. Christine then took the witness through a series of foundational questions, then proceeded into the details.

"Now, Dr. Singh, you've told us that you have a Ph.D. in aerodynamics from UC Berkeley, is that correct?"

"That is correct."

"And you've told us that you have worked at Lockheed Martin for the preceding fourteen years, correct?"

"That is correct."

"Did you participate in or lead the investigation into

Lockheed Martin's missing information once the FBI had informed you that Nancy Bergholzer had been arrested?"

"Yes, I led the investigation."

"Please tell us about that investigation."

"Well, I received a call from SAIC Damon McDowell, and he explained the situation to me. He also explained that not only had Ms. Bergholzer provided a thumb drive containing a thousand gigabytes of information, but that it had also happened maybe another dozen times previous to that. Knowing this, the system administrators and I looked into the server's timeline where Nancy's project was kept. We studied all access made to that data from all employees wherever situated in the company. Of course, we can pinpoint which employee accessed the files on the AN/SPY-1 Radar System on what date, time, and location."

"Beyond the access, was there anything else you learned?"

"Yes, we were able to determine that Nancy Bergholzer had written a piece of code that disguised her access to certain files that were downloaded to an external disk. Knowing this, we have been able to piece together what information has been stolen by her and removed from the premises of Lockheed Martin in San Diego, California."

"Please tell us the nature of the files that were accessed and downloaded, without going into specifics of the secret nature of those items. I'm not asking you to violate any governmental or internal secrets by my question."

"On the first thumb-drive illegal download, Ms. Bergholzer got away with ship integration and test practices, data analysis and automated testing techniques, and information about fiber-optic, cable, power, and cooling issues in the radar equipment in question. Should I go on to incident number two?"

"Please do."

Dr. Singh then consulted his notes before continuing. He then drew a deep breath and said, "On the second round, she acquired radar system status reports to the AWS lead engineer and tech directors and also acquired test procedures, recommended changes, and document test procedure discrepancies that were going to be looking at future revision for the AN/SPY-1 radar system. Should I go on?"

"I think that's enough if you can confirm that the rest of your testimony regarding the assets taken from your company would be in much the same characterization as you have provided."

"Yes, similar and sometimes repetitive since it appeared that, at some access points, she wasn't aware she was copying information for a second time, or she didn't care, or she intended to. We don't know which."

Christine then asked the question that had to be asked, which was, "Concerning the information you are claiming Ms. Bergholzer accessed and downloaded and removed from the premises of Lockheed Martin, what part of that information was rated secret either by the U.S. government or Lockheed Martin or both?"

Vijay Singh did not hesitate. "All of it. Every last document, every last word, every last equation, and every last rendering. It was all secret information."

Christine hesitated. She appeared to be in deep thought. Singh was afraid just then he might know what was coming. And he was right.

Christine said, "Thaddeus, do you have any questions of your own for this witness?"

Thaddeus looked down at the notes he had been making and slowly nodded. "Dr. Singh, I'm wondering how you know it was Nancy Bergholzer who was operating her computer at the time the accesses and downloads were made."

"We know because her password was used."

"Yes, I understand that, but isn't it possible someone else had access to her password and her computer and was doing the actual downloading of the secret documents?"

Dr. Singh squinted his eyes and leaned to his right as his attorney whispered to him. He then came back upright and said, "I guess anything is possible. But we do have Ms. Bergholzer on CCTV on each date and time bent to her computer with her fingers on the keyboard. We keep all of our employees under such surveillance, and they know it. They have consented to it because important military secrets outweigh the privacy rights of people who come to work for us."

Thaddeus sat back from his paperwork, thoughtfully making notes, before looking up and saying, "Let me ask you this. If a programmer were engineer enough, would he be able to inject code into the access times that would make the downloads done at a later time look like they were done at the time when Nancy could be seen on the CCTV?"

Dr. Singh said, "Are you asking me whether it's possible someone took the documents that night when everyone was gone from the building and yet made it look like it had been done that afternoon when Nancy was at her keyboard?"

"Yes, that's exactly what I'm asking."

Dr. Singh again whispered to his attorney, who whispered back to him. Then he said, "I suppose it's possible. I don't know who would have those chops, but as a computer scientist, I can only answer your hypothetical in the affirmative. Yes, it is possible. Not likely, but possible."

Christine then retook charge, saying, "All right, I think

we're done here. Counsel, would your client wish to read and sign?"

Smiling graciously, the attorney in the pinstripe suit spoke up. "He will read and sign, thank you."

Christine then turned to Thaddeus and said, "I'm sorry, were you finished?"

"Yes, I was."

"Then we're done here," said Christine.

The parties began packing their tablets and papers into their folders and leaving the room with nothing further said.

In the hallway, Christine said to Thaddeus, "My office, please."

"Let me hit the head, and I'll be right there."

"See you in five."

Christine and Thaddeus reassembled in Christine's office a few minutes later. She was seated behind her desk, drinking a Diet Coke, when he sat down in a client chair across from her.

"Did I screw up again? Am I in trouble?"

"No, no, honey, you did quite well. I was quite amazed at the theory you came up with regarding the timing of the document downloads. Pretty damn amazing, I can tell you."

He smiled. "Does it help us all that much?"

"Well, we know from the documents, and things turned over by the FBI that they have Nancy on nine different occasions on CCTV hiding thumb drives in the same place and receiving cash moments later. I'm afraid that's pretty damning, but that still doesn't take away from how well you did in there today."

Thaddeus shuffled his feet, thinking, then said, "I might have done pretty well, but we're no closer to walking my sister out of this case than we were before breakfast today, am I right?"

Christine nodded and took a drink of her soda. "I'm afraid you're right. We're going to have to go with the affirmative defenses of 'defense of another' and 'duress' if we're going to win this thing."

"Our chances? Did I help improve our chances?"

She died inside, seeing how unsure he was about everything.

"You helped improve our chances. Ready to skedaddle home? Maybe some soccer?"

"Yep."

Chapter 59

W
hile discovery went on in the case for several more weeks, it was tranquil around the Murfee household.

Christine and Thaddeus were talking, although she was kicking herself for not letting go of her anger and being there for her husband. She knew he was dying inside at his bumbling and general uselessness at the office. Worse yet, for two days now, he no longer went to the office but instead spent his days riding Coco around the hills. When she came home at night, there was just a perfunctory hello—an ill attempt at showing the kids Mom and Dad were okay.

Nancy had come by several times to see Thaddeus and had told him how sorry she was that he was having problems. She wondered with him—when he confided in his sister—whether he would ever regain the abilities he'd had before the injury to his head. He believed he would not; she encouraged him to stay open because it would be a slow recovery, but he would recover 100%.

Marcel was encouraged by Christine to spend time with

Thaddeus. Some days, they would go to the shooting range and put 1500 rounds of 9 mm through their Glocks. On other days, they would take the small yacht into the Pacific and while away the hours fishing and drinking iced lemonade. These were the best times for Thaddeus, as he felt insulated from whatever problems he was having back onshore. During these times, Marcel was careful not to bring up law matters, not to discuss cases, and not to discuss his injury. Instead, he kept Thaddeus focused on the small things, such as horses, guns, inboard-outboard motors, and preferences in motor yachts.

During these days, Thaddeus visited with two different psychiatrists. They assessed him, tested him, and determined the extent of his head injury. Then they sent him to a psychologist for general counseling, including where he would soon be living.

Thaddeus also began spending more time with the children, especially the younger ones, helping them work with their ponies and taking them for rides after school, as well as slipping on their life jackets and taking them out on the boat for joyrides. The kids responded, and Thaddeus began feeling useful again. His intense depression began to lift somewhat.

One night after work, Christine asked him, "I see you spending a lot of time with the kids. How's that going for you?"

"I think the kids are eating it up. I think they needed more time with their dad. It's a good thing."

"No, you didn't answer my question. I meant, how's it going for you?"

"For me, it's exactly what I needed. Keeping up with the kids is something I can do, and engaging in horseback riding and shooting basketballs and surfing and taking boat rides is ground that I can meet them on and be with them successfully. The other half of my life, spending time in the law practice, not so good."

"Do you miss it at all?"

"I miss what Thaddeus Murfee could once do. I don't miss what he can't do now."

———

TWO DAYS LATER, Christine came home with a pleading entitled *Motion to Strike Defendant's Affirmative Defenses Based on Insufficiency as a Matter of Law*. Earlier that day, she'd had a talk with Marcel about the government's motion to strike defenses.

"I'm holding in my hand the government's *Motion to Strike Defendant's Affirmative Defenses Based on Insufficiency as a Matter of Law*. I can tell you that winning this thing is a no-brainer. It appears to have been written by a first-year Assistant U.S. attorney, and it somehow got past the supervisor's review because it's that ridiculous. Are you thinking what I'm thinking?"

Marcel frowned and shook his head. "I don't like it one goddamn bit. Please don't tell me you're going to give this to Thaddeus to defend because it's a no-brainer, something he can't lose. Please tell me you're not doing this just to bolster his self-confidence."

"Why shouldn't I?"

"Because it's artificial. If it's something he couldn't possibly lose, then it might bolster his confidence but give him a false sense of confidence that he shouldn't really have. Are you reading me here?"

"I am, but I think the possible good it might do outweighs what you're talking about. I'm going to give it to him, number one, and see if he wants to work it up, number two, and then stand right next to him in court if he decides he wants to argue the defendant's response."

When she handed the motion to Thaddeus that evening, she told him it was something she wished he would look at and let her know if he would feel like being involved with defending the motion. At first, he pushed it away and said he wanted nothing to do with it. But she persisted and finally convinced him she could really use the help.

"All right," he said. "I'll take a look, but that doesn't mean I want anything to do with this. But I will look at it so I can give you whatever feedback I can give you, whatever that might be worth."

"Hey, if that's the way you want to do it, that will be perfect. I will certainly appreciate your input."

"I'm going to my office. I'll do some research, write a little memo, and get back to you in the next day or two."

———

FIVE DAYS LATER, she had her answer. Thaddeus had reviewed the motion and had given her a memo covering the applicable federal rules of criminal procedure and the court cases that applied. However, he told her that he would not be willing to argue the motion in court, although he would be willing to write it. What did she think of that?

"You know what I think? I think it's a start. I think I appreciate you giving me a hand with this. And maybe that's a perfect way for us to begin, with you writing the brief and me doing the argument on it. I can see us going a long way in that formation."

"Good. Then I feel comfortable. I don't know that I'll ever again feel comfortable being turned loose in the courtroom to make arguments on my own, to examine witnesses on my own, to make closing arguments to juries on my own, or to select juries or any of the other jillion things a trial lawyer has to do. I'm ninety percent convinced those days are gone."

"Dr. Miller called me today, incidentally. He tells me you haven't shown up for your last two appointments. Is it just because you're feeling that much better that you're not going to Antonella? Or is it because you've given up?"

"First of all, it's medical negligence for him to discuss my case with my wife. I'm thinking of sending him a strongly worded letter in that regard."

"Sure, Mr. Big Shot, go out and flex your muscles around some seventy-year-old psychiatrist who's only been trying to help you. A hell of a lot of good that will do anybody."

Thaddeus looked away. He was quiet several moments, then, "You're right. I would be legally justified, but I would be stupid as hell to do that. I haven't been going because I feel like I've been spinning my wheels. I don't see myself getting any better. I don't know if I ever will. And I'm sure Dr. Miller doesn't know how much recovery there is for me because I've asked him. Maybe I'll start going again in a year, and maybe I won't. But for now, I'm finished."

"Okay, then please call him and tell them you won't be returning."

"I will. I'll call him tomorrow as soon as his office opens. Thanks for letting me know."

Chapter 60

T he trial began two weeks later on a Monday when Judge Hortense Franklin walked into the court-room at 9:01 a.m. and took a seat high above the crowd. He cracked his knuckles, arranged documents and books on the desk before him, looked over the crowd and smiled. "Ladies and gentlemen, welcome to the first day of trial in the case of *United States of America versus Nancy Bergholzer*. I'm going to give you the rules of conduct for my courtroom."

The judge then went on to talk to the jury panel about not discussing the case amongst themselves, not reading newspapers, watching TV, or reading magazine articles about the case.

At the end, he told the jury they would be drawing enough names to fill the jury box plus alternates, and then he would begin qualifying the jury.

He next went around the jury box, probing for possible prejudice. He dismissed two jurors who admitted that they could not be unbiased in a case involving treason in which the defendant could be facing the death penalty.

Other venire members also expressed concerns, upon further questions, about the crime of treason in light of the fact they were such strong patriots and wanted any such acts of treason to be punished by the maximum penalty. However, in the end, they were all able to say that regardless of their biases, they would still be able to render a verdict based on the facts, and evidence, and testimony in the case.

Once he was satisfied with the jury, Judge Franklin had them sworn in, denying a request by counsel to question the jury directly themselves. Thaddeus explained to Nancy that *voir dire* was rarely allowed to be conducted by counsel in federal court. Judges were cautious there to keep their jury unblemished regarding any prejudice or prejudgment the attorneys might try to get the jury to commit to. It just wasn't going to happen in federal court, unlike state court, where the *voir dire* could often be a feeding frenzy in the back and forth of questions asked by the attorneys.

It had been decided between Thaddeus and Christine that Christine would give the opening statement in the case, as Thaddeus did not feel up to it.

The government proceeded first, building a detailed case against Nancy based on the facts it thought it could prove.

Then it was Christine's turn. She humanized Nancy and talked about the kidnapping of Simon and the duress Nancy was under when she delivered the military secrets to the company she referred to as CSID.

Chapter 61

The Assistant U.S. attorney prosecuting the case was Muriel Newsom, a ten-year veteran in the prosecution of intelligence breaches and the illegal distribution of secret documents and related files such as what Nancy had turned over. Muriel Newsom was thirty-five years old, a black woman raising her children with a husband who was a chemical engineer at a Long Beach refinery. She was 5-10, slender, with short black hair cut into a pageboy. She habitually wore black suits with white blouses and a small gold necklace in the form of the Earth being held by two hands and inscribed underneath with the words *My Light*. Muriel Newsom called as her first witness Damon McDowell.

McDowell took the witness stand, was sworn in by the court clerk, and then gave the jury the obligatory FBI smile. He then looked back at AUSA Newsom, ready to crush Nancy Bergholzer, where she sat at counsel table between Thaddeus and Christine.

"I'm now going to direct your attention to August twelfth. What, if anything, on that date did you see and observe involving Nancy Bergholzer?"

The FBI agent nodded slightly, then said, "I was there on that day at the Avion Kite Store in Seaport Village. Through the glass window, I witnessed the defendant place an object above a display of kites on the top shelf and walk down to the other end of the room. I then observed FBI Special Agent Ricky Martinez retrieve the object from the shelf, then follow Bergholzer to the other end of the store and drop a packet of cash into her open coat pocket."

"You observed all of this from where?"

"Another agent and I observed it from the sidewalk immediately outside the store. We peered through the window at the moment defendant Bergholzer made the placement. '

"Were you able to identify what object was placed?"

"I was. The object was a computer thumb drive, capable of holding 1000 gigs of data."

"Were you able to determine what data was contained on the thumb drive? "

"Yes, I determined, in consultation with security agents from Lockheed Martin, that the information contained on the thumb drive was secret schematics and drawings and discussions regarding the AN/SPY-1 radar system."

"And you determined this information in consultation with security agents from Lockheed Martin here in San Diego?"

"That's right."

"Were you able to learn where the actual data came from?"

"Yes, it came from the computer servers of the Lockheed Martin Corporation in San Diego, California. The data was downloaded from the San Diego Lockheed Martin computer servers by the defendant, Nancy Bergholzer. Should I go on?"

"Yes, please do, as long as it is germane to the question which I asked."

"I also learned that Nancy Bergholzer had written a computer algorithm capable of masking the fact that she was downloading data from the Lockheed Martin servers into her thumb drive. It was quite a sophisticated operation."

Muriel Samson then paused, consulted her notes, and looked up from the lectern. "Your Honor, the government has no further questions for this witness at this time."

"Very well, counsel, please be seated. Defense counsel who will be questioning the witness on cross-examination, please come forward and take your place at the lectern."

Christine proceeded to the lectern, placed her notepad before her, and began asking questions.

"Agent McDowell, did you see Nancy Bergholzer place thumb drives or any other objects on the shelf at any time before or since that day on August twelfth?"

"I have not. I'm not aware of any reports, either, where this has happened."

"Were you able to see the item Nancy Bergholzer left on the shelf?"

"No, we could not see the actual object."

"So, you are assuming that the thumb drive retrieved from the shelf by Ricky Martinez had, in fact, been placed there by Nancy Bergholzer?"

"I'm assuming that, yes, but it's a powerful assumption based on the fact that she came away with $5000 as payment for the item she had placed there."

"I can tell you that Nancy Bergholzer is going to raise the affirmative defense of duress. She is also going to raise a second affirmative defense, known as the defense of others. She will claim these defenses based on her testimony that her four-year-old son, Simon, had been kidnapped by the party making her place the stolen secrets on the shelf. Are you aware of any evidence tending to prove that her son was not kidnapped?"

"I am not aware of any evidence that her son was not kidnapped. However, I am also not aware of any evidence tending to prove that he *was* kidnapped. Our investigation has uncovered no facts about the alleged kidnapping."

"Hold on, are you telling me that you did not assist Thaddeus Murfee with information to locate his kidnapped nephew, Simon, son of Nancy Bergholzer and Jeff Bergholzer in Bogotá, Colombia?"

The special agent's face tightened, and he became thoughtful. Then he said, "The FBI received pictures from the DEA of children possibly being held in Bogotá, Colombia for human trafficking. We knew that due to Mr. Murfee's actions, the arrest of a human trafficker, Franco Cárdenas, might be possible. So, we offered him the information we had. We could not confirm whether the picture of the child was indeed his nephew or not, so we left it up to him to make that call."

Christine dropped her eyes to the wooden shelf and began flipping through her notes. Her lips were pursed, and her forehead wrinkled as she concentrated her attention on a particular note that she wished to ask questions about. Finally, she located what she was looking for and then continued.

"Nancy Bergholzer is also raising the affirmative defense of defense of another. As you may or may not know, this defense is often raised where an actor claims that another person was being threatened with harm and that she acted, maybe even illegally, to prevent harm to that person. Hence the title 'defense of another.' Is there anything in your investigation that would disprove that Nancy Bergholzer acted in defense of another person when she turned over the secrets?"

The Special Agent slightly shrugged, saying, "There's nothing in my investigation proving that she was not acting in defense of another. However, there was nothing in our investigations to prove that she *was* acting in defense of another. As far as we were concerned, it was all hearsay and not actionable. The FBI will not waste resources and people to follow down hearsay leads. There must be more than that."

"If Nancy Bergholzer testifies before this jury that her son had been kidnapped and that she was removing secrets from Lockheed and turning them over to a third party because she was afraid for the life of her son, would you have any evidence tending to disagree with her?"

"We have no such evidence. But again, we consider that to be hearsay only and wouldn't have gone out to collect any evidence one way or the other."

"Of course, you do have the fact that the FBI cooperated with Thaddeus Murfee and placing him with the location where Simon had purportedly been taken. Isn't that correct?"

"I repeat, our cooperation was in no way predicated on helping Thaddeus Murfee retrieve a child which we didn't even know to be kidnapped. There is no way we would've cooperated with Mr. Murfee based on that hypothetical alone."

Christine leaned to Thaddeus and whispered. "What? Didn't he tell you about Simon?"

He shook his head. "I have no recall."

Christine looked up at the judge and said, "I believe that's all I have, Your Honor."

Judge Franklin then excused the witness and told AUSA Newsom to call her next witness.

Chapter 62

Before the government's next witness going up to the witness stand and being sworn, Christine nudged Thaddeus and asked if he would like to handle the coming cross-examination. She watched as his face turned white, and he imperceptibly shook his head. "I can't do it," he whispered. "There's too much riding on it, and if I hurt my sister's case, I could never forgive myself. You're doing great. Please keep it up. I love you for helping."

Christine nodded, indicating she understood where he was coming from, and deep down, she had expected that response anyway. But she had asked him the question to at least allow him to help his sister's case if he felt up to it. After his refusal, she had to admit to herself that she was still hoping the Thaddeus of old would step forward and save his sister. But it appeared that it was not going to happen. What was going to happen was up to Christine and Christine only.

She began looking through her notes for the upcoming witness. At the same time, she found herself becoming resentful of Thaddeus. Still, she immediately reminded herself he was declining to help, not because he was mean or uncaring, but because he lacked the self-confidence to do the job without condemning his sister to prison.

AUSA Newsom called her next witness, Stanley Diemer, and put him under oath and quickly let the jury know through her questions that Special Agent Diemer was the supervisor of Special Agent Damon McDowell.

"As Agent McDowell's supervisor, did you play a part in the decision of the FBI as to how to treat the claim by Nancy Bergholzer that her son had been kidnapped?"

Stanley Diemer, a stout man wearing a light brown three-piece suit, said, "Actually, it was my decision and my decision alone not to follow up on her claims of kidnapping. My thinking was that if her son had been kidnapped ten hand-to-hand sales ago, she would have reported his kidnapping to us earlier to enlist our help. It just seemed illogical to me that she would wait until it was her butt on the line before reporting her son missing. It sounded more self-serving to me than it did factual. Can you blame me, counsel?"

Christine shook her head. "Special Agent Diemer, I know you've testified probably thousands of times before, and I know that you know the rule about not asking questions back when you are being asked the question. So, let me ask, why are you breaking that rule in front of this jury?"

"I didn't think I was breaking the rule as much as I was trying to get more information to answer your questions properly. So, I'll ask again, why would your client wait so long to inform the FBI?"

Christine looked up at Judge Franklin for help. "Your Honor, would you please instruct the witness that he is not to be asking the questions but only answering those questions put to him?"

Judge Franklin said, "Special Agent Diemer, I'm going to order you to stop asking questions, as this is neither the time or the place. If it happens again, I'm going to instruct the jury to ignore all of your testimony as if it never occurred. That is all. Counsel, please continue with your cross-examination."

"Agent Diemer, is it the FBI's policy not to investigate claims of kidnapping because those claims had not earlier resulted in requests for FBI assistance to locate the kidnapped person? In other words, is it the FBI's policy to ignore such claims across the board?"

Special Agent Stanley Diemer shook his head vigorously. "No, because the FBI investigates all believable kidnapping claims."

"Yet, in this case, you alone determined that the kidnapping claim was not supportable, and you, therefore, let a four-year-old boy remain in the hands of kidnappers because you were unwilling to have a look. Isn't that correct?"

"That is not correct for the reasons I've previously given."

"That is all I have, Your Honor, at this time for this witness. But the defense does reserve the right to call this witness in its own case."

Christine returned to counsel table, where Thaddeus whispered to her, "These guys can be such hard-nosed bastards. You did well without much to work with."

"I only wonder how much better you would've done," she said with more than just a hint of irony in her voice. Thaddeus didn't respond to her, and the court moved ahead.

AUSA Newsom went through several more witnesses, some of whom had been interviewed by Thaddeus and Christine, and some of whom had not been. They included laboratory personnel and computer science personnel who were called to explain different facets of the case, all of which Christine felt was testimony that only moved the case sideways rather than ahead. For that reason, she ignored it.

The government then rested its case. Christine made an oral motion to dismiss the charges, *pro forma*, which was denied.

The court then told Christine to call her first witness.

Chapter 63

I t happened after the second day of the trial at 9:22
Tuesday night when Christine received the call from
her sister's husband in Orbit, Illinois. Her sister had
suffered a terrible auto accident, train versus car, and was
given only a 50-50 chance of surviving the next forty-eight
hours. Christine kept her own Gulfstream aircraft and was
down to San Diego airport and in the air before eleven p.m.

Before she left, she tried to calm the panicked Thaddeus, whose role in his sister's defense was now lead attorney. He was stunned and, for the first half-hour, unable to
speak. Then, as Christine was throwing some things into a
suitcase spread out on their bed, he managed to ask, "Could
we get the trial continued since you're going to be
unavailable?"

"Not on your life," Christine replied. "Federal judges
coddle their juries. He won't make them take days or weeks
off while I'm away. It's come down to it, Thaddeus.
You're it."

He tried a compromise. "Tomorrow begins Nancy's

284

testimony. Can you at least wait and get her testimony in before you leave for Illinois? Please?"

She wheeled on him. "Thaddeus! Collect yourself! My sister might be dying! I'm going tonight. You take care of *your* sister tomorrow."

After she was gone, he was up half the night laying out direct examinations, possible objections to cross-examination questions, and re-direct examination questions. By the time the sun was coming up, he felt ready, insofar as planning could make him. But there remained that huge unknown: how would he perform? When the government objected or made arguments, would he be able to hold up his end of it? Or would he blank out and make spurious responses and be laughed out of court? Would he even get his sister convicted with his injured brain?

He honestly did not know, and that was his frame of mind that Wednesday morning, the third day of trial.

Chapter 64

C ourt began the next morning at 8 o'clock sharp. Judge Franklin took his seat on the bench, counted noses in the jury box, and then told Thaddeus the defense could proceed with its first witness. Thaddeus called Nancy Bergholzer to the witness stand, where she was sworn in and took a seat.

"Tell us your name for the record."

"Nancy Bergholzer."

"Nancy, what is your business, occupation, or profession?"

"By training, I am a master's level computer engineer. I program in C++, C#, Java, several scripting languages, and I am a Microsoft Certified Systems Engineer as well."

"Anything else?"

"I also program in assembly language."

"Give us some of the high points of your resume, please. Tell us where you have worked in the past."

"Let's see, I have worked at Intel, Allstate, Jet Propulsion

Laboratory, and most recently at Lockheed Martin in San Diego."

"Have you ever been accused at any of those prior places of employment of any employee wrongdoing?"

"Never."

"Have you ever in your life been charged with any crimes or been sued for anything before the matter we're here about today?"

"Never. This is the first time I've ever been to court in my life."

"I want to ask you some questions about the ten incidents contained in the indictment where you have been charged with trafficking in stolen government secrets, in various shapes and forms, all of which underpin the government's charge of treason. Concerning those ten incidents, please look over at the jury and tell them why you agreed to commit those transactions where government secrets were traded for money."

"First of all, I did none of it for money. The other party insisted I take money. I never wanted it. And the reason I did the things I did was that they had kidnapped my four-year-old son, Simon, and had threatened his life if I failed to cooperate."

"Hold it right there. In this court, the FBI agents testified that you did not ask them for help when Simon was first kidnapped. Can you please tell the jury why you didn't ask?"

"I didn't ask because I didn't trust the FBI. I didn't trust anyone. I only wanted my son back, and I was willing to do anything they said to get him back. In hindsight, maybe I did the wrong thing. But my husband and I discussed how confident we were with the FBI and decided not so much. So, we tried it as the kidnappers demanded. I was told I would be required to make ten turnovers and that my son would then be returned. Right or wrong, I had no option but to go ahead with that."

Thaddeus looked down at the lectern and studied the page upon which he had mapped out his direct examination. He decided that so far it had gone quite well. None of his questions had been objected to, and the answers his sister was giving were logical and compelling. He felt quite good."

"Ms. Bergholzer, your son was returned to you?"

"Yes, from the country of Colombia, South America. He flew back to California with a man named Marcel Rainford."

"Has anyone told you how that happened?"

"Yes, you told me."

"What did I—"

"Objection! Calls for hearsay."

The judge looked down at Thaddeus and said, "Objection sustained. Please refrain from asking the witness what she has been told, Mister Murfee. If you have the testimony of witnesses as to what happened in Colombia, you may call them. This is assuming you have listed any such witnesses in pretrial discovery as people you might call at trial."

Thaddeus thought about the court's ruling before saying, "Then the defendant moves to amend her pretrial discovery responses and add the name of Elizabeth Janes to her list of witnesses. Elizabeth Janes is a map specialist and was a member of my task force in Colombia. She can prove—"

"Hold it Mister Murfee!" interrupted the judge. "Counsel, approach the bench, and we will speak out of the jury's hearing. Approach now, please, both of you."

Assistant U.S. Attorney Newsom and Thaddeus moved to the far side of the judge's perch while he leaned forward, where they whispered among themselves.

"Mr. Murfee, exactly what would you attempt to prove through this Elizabeth Janes?"

"Your Honor, Elizabeth Janes is ex-DEA and a specialist used by Interpol. She was a key player in my extraction team in South America. I handed her Simon Bergholzer during a firefight in the Colombian jungle. She can testify that Simon was being held hostage in the jungle at a location under the control of a drug lord named Franco Cárdenas. As the court is aware, the prosecution has denied that there even was a kidnapping. Through the testimony of Elizabeth Janes, I can prove that there was, indeed, such a kidnapping. We need this witness, Your Honor, so I asked that the defendant's list of witnesses be amended accordingly."

Assistant U.S. Attorney Newsom then presented her position. "Your Honor, first of all, the government has not had the opportunity to interview Elizabeth Janes. To allow her now would be a clear surprise to the government and create prejudice warranting a new trial. Moreover, calling this witness could take days or even weeks, which would provide great hardship and disservice to the jury, and I know the court will not want to do that."

Judge Franklin looked again at Thaddeus. Thaddeus realized he would be asked to respond to what the government had just said, and his heart pounded in his chest, and his mind went blank. But the judge went right ahead and said, "Mr. Murfee, two objections by the government. First, surprise. Second, delay. How do you respond to these objections?"

Before Thaddeus could answer, the bailiff asked in a loud voice, "Ms. Bergholzer, do you need a drink of water?"

Thaddeus turned and saw his sister sitting alone at counsel table, dabbing her eyes with a piece of white tissue paper. In just that moment, she was vulnerable, and he saw she was very small and up against the might and power of the United States government by herself if he failed her. She was in the grip of the social workers again, just as when they were children and being torn apart. He had no choice, at that moment, but to rear up and stiffen his spine and fight back.

Without hesitation, he said to the judge, "Your Honor, it is ridiculous for the government to claim surprise as to one of its own employees. As a matter of law, the government is charged with knowledge of everything about its employees. The government is charged with knowing what Elizabeth Janes has been doing in South America since she arrived there. So that part of the objection must fail. As far as the second part of the government's objection, that any delay will unnecessarily burden the jury, I can avow to the court that by Friday, the day after tomorrow, I will produce Elizabeth Janes in this courtroom and obtain her testimony. Suppose the court were not to allow my client the opportunity to fully defend herself against the government's ridiculous claim that Simon wasn't kidnapped. In that case, the prejudice that would result to my client is huge compared to the petty prejudice that would result to the jury by a day spent waiting."

Judge Franklin then returned the attorneys to their tables, removed his eyeglasses, and cleaned them with a bit of cloth. He then said, "Ladies and gentlemen, we are in recess until the day after tomorrow, Friday morning, at 8 a.m. Court stands adjourned."

Thaddeus was at his desk aboard his Gulfstream jet two hours later, headed south to Bogotá. As soon as he was airborne, he found himself smiling from ear to ear as he recalled his whispered argument. It was strange that the real Thaddeus had returned in a whisper, but he had.

He was back.

Chapter 65

Thaddeus called Elizabeth Janes en route from his airplane. They caught up for a few moments, and then she asked him what in the world happened when he disappeared after the Monkey's Paw raid. He explained to her that he lost it over Anna's death and was trying to get help for her away from the insanity of central Colombia when he was shot off his motorcycle. *What of Anna? she wanted to know.* He told her that as far as he had been able to tell, she had died by the time he returned to the Monkey's Paw.

"I'm getting mixed up," she said. "If you knew she was already dead, why would you take her with you on the motorcycle?"

"That, Elizabeth, is the question I'm still asking myself when the night is quiet, and everyone in the house has gone to bed. I can only think that I had mentally lost it and was reacting rather than thinking."

"Well, when you didn't return to Bogotá with everyone

else, we all just figured you had been shot or taken captive or died some other way and that we would never know.

Thaddeus looked out the window of his airplane from 36,000 feet. The time of telling lies was over. "Truth be told, I felt responsible for Anna since she'd been partnered with me. I totally lost it and strapped her dead body onto my motorcycle and went God only knows where to find help. It was going to take a resurrection to help Anna at that point. But I was too screwed up in my mind to know it. It was just a terrible situation. To keep things short, Colombia was not a good experience for Thaddeus Murfee. Too many things went wrong, but at least one thing went right, and that was we found my nephew Simon, and you helped me get him out of that hellhole. Do you remember that night? That's actually why I'm calling you."

"Of course, I remember. You handed your nephew to me, and I ran with him to the Huey and climbed in. We were the last two on that flight. He stayed with me back to Bogotá and then stayed in my room for two days while Marcel and I made travel arrangements for him. I think he felt more comfortable with a mother figure than a scary-looking Marcel. He knew his mother's name, his father's name, and he knew the city he lived in. Rather, he knew the beach's name where he went to wade and played in the sand. It was enough, Murfee—I mean, Murfee. A day later, Marcel took him back to California on your private jet."

"Well, here's my problem now. Simon's mother—"

"Nancy."

"Nancy, that's right. Anyway, she's been arrested for selling military secrets, which she did when Simon had been kidnapped, and they were holding his life and threatening to kill him if she didn't turn over the information."

"Oh, my God, so that's what he was doing at the

Monkey's Paw. He was being held as ransom to steal government secrets. Oh, my God."

"And now I'm defending her in federal court on ten counts of trafficking in governmental secrets. These are treason charges, and she is looking at the death penalty."

"Hmm. And you want me to come to testify for some reason. Am I right?"

"That's exactly right. Right now, the government is denying that Simon was kidnapped. They've taken the position that Nancy was making it up as an afterthought and an excuse. I'm in the air right now as we speak, headed for Bogotá, and I'm hoping to steal you away for one day so that you can come into the court and testify that you saw Simon pulled out of the Monkey's Paw where he had been held as a captive. Also, testify that he was a kidnap victim, meaning that he could not leave if he wanted to, which is a stupid thing to say because he was only four years old. Nevertheless, that's what the law requires."

"Let me make sure I understand, Thaddeus," she said. "You're asking an ex-government agent who had acted as undercover narc for the DEA to come into court and testify against a sister agency, being the FBI. Does that sound to you like the right thing for me to do?"

"I like to think of it less as testifying against the FBI than as testifying against the Special Agent in the FBI who made the initial decision there had been no kidnapping and that my sister was lying. To my way of thinking, your testimony would be more to offer an alternative to what the FBI *is* saying, based on facts that you know to be true. Let the jury decide if what you will tell the court constitutes kidnapping. This is the way it must be done, rather than letting a solitary FBI agent make that decision for the jury. I know I'm asking a lot, but it means a lot. It means allowing a five-year-old boy to grow up knowing his mother and having her loving care and affection versus having her languish in some federal facility a thousand miles away while he grows up never to see her again. Given the circumstances and given what you and I both saw at the Monkey's Paw, I don't think either of us has an option except to tell the truth and let the jury make up its mind. Can I count on you?"

There was a long pause. Then she said, "Count me in. What's your ETA at the airport so I can be waiting for you in general aviation?"

Our ETA is at ten a.m. Thursday. I cannot thank you enough, Elizabeth."

"Don't tell anyone, but I've never much cared for the FBI. That's not for repeat. See you in the morning. Little black dress? I thought so. It'll be in my bag."

* * *

At 11 a.m. Thursday, the aircraft took off, transporting Thaddeus and Elizabeth Janes back to San Diego to continue trial the next day. Elizabeth slept much of the way while Thaddeus worked on his witness questions and closing argument. As far as he was concerned, the trial now belonged to him.

In the early afternoon, Thaddeus finally managed to connect with Christine. Her sister was out of the woods, as she put it, but Christine planned to stay on and help nurse her back to health once she was released to go home. Thaddeus told her no problem, that he had the trial nicely under control.

"Seriously?" she wondered out loud.

"Thaddeus Murfee has returned to the building." He then ended the call and went back to his laptop.

Chapter 66

Elizabeth Janes came to court Friday morning freshly scrubbed and with a new haircut and wearing her little black dress. A fine-link gold necklace was around her throat, and she was wearing a wedding ring and an engagement ring, neither of which Thaddeus had ever seen on her hands before. When she came into the courtroom, she appeared relaxed, calm, and collected and gave the jury the obligatory government agent's smile as she took her seat in the witness box.

Thaddeus went over all of the preliminary questions, including her name, age, employer, and education. He did not go into the secretive nature of her work, of course, nor would the court force her to divulge that on cross-examination.

She testified about the night in question at the Monkey's Paw. She testified to the jury in clear, unequivocal statements that she had seen Simon when they first entered the dormitory. She testified she saw Simon a second time when she was charged with counting noses and radioing to the

Huey helicopters how many seats they needed for all the children to be exfiltrated. She left no doubt that Simon was one of the first children she had seen upon entering the second-floor dormitory sleeping area. She said she knew that because he had been sitting up in bed, wild-eyed at all the noise from the helicopters and the machine-gun fire. She remembered him, too, because he had been quietly crying and saying over and over again, "Mama, come get me. Mama, come get me." She testified she had only taken him in her arms later when all the children had been located.

When she said these things, it was hushed in the courtroom. Thaddeus knew there was no longer any doubt in the jury's mind that a kidnapping had occurred. Janes was an utterly believable witness, relaxed, and perspicuous in her approach to answering questions in a very logical, straightforward manner. As he looked up from his notes, ready to continue the line of questions in a new area, he noted several members of the jury dabbing at their eyes and leaning forward in their seats. He knew they were anxious to hear how Simon had been removed from the compound and made his way back home to his mother and father.

Thaddeus then provided that information, getting Janes to testify how the boy was helped to get back to America and be reunited with Jeff and Nancy Bergholzer.

The Assistant U.S. attorney knew going in that government law enforcement agents were exceptionally well trained in providing courtroom testimony and would never be rattled or made to look bad. So, she kept at her cross-examination for only five questions, none of which went anywhere, and then she sat back down and said she was done.

***

The parties finished with their direct and cross-examinations of Elizabeth Janes before noon. Unwilling to waste any court time, Judge Franklin then instructed Thaddeus to call his next witness. Thaddeus called Dr. Michael Stoner, who had been waiting outside in the hallway cooling his jets at the rate of $1000 an hour. After the clerk of the court had sworn him to tell the truth, and after he had taken a seat in the witness stand, the doctor testified that he was a psychiatrist. He explained that he was trained at Stanford University, that he was board-certified, and treated Nancy Bergholzer since her arrest.

The doctor was able to testify that Nancy had suffered the emotional and mental injuries that would naturally follow a kidnapping of one's child. This meant much argument back and forth between the attorneys. Still, Judge Franklin finally allowed Dr. Stoner to testify that, in his professional opinion, Nancy Bergholzer had been forced against her will to participate in the exchanges of military documents and government secrets. Had he invaded the province of the jury? Thaddeus didn't care. He had his ruling.

Nancy testified next. Thaddeus thought it was vital for her to testify there were no prior arrests, not even for traffic tickets, and about her motherhood and about the kidnapping of Simon and how it had destroyed her. And its impact on Jeff, who had attended court that day and was sitting right behind the bar, as close to his wife as possible. When she was finished testifying, there were no dry eyes. The impact of Simon's disappearance, the picture of the little boy with his eyes stitched shut—all of it made for a decisive moment in court. Nancy then underwent a half-hour of cross-examination, but Newsom knew not to take off the gloves because Nancy was now seen as a victim herself, thanks to Thaddeus and how he had presented her testimony and the iPhone picture. Nancy then returned to her place at the defense table.

Jeff Bergholzer was listed as a witness and was called to be asked whether his son had been kidnapped. He so testified, and there was minor elaboration that Nancy hadn't already provided. Thaddeus had only one or two more questions regarding Nancy and her—and his—mental state when Simon was kidnapped. Anything else would have been cumulative, so Thaddeus stopped. There was no cross-examination, so Jeff then sat back down with the spectators.

Thaddeus then whispered to Nancy at the defense table, asking whether she had any other testimony or exhibits or anything else she wanted him to introduce at trial. He was covering all his bases in case the very worst happened in the end. She told him no that she was well satisfied with what he had done, and there was no need for any further witnesses or exhibits that she was aware of. For that reason, Thaddeus then let the judge know that the defense was resting its case. At that time, Assistant U.S. attorney Newsom shot up to her feet and advised the court that the government had an impeachment witness to call. The court told her that she could begin with her impeachment witness after lunch at 1:30 p.m..

Chapter 67

Directly after lunch that Friday afternoon, once the court had taken up again, Assistant U.S. attorney Newsom called to the witness stand a woman named Guelda Fischer. She was a stocky woman with fleshy bracelets and hair fixed in place with combs. She looked lovely, a mature face that seemed to smile from any angle. She took the witness stand and began answering questions.

Asked Newsom, "Your name is Guelda Fisher, and you work at Lockheed Martin and have worked there since 2011, is that right?"

"That is correct. I began there the day after New Year's."

"What is your current role with the company?"

"I am a digital librarian. That means I am responsible for organizing and tracking all Lockheed Martin documents on the AN/SPY-1 project."

"And while you were working as a digital librarian on that radar project, did you happen to have contact with the defendant, Nancy Bergholzer, at any time?"

"Oh, yes, many times. We interacted with all of the team, Nancy no more no less."

"Directing your attention to August fifteenth, did you have occasion to meet with Nancy on that date?"

"After the FBI came to see me and interviewed me, I provided the date of August fifteenth myself. It was the date Nancy Bergholzer came to my desk and invited me for drinks after work. We went out that night, just down the street from the plant, at a bar called the Radar Room, and we each had a white wine. We were into a second-round when Nancy offhandedly asked me whether I had considered making extra money by turning over documents to other companies."

"How did you react?"

"I was shocked. For the life of me, I could not believe my ears. Don't get me wrong, I didn't know that much about Nancy, but the fact that any of our employees would make that kind of a pitch to me was shocking. I became frustrated and began crying and ran out of the bar. I called a cab and left my car in the parking lot while the cab took me home that night. I had to call a cab to get back to work the next morning. The whole incident has haunted me ever since. I was not surprised when the FBI came calling."

"Between the time when she made her pitch to you and when the FBI came calling, did you ever go to your employer or your supervisor and tell them what happened?"

"I thought about it but decided not to. We had been drinking, the bar was noisy, and while I was mostly sure that's what she had said, there was a slight question in my mind, but most of all, it would've been my word against hers. Those are very poor odds, and I didn't want to jeopardize my job when coming forth would probably have made very little difference."

Several other areas of inquiry were pursued, and then the witness was turned over to Thaddeus for cross-examination. He stepped up to the lectern, planted his feet, and told himself that he was going to go after this one.

"Ms. Fisher, isn't it true that you have made all this up?"

"No, no such thing. What I've said here today is the absolute truth, so help me God."

At that point, Thaddeus had an exhibit marked and asked the court to allow him to present it to the witness. The government objected, claiming that the exhibit had not been listed in the pretrial disclosure and, therefore, it should be barred from coming into evidence. Thaddeus replied that the witness herself had been undisclosed and that he hadn't objected to her, and that justice now required the court to allow him to use the exhibit. After batting the ball back and forth a few more times, the parties looked to the judge for his decision. He told Thaddeus to go ahead and use the exhibit, to have it marked, and to pass it to the witness. When those things had been accomplished, and the document was given to the witness, Thaddeus continued with his examination.

"Ms. Fisher, can you tell the jury the nature of the document you are holding in your hand?"

"It is a letter written by Lockheed Martin to Nancy Bergholzer."

"Why don't you go ahead and tell the jury what the letter says—read it out loud, please."

The witness read the statement: "Dear Nancy Bergholzer, it has come to our attention that you have been arrested by the FBI and charged with providing company secrets to other countries, companies, or people. You are hereby notified that your job at Lockheed Martin is terminated, that your passcodes have been erased, and that your badge ID will no longer gain access to any company property. Your final paycheck will arrive on the fourth Friday of this month, as usual. You are to have no further conversations with any Lockheed Martin employees." Finishing the letter, Guelda Fisher then looked up, her face frozen in her customary smile despite the moment's seriousness.

"Ms. Fisher, please read the date of that letter."

"August third."

"So, let me get this straight. You previously testified that on August fifteenth, Nancy Bergholzer approached your desk inside the Lockheed Martin building. Yet you are holding a letter confirming that she was terminated by Lockheed Martin on August third and had no way of re-entering the premises as all of her passcodes and ID cards had been deactivated. So, let me ask you, is it you who came up with the story about the wine and the pitch, or was it the FBI who came up with that story?"

"To-to-to be honest—"

"That would be nice. Please keep going."

"I don't remember."

"You don't remember what? Whether it was you who made up the lie or the FBI who made up the lie? Is that what you don't remember?"

"I don't remember."

Thaddeus turned to the judge and said with evident disgust, "Nothing further for this witness, Your Honor."

At that point in the trial, the judge asked the parties whether they had any further witnesses or exhibits to take up with the court. They both replied negatively, so the judge took a thirty-minute recess to give them time to work on their closing statements to begin at 3 p.m..

The jury worked the rest of Friday and begged the court to be allowed to deliberate over the weekend so they wouldn't get into the next week. The judge agreed, and the jury worked Saturday and then at ten a.m. Sunday told the court they had their verdict. They were then excused to return to their homes.

Chapter 68

Thaddeus stood with Nancy to receive the verdict Monday at nine a.m. Thaddeus put his arm around his sister's back and pulled her close to him. He turned to her and whispered, "I'm right here with you. You're not going through this alone. I'm going to get you out of this, so take a deep breath."

The jury foreperson spoke, "We the jury, find the defendant, Nancy Bergholzer, not guilty of Count One of the indictment…" and then continued through Count Ten, all not guilty. Nancy collapsed against Thaddeus and then fell into Jeff's arms, weeping, for several minutes as the jury filed past, all smiles. Thaddeus saw one juror, a woman of about thirty, reach out and touch Nancy's shoulder as she walked past. Others reached as if to touch but didn't quite, content with the impression they left. Then the courtroom was empty but for Nancy, Jeff, and Thaddeus.

He packed up his rolling case of trial books and headed for the courtroom double-doors. "Coming?" he stopped and said to Nancy and Jeff.

"I can't get out of here fast enough," she replied. "Never, ever again."

Thaddeus smiled and nodded.

An hour later, he drove her home after sending her husband Jeff on his way in his car. Thaddeus had told Jeff that he wanted to talk to his sister, and would he mind him having the time alone with her?

They were merging into northbound traffic headed toward her home in Pacific Beach when Thaddeus said, "I need to understand why you didn't come to me when they kidnapped Simon."

Nancy slowly shook her head and adjusted her sunglasses against the low-lying ten o'clock sun. It was that time of day in San Diego when the marine layer had not yet burned off, and swatches of fog and clouds cast an orange-gray color over the landscape.

Nancy turned to Thaddeus. "I didn't come to you because I knew what you would do."

"I really don't understand that at all. What would I have done?"

"You would have gone after Simon's kidnapper's tooth and tong. I was afraid you would get my little boy killed."

"I see. Well, if something like this ever happens again, will you at least come and talk to me about it if I promise you I won't take up arms and go after someone?"

Nancy smiled, and it was a kindly smile. "Brother, I can't make that promise because that wouldn't be you. You always have been aggressive and overwhelming when your family is threatened. So I can't make that promise."

"Aw, shucks," said Thaddeus. "You just made my day."

"No, I just told the truth. You just made my day. You've always been there for me. Today was no different."

Chapter 69

Christine continued with the lawsuit against CSID for the next six months. It soon was clear that each time she took a deposition or received a new batch of documents in discovery she was going to have a new name for the FBI to investigate.

On the victim side, the names of two-dozen children were located, hidden in code, inside the company's personnel roster, of all places. Twenty-four children had been kidnapped and sent to the Monkey's Paw from across the country. Twenty-five children had actually been transported out. The additional one was from someplace else, but she was old enough to call her parents from San Diego and tell them to come and collect her up.

Trial was set six months off when, without warning, CSID filed a Chapter 11 case in the U.S. Bankruptcy Court for the Southern District of California. The officers and employees then scattered to the four winds and the case that Christine was litigating was over.

In all, six company officers and agents were indicted by

the U.S. Attorney for their role in stealing classified documents from defense contractors. Eleven others were under investigation when Christine closed the file for the last time.

Three low-level security officers with CSID were mysteriously murdered after the company had ceased operations. This was after all twenty-five children had been flown home out of Colombia. The security officers were, Dennis Mackey, Jr., Travis E. Armstrong (ex-CIA), and Nathan Jennings. The murder victims were, posthumously, discovered to be the men who had actually pulled off the kidnappings of all twenty-five children.

After the last murder, the FBI announced that it had investigated no less than eleven fathers of the children kidnapped in relation to the mysterious murders.

None of the fathers was ever indicted.

Chapter 70

Elizabeth Janes awoke one day to find she owned a Swiss Chalet valued at over fifteen-million dollars. She learned of it by watching a video slipped beneath her apartment door while she slept. Along with it came a Swiss numbered bank account. She was speechless when she called Zurich and got the balance. The phone fell from her hands onto the floor, and she didn't return to work that day. Or ever again.

John Blackletter received a letter from the Bank of the Cayman Islands. His retirement account was in place and waiting to be activated by his call. He would never work again, and a week later was back in the arms of his loving family stateside. He didn't know how or where the funds came from, but he was asking few questions. It was time to golf and fish and shoot baskets with his growing boys.

Lamont Wilkinson received the same, a bank account in the Cayman Islands with 5 million U.S. dollars waiting for him when he wanted it.

Huey the helicopter Huey was testing the "Jesus nut" on

his Huey chopper—the nut that holds the rotor on or else one meets Jesus—when outside his hanger there came a thundering roar as only Blackhawk helicopters make. Two of them, settling down just beyond his hanger, two men approaching with ownership documents and keys. He was in shock when the men asked could he call a taxi for them, that the two helicopters now belonged to Huey himself. Even the owner's manuals were still sealed in plastic.

Miss Kitty of tent city found herself approached one day by a private detective who talked her into taking a ride with him. She also was allowed to bring her two closest friends. They wound around downtown Bogotá until coming to a swank apartment complex complete with a doorman. The detective parked underground and took the trio up to apartment 1202. He handed Miss Kitty the keycard and told her to open the door. Inside they went.

"Three bedrooms," said the detective. "One for each of you. And here on the counter is your passbook. First United Bank of Colombia. Twelve-thousand dollars, enough to live for a year while you find a job, all of you. There's soap in the bathroom and shampoo. There are money envelopes in each closet to buy new clothes. There's food in the kitchen and enough coffee to last two years. Plus a cupboard full of cigarettes and a drawer full of cigarette lighters. Am I leaving anything out?"

Stunned, the trio was speechless.

"Good. Now get cleaned up and find jobs. If you don't, it's on you. If you need drug and alcohol counseling, call me —here's my card—and it will be arranged. Even hospital care for withdrawing from drugs. Okay, that's it."

He disappeared, leaving Miss Kitty dumbstruck. She then took a long shower. She'd start looking for a job right away.

Thaddeus did return to Colombia, but the first thing he did was go looking for Anna. Thaddeus found her grave in a small, shaded graveyard behind an adobe church with two turrets. The town was a Colombian name he couldn't pronounce. But her name was pronounceable, and he knew Keystone had been there before him and had made arrangements for her final resting place.

He sat beside her grave, green grass and monarchs flitting north. He told her about Simon and Antonella, about Christine and Nancy. Then he said, "I couldn't leave Colombia with you alone out here. For all that you did for me. For all that you did for my family." Then he stood up, ran his finger around the inside rim of his Stetson, and stepped away, refusing to turn his back on her.

He purchased the out-patient surgery center with American dollars, which brought the price down considerably on the Colombia price tag. It was outfitted with the most up-to-date, modern, available surgical instruments, scanners, tools, devices, and medical equipment the world had to offer. He told the agents cost was no object. He would spend every penny he had to outfit it for her. Four surgeons could operate in four different surgical suites at the same time. Then he sent her the keys.

———

THADDEUS APPEARED one night at the seaside home of the doctor whose patients called her Dr. Antonella. He rang the doorbell at ten o'clock, and Cavonna, his old friend and housemate, greeted him with a bear hug and pulled him inside.

"She was in surgery all day. But I know she would kill me if I didn't wake her. I'll be right back."

Thaddeus walked into the kitchen for water. There, on the corkboard wall, were pictures, dozens of them. All Thaddeus. Then he heard the voice behind him, and tears washed into his eyes as he turned.

"So," she said, "you came after all."

"I came."

She hesitated, standing apart. "Did you go to three doctor's meetings first?"

"Many more than that."

She came forward three steps.

He stepped back.

Chapter 71

Six Months Later

He loved snorkeling. He loved the Pacific Ocean and everything that he saw under the surface. Fish of every description—shape, size, and color —a sandy bottom, turbulent and reflecting the sunlight in boils of light, the feel of the saltwater on his skin, and the strength that he felt as he made his way through the water with the fins on his feet, his arms pinned at his sides, and his eyes through his face mask taking in this wonderful world.

At these moments, he felt carefree, didn't feel like he had growth to do as the doctors said, and he was at peace. Which is why he came to the beach and the ocean every day at noon. He looked at the rubber watch on his wrist and saw that it was five minutes until one, time for lunch. She would be sitting on the beach towel, looking toward the ocean, waiting for him to surface. She had told him that she worried about him being in the water alone. It wasn't because she doubted his skills but, rather, because she loved him so desperately.

He surfaced and looked around. Farther out to sea, he could make out an oil tanker headed for the refinery. From his porch, he made out several of these every day through his field glasses, which waited beside him on a white plank table even though there was rarely anything more exciting than pelicans and seagulls. But it all excited him and made him glad to be alive. He often dozed between sightings.

Lunches were usually seafood with avocado and onion, iced tea, and tortilla chips with plenty of salt. Naps would come later. He had noticed that he always felt less confused after his nap than before. The doctors told him that sleep was healing, that sleep was the best medicine for him, and that he required a good nap every afternoon.

He began swimming to shore. His arms felt strong, and the muscles in his shoulders were responding to the weightlifting he did every morning at the gym. He was again running, five miles every morning before the sun came up, and his legs were getting much stronger. He could get up out of his chair without grunting, and he felt much more stable on his feet.

As he swam toward shore, he reached that point where his feet touched the sand, and he stood, pushed the snorkeling mask back on his head, and began slogging his way through the knee-high foamy water. He stooped, removed his fins, and then walked up onto the sand, hot on the soles of his feet and between his toes.

She patted his towel and told him to come join her. As always, she had brought along two bottles of iced tea inside a cold bag. She removed them from the bag and then twisted the tops and handed him one.

She said, "Are you glad to be here?"

He smiled and sat back on his hands behind him. "Tell the truth, I'm glad to be anywhere."

"31 Flavors on the way home?"

"Can we gather up our kids and take them with us?"

"Of course," she said.

"All right, then. You've got yourself a deal."

She stood and shook out her hair. Then she put her Padres cap on backward. He helped gather their beach gear and stow it in a backpack, which he then slung over his shoulder.

"I love La Jolla, Chris."

She smiled and led them off across the sand.

THE END

The Michael Gresham Series

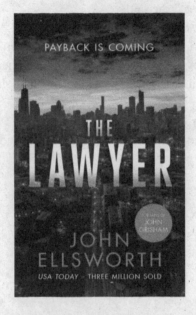

If you enjoyed The Thaddeus Murfee series, you might enjoy The Michael Gresham series - a gripping legal thriller series.

vinci-books.com/thelawyer